along

comes a

Wolfe

a SHEPHERD & WOLFE
mystery

COUNIOS & GANE

ALONG COMES A WOLFE
© Angie Counios & David Gane, 2016
All rights reserved.

Published by Your Nickel's Worth Publishing.
November 2016

While this book is suggested by actual events, it is in its entirety a work of fiction. All characters names have been invented, all characters have been composited or invented, and incidents have all been fictionalized.

Shakespeare, William. *As You Like It*. eds. David Bevington and David Scott Kastan. Act 2, scene 7; Act 4, Scene 1. New York: Bantam Dell, 2004.

Library and Archives Canada Cataloguing in Publication

Counios, 1968-, author
     Along comes a Wolfe / Counios & Gane.

(Shepherd & Wolfe)
Previously published by the authors.
Issued in print and electronic formats.
ISBN 978-1-927756-78-2 (paperback).—ISBN 978-1-927756-79-9 (epub).—
ISBN 978-1-927756-80-5 (mobi)
ISBN 978-1-988783-92-5 (POD)

     I. Gane, 1973-, author II. Title.

PS8605.O8937A64 2016   C813'.6   C2016-906090-X
                                           C2016-906091-8

Printed in Canada.
26 25 24 23 22   1 2 3 4 5

Cover © istockphoto.com\BIMKA1; © istockphoto.com/kirstypargeter; and © Angie Counios.
Book design by Heather Nickel.
Proofreading by Nathan Mader.

YOUR NICKEL'S WORTH PUBLISHING
www.ynwp.ca

prologue

1

**Erika told Sarah she thinks
u'll be mad if she goes 4 Derek**

Jayce Morgan stands in the hallway of Gardiner High, staring at the text on her phone. Erika has the whole school to pick from and she goes after Jayce's ex? Of course she's mad. She fires off a response.

Hell yeah

She heads toward the girl's bathroom on the second floor, in absolutely no rush to head back to class. She's looking for any excuse to wander the halls instead of sitting in English and this message gives her one more reason to stay away. She needs a minute to cool off. No one ever really needs to go to the bathroom anyway.

The corridors are clean, empty, and quiet.

Bzzz. The phone vibrates and she pauses at the bathroom door.

It's her bestie, Molly, in Level Three Science on the main floor, making a dumbass face. Molly always makes her smile, and Jayce snaps her own dorky pic and sends it back. Leaning against the heavy bathroom door until it opens, she goes inside.

She stops at one of the mirrors for a moment, but finds herself indifferent to her looks, neither pleased nor displeased with her complexion, the long fall of her brown hair, or the way her clothes shape her curves, so she moves on.

The corner stall is the one she always goes to, and she sets her phone on the small ledge above the toilet paper. Last time she forgot her phone was there and nearly knocked it into the toilet, fumbling for it as it clipped the edge of the seat and hit the floor.

She settles in.

The door to the bathroom swings open. Footsteps. The stall closest to the door bangs open and then locks.

Bzzz. Another photo from Molly. Mr. Fleet's in the background pointing to a chart of a frog's reproductive system. She stifles a silent giggle.

A toilet flushes and the other person leaves the stall. The door squeaks open and the sound of Ms. Maple's history class across the hall spills into the silence.

The bathroom door hisses closed.

Gross—they didn't wash their hands. Who doesn't wash their hands? Jayce shakes her head, scrunching her face in disgust. She looks at her phone again. Time to get back before Mrs. Drake busts her.

Standing, she tugs her jeans over her hips and zips them up, then shoves her phone into her back pocket. She flushes. She steps out of the stall and moves toward the sink. She hates washing her hands with the pink soap that stinks like a hospital and leaves her skin dry and ready to crack, but the germs around here are nasty. She pumps the dispenser several times and rinses her hands thoroughly, drying off with the paper towel and wishing the school would buy some decent hand dryers. She reminds herself to stop at her locker and moisturize before getting back to class.

Leaning into the mirror, she combs her fingers through her hair, and waits until it once again flows smoothly around her face before inspecting her dark eyeliner. Carefully she drags her middle finger beneath each to clean up the edges. Jayce leans back, assessing her reflection. She's satisfied—she's wasted enough of this class period with her fake break. Time to head back to English.

2

He presses a closed fist against the bathroom door's metal plate, making sure to swing it hard and let it bang against the wall to signal his entrance. It's tidy. No scraps of paper towel litter the floor. But it's early—he knows the place doesn't look like this at the end of the day. He also knows that a clean space is a more efficient space.

He bends down. Only a single pair of trendy red Toms are visible under the stalls. He rises, moving into the stall closest to the exit. It's cleaner than the guys' washroom, and lacks graffiti. Smells better too.

He gets down to business, pulling off his backpack to put it down by his feet. He lifts one foot, working to avoid touching the walls, and slips off his shoe. He shifts his weight and pulls off the other one, dropping them both into the open backpack. He stands still, waiting, preparing himself for the next moment.

Bzzz.

He listens. A slight hiccough of breath. Is she laughing? Is she texting while sitting on the toilet? His face twists in repulsion.

He reaches out and flushes the toilet, walking out of the stall and across the bathroom before the noise fades. He yanks the bathroom door open—it swings easily enough and he releases it. It closes with a slow, hissing whisper. Turning back into the room, he steps swiftly and silently toward a middle stall, gently pushing the door open with his knuckles, careful not to bang it against the partition or leave any fingerprints. Inside, he rotates on the ball of his foot, catching a glimpse of himself in the mirror as he pulls the door shut.

A smile crosses his face.

He doesn't lock the door and leaves it slightly ajar. He lifts the toilet seat and sets his right foot on the porcelain edge. He ignores the thought of what may have splashed against the cold rim—what his sock might soak up—and focuses on his goal. Now the left foot is up too, and he perches on the toilet, pressing his forearms gently against the walls for stability. He takes a silent breath. And waits.

Swoosh. A toilet flushes. He hears her zip up. A lock unclicks and the stall door thumps open.

He looks through the thin opening between his door and the stall partition and sees her move over to the sink.

She runs the tap and pumps the soap—a lot of soap—and washes her hands. While the water splashes in the sink, he eases himself down from the toilet seat, watching her through the crack between the door and the partition. She crosses over to the far wall and pulls paper towel out of the dispenser, then crumples it up and throws it away.

He readies himself, reaching behind to tug gently at the plastic bag in his back pocket. He slides it out silently, the black letters from the local grocery store legible in its creased folds. He tightens his fingers in its handle straps, careful to make no noise.

She pauses at the mirror again, and he watches as she checks herself one last time. Her hair spills down her back as she plays with it. He can't fault her for her vanity. She is tall and brunette, just like the girl he hurt in Grade 8. Her faded blue jeans are tight against her ass, the way all the girls buy them now, and they look good on her. She never quits watching herself, absorbed by her reflection, and he must clear his mind. He can't let those thoughts in—not when his moment is so close. He takes a slow, calming breath.

It's time.

He opens the door and is out of the stall in one quick motion.

She doesn't even see him coming.

He makes no sound, raising the plastic bag over her head and pulling it down quickly. Her dark hair hangs out the bottom, and he pulls back, the bag sinking deep into the folds of her neck. He can see her in the mirror, face pressed firmly against the inside of the bag, her mouth sucking plastic with every breath.

She panics, hands flailing at her face, struggling to tear it away. She's stronger than she looks and he pushes his knee into her back for leverage. She bucks against him and he stumbles, banging his thigh hard against the porcelain sink. He grunts in pain.

He pulls the bag taut and her fingers tear at the stretched plastic... but then her knees give way and she crumples to the floor. He struggles to stay standing.

He doesn't know it yet but girls are taught to fall in self-defense, and though he's on top of her, she's got the upper hand now. She kicks blindly, striking him sharply on the side of his shin. He stumbles and she kicks out again, nearly making him fall.

He's losing. He's got to get away.

She's still kicking, clawing at the bag, and before she can free herself, the bathroom door opens with a bang and he's gone.

3

"Can anyone tell me why Scout thought the world was ending?"

The class sits in silence.

Mrs. Drake smiles, patient. "I know you guys read this."

A girl in the second row begins, "I think Scout—" but she
stops short, staring at the door.

Jayce stands in the doorway, holding a white plastic bag
loosely in her fingers. The colour is gone from her face, her
hair a tangled mess. Eyeliner streams down her cheeks. She
can't seem to speak.

"Jayce?" Mrs. Drake asks.

Jayce says nothing.

All the students stare as Mrs. Drake moves to the girl at the
door. She speaks louder, adamant. Worried. "Jayce, what's
wrong?"

Jayce looks up into Mrs. Drake's eyes and shudders, her
breath catching.

"You're okay," Mrs. Drake says. "Tell me what's wrong."

Jayce looks at the plastic bag in her hands. She chokes, gasping in panicked moans that burst into a wailing cry.

It sends a shiver down Mrs. Drake's spine, and she scrambles to catch the girl as Jayce collapses to the floor.

Jayce's friend Deb, on the far side of the room, pulls her phone out.

Shits going down with J. Come quick.

4

Bzzz. Molly's phone vibrates under her science notebook.

She peeks at it, expecting something about Erika going after Jayce's ex, but instead there's a photo of her best friend on the floor beside Mrs. Drake.

Molly doesn't hesitate.

"Molly, where are you going? Molly!" Mr. Fleet calls out as she rushes for the door.

She doesn't stop.

She bolts down the hall and through the indoor courtyard, rushing past a senior sitting on a bench putting on his shoes.

Mr. Coogan, the vice-principal, steps out of the office and Molly knows she's about to catch hell.

"Slow down!"

"Sorry!" she calls over her shoulder. But she keeps running, all the way to Jayce's period two English class.

Kids crowd in a circle and from somewhere in the middle, Mrs. Drake yells, "Owen, grab my water."

As Owen moves to the desk, Molly slips inside and sees her friend. She's not really prepared for how bad Jayce looks.

Owen comes back with the water bottle and Mrs. Drake gives it to Jayce. "Calm down. Breathe. You're okay."

Molly kneels down beside her and takes Jayce's trembling hand. Her friend's breath hitches as she fights to talk through the tears.

"Tell me what happened."

5

He goes to the nearest stairwell. He needs distance from the upstairs bathroom. This isn't what he'd planned. The girl fought too hard and now his leg hurts—and he hasn't finished what he'd intended to do.

He steps into the empty indoor courtyard, breathing slowly. He can't let the stress show. He's a hundred feet from the exit and he needs to hold it together.

He slips his shoes out of his bag to get them on before anyone notices he's in sock feet. When he glances up, he realizes he can see right through a large window into the administrative office. A man wearing a suit stares out at him.

He stands, his laces still dangling loose, and acts casual, wandering over to the vending machines. He tries to keep cool, digging in his pocket for change. He turns away from the man in the suit, pops in a few coins, and chooses E5. His favourite nutty chocolate bar drops down. As he reaches for it, he looks over his shoulder.

The man is watching him.

This can't be about the girl in the bathroom already; he's probably just concerned about seeing a student—himself—wandering the halls during class.

He could head for the exit but that only makes him more suspicious. He needs a new plan.

Stuffing the chocolate into his backpack, he sits on the nearest bench. He's leaning over to tie the first shoelace when a girl rushes past.

Now, *that* might have something to do with him.

"Slow down!" the man in the suit yells, and hurries out of his office to chase after her.

The inner courtyard is silent, except for the quiet hum of the lights above. He ties the other shoelace and sits up. He pulls out the candy bar and unwraps it, takes a bite and closes his eyes, enjoying the crunch of chocolate and peanuts.

Next time he needs to be better prepared. To think his actions through more clearly. He has to take into account how hard the girls will fight.

He stands, slinging the backpack over his shoulder. With time, it'll get easier. The more he does it, the more it'll become routine. His mind will be ready and he'll work on instinct.

The bell sounds, signaling the next class. He savours the last of the nougaty goodness and tosses the candy wrapper in the garbage. He slips out the door.

Today was his first try and, with time, he'll get better. Practice is all he needs. What is it they say? Practice makes perfect.

The sun is warm on his face and he feels a smile form.

It'll be a good summer.

[illegible]
[illegible]
[illegible]
[illegible]

[illegible]
[illegible]
[illegible]

[illegible]
[illegible]
[illegible]
[illegible]
[illegible]
[illegible]
[illegible]
[illegible]
[illegible]
[illegible]

part 1

chapter 1

"Anthony, you're up next."

Coach Davies has had us busting our asses running lay-ups for the last half hour. Even though we won our last game, he says we missed too many opportunities, and Coach's philosophy is that practice makes perfect.

I'm facing off against my buddy, Mike, who's defending. This is easy stuff, and I'm pretty good using either of my arms, so I've already got a plan. I drive the ball down the court, pushing strong to the hoop. I'm not even thinking about it, my mind zeroed in on the backboard. I easily dodge Mike and move past the basket. I plant my foot and push off. I feel the spin I have on the ball and I know it's going in without even looking.

I'm feeling pretty good about it, but it doesn't last long. Coach is on me right away.

"What the hell was that?"

"Reverse lay-up."

"And why'd you do it?"

I'm not exactly sure how to answer. "To guard myself with the net?"

"No! Why the hell did you do a reverse while the rest of us are doing standards?"

"Come on, Coach, this is easy stuff." I know I've screwed up as soon as it comes out of my mouth.

"Well, I'm happy for you. And when you get your ass handed to you by Cornwall next Friday, I'll be the first to remind you about this little chat of ours."

Cornwall High currently ranks first in points and rebounds—they've destroyed us in our last two games.

"Quit thinking about what's just in front of you. You've got to start thinking about what's coming up from behind that might blindside you."

Coach looks at the whole team now. I'm grateful.

"You guys need to respect the fundamentals. It's what'll get you out of a jam when things start falling apart. Now, hit the showers. We're done here."

chapter 2

I step out of the shower, wrapping a towel around my waist.

"Just had to show off, hey, Shepherd?"

Mike's at the mirror shaving his three chin hairs while I sit on the bench, drying off.

"Well, I knew you'd be too slow to catch me—"

"Don't need the speed when I got the shots." He air-swishes an imaginary ball.

"Not if you can't get to the basket." I'm beside him at the mirror now and watch him finish. "I don't know what you're even trying to scrape off there."

He grabs his towel and wipes his face clean. "You're just jealous that I've got something to shave." He admires his jawline then heads to his locker.

I stand in front of the full-length mirror, pleased with my well-formed six-pack. Every sit-up, every crunch, every chin-up that my drill sergeant of a coach has us doing is worth it. I barely have to flex. My abs are solid.

I look back at Mike, gesturing at my reflection. "Now *that's* a form to be admired."

Mike shakes his head as he pulls on a shirt. He's a big guy for being white, but he's still got a bit of baby fat on him that he can't seem to shake. In twenty years he'll be that chunky guy in an office selling life insurance. But these abs of mine are a little preventative medicine for my own mid-life crisis.

"Save it for your girlfriend, buddy."

I go over to my own locker and start getting dressed, letting my boxers hang out just enough to tease over the belt of my Hollister jeans. I grab my tee-shirt, even though it seems a shame to cover up this magnificent stomach.

Mike catches me rubbing my abs in admiration.

"Do you need to get yourself a room?"

Maybe.

chapter 3

On the way home, my phone launches into "Pumped Up Kicks" by Foster The People. It's my girlfriend, Sheri. She's on the track team and she's fun and easy-going, so the ringtone suits her. She's sent me a picture on Snapchat, one of those image apps that self-destructs, of her holding a photo of me. Her eyes are shut tight and she's got the biggest pucker. She's adorable and goofy and I can never figure out why this combination makes her the hottest damn girl.

I let out a quiet laugh and a little shudder runs up my spine. The image disappears. I should have taken a screenshot.

Send another.

A moment later, and Sheri's ringtone plays again: *run baby run, faster than my bullet.* I open it and she's holding her hands in the shape of a heart, and I feel lucky and happy. This time I'm ready and save it to my collection.

A split second later, my phone vibrates.

You screenshot that didn't you?

Maybe? :-P

I move across Albert Street, ankles nearly skinned by an impatient asshole in a car turning north. I step onto the curb, look over my shoulder, and see he's already half a block away. I adjust my gym bag on my shoulder and text back:

How'd the test go?

Good enough.

And the track meet?

The typing indicator bubbles away. This reply is longer, because she loves being competitive.

**It went well. Made great time. Need to pace myself
better but I don't think Broadhill will be real competition.
Track isn't their thing. Coach said there may be
some university scouts at the next race.**

I'm so proud of her.

That's great babe.

You?

I want to reply in my smartass way, but I hesitate. She deserves a real answer once in a while.

> **Practice was hard, but good.**
> **No pain. No gain.**

With all the texting, I don't realize how far I've walked. Though I'm already in my neighbourhood, I want to chat more. But like me, Sheri is busy, and I know she's likely itching to get to her run. She's not one of those needy girls always looking for her boyfriend's attention, and I love her for it.

Bzzz—another text.

Hanging out with Brody tonight,
maybe help him with science. You?

Sheri's the oldest in her family and Brody is her younger brother. Since I'm the youngest in mine, they (whoever they are) say that this is a good match for a couple. Just one in a long list of reasons why we're a good match, in my opinion.

> **Almost home. Supposed to be reading a**
> **couple chapters of Catcher in the Rye for**
> **English, but have science test coming up.**

Send me a pic?

I smile. I suppose I owe her one. I turn my hat around and duck face the shit out of the camera.

Bzzz.

**BAHAHAHAHA! Get yourself home babe.
We'll talk later.**

I text her back quickly:

Let's make plans for the weekend?

It's only Wednesday, but it's good to plan ahead. I send it and slide the phone into my pocket.

chapter 4

I cross the street to my house. We're west of the school and the neighbourhood always gets nicer. Although the area was developed at the turn of the last century, our house is one of the newer ones on the block. It's a white two-storey, constructed to blend in with the older homes around it. It has the big pillars and the porch, but not the dark, leaky basements all our neighbours have.

I run up the steps and go inside to find Dad on the couch. He smiles as he puts down the book he's reading.

"You're late for supper."

I pull out my phone and look. "Almost late."

"Tell that to your mother."

Mom hollers from the kitchen, "Is that Anthony? Tell him he's late for supper."

Dad yells back at her, "Geesh, woman, you in my kitchen? Leave my food alone. You're the breadwinner and I'm the cook."

We are traditional in a lot of ways, but Mom and Dad carved their own path a long time ago, back when they started dating in college. Grampa was from Jamaica and freaked out when he learned Mom's new boyfriend was white. Dad tried to cook every holiday meal for three years—including Grampa's favourites of ackee and saltfish, which is a little challenging to get the ingredients for in a city like this. But Dad wanted to prove to him that family and tradition were something special to him, too. The two of them still laugh about it, Grampa admitting he liked Dad after the first year but didn't want to lose out on all that good food. Back then, interracial relationships were a big deal, but now that label is mostly gone—Mom and Dad are just a couple and my mocha skin is a blessing.

Dad looks at me and wrinkles his nose. "You stink."

Mom calls again, "Tell him to change his shirt. He probably stinks."

"How do you guys do that?"

Dad holds up his ring finger with a knowing nod. "Gives you magic powers, son."

I know a little interest in my parents goes a long way, so I nod at the book spread open on Dad's chest. "What are you reading today?"

"Le Carré."

"Ah." I nod but don't really know who that is.

"How was practice?"

Seems Dad uses my tricks too.

"Good."

"What'd you do?"

"Lay-ups."

"Coach work you hard?"

I nod.

He picks up his book again. "Go get changed before your mom gets a real whiff of you."

"You just want to finish your chapter."

"Maybe, but I wouldn't debate that with your mom."

My sister Heather comes out of her room as I head up the stairs. "Did you listen to that download I shared?" she asks.

I nod. "Yeah. It's good. Your taste in music is improving, College Girl."

I think all those pre-law classes have got her thinking differently. One day, she'll end up working for some high-priced firm far away, and I'll miss her when she does.

"Shouldn't you be at some sorority thing?"

Heather's two years older than me and we're finally starting to click as siblings. The banter is fun—way better than the cat and dog fights we used to have, and I'm sure Mom and Dad are grateful too.

"That's just in the movies, smart ass."

"Easy or I'll give your number to Mike." All my friends think she's hot, and I'm grateful that this didn't happen until after she graduated—no guy wants to deal with that growing up. Just way too weird.

Mom yells up the stairs, "Are you two ever going to make it down here?"

Heather turns back to me. "I think supper's ready."

"A magnificent feat of deduction. You'll make a great lawyer someday."

Heather winks and goes downstairs.

In my room there's a laundry basket full of fresh, clean shirts on the chair next to my desk. Nice—Dad makes a good housewife.

I pull out both a red tee-shirt and a yellow tee-shirt, trying to decide.

Mom yells from downstairs, "White."

How the hell does she do it?

"You heard your dad. Magic powers."

Damn.

I dig a little deeper and, sure enough, there's a white tee. I take off my pit-smelly school shirt and pull it over my head, then check my messages. One from Mike and a couple from Sheri.

"Anthony!"

Ah, yes, the call of a mom telling you to get your ass in gear.

The texts can wait. I toss my phone on the desk and head downstairs for supper.

chapter 5

Standing on the path, Sheri folds into a forward bend. With very little effort, her face is nearly against her legs, her palms reaching around her Asics runners to grasp her calves as she pushes into the pose. It's the end of a beautiful fall day. The leaves haven't started to turn and she wants to take advantage of the warm weather to practise her race strategy before the next cross-country meet.

She comes up, feeling the stretch along her straightening back. She wears short, black spandex running shorts that hug her long, strong legs, and a white sports bra peeks out from beneath the shoulders of her loose, grey tank top. She is fit, firm, and naturally athletic.

She pulls her long hair back into a ponytail at the top of her head and ties it with a white bandana. She snuck it from Tony's drawer because he's a boy and a slob and probably won't notice it missing, and she likes to keep him close. Besides, it helps hold back the little hairs that tickle and annoy her, and keeps the sweat out of her eyes when the run is long and concentration is crucial. Today is all about focus and she doesn't want anything to distract her.

Two older men jog by and give her a wave. She smiles. It's a lovely courtesy to acknowledge other runners and keeps her going when the distance is long. Today her goal is six miles. It's a little farther than a regular practice run, but she wants to push herself all the way to the tracks outside the city. Her goal is to finish in fifty-one minutes. After all, she is still training.

She hopes that when she gets back to the car, there'll be a text message from Tony. That'd be perfect. What she doesn't want is a text from her ex, Dillon, who keeps trying to rekindle things. It's irritating but she hasn't figured how to cut him out completely.

She clears both boys from her mind and presses into long lunges until her hams stretch and she feels a surge of blood in her veins. She comes up, slips earbuds into her ears, and hits play. Green Day's "Jesus of Suburbia" starts up as she takes the first few strides. It's easy and smooth and she quickly puts distance between herself and her starting point.

She jogs past a woman in her forties who keeps a good pace. Sheri imagines she'll be like her later in life, still running, still happily taking care of herself—maybe with a special someone like Tony. As she travels along the golf course, she passes the Ferguson memorial bench, her personal reminder that her warm-up is done and now the serious workout begins. The creek twists away from the city and she picks up the pace.

A Tiesto mix of the love song "All Of Me" by John Legend plays and she smiles inwardly as thoughts of Tony slip between the *thup-thup* rhythm of her feet on the pavement. He hates her choice of music, dismissing anything even slightly mainstream as crap. He likes hip-hop and anything that's never graced the top twenty. He's a music snob, and his strong opinions put people off, but it was his manners that drew her in.

They'd met at the gravel pits; a bunch of people from different schools hanging out to party. He didn't use any cheesy pick-up lines and didn't try to get her drunk. He swept in while Ross from her English class was attempting to ply her with drinks and absolutely no good intentions. Then this guy had appeared out of the crowd and grabbed the bottle out of Ross's hand before he'd even known what was going on.

"Hey, it's Mr. Unsportsmanlike Behaviour!"

"Back off, Shepherd."

Ross had gone for the bottle but Tony towered over him—he was tall for a sophomore.

"Oops! Sorry! Was this for her? Did I break up your thang?"

That's when Tony had looked at Sheri, and she realized he had the sexiest eyes.

"Was this yours?"

She'd been about to answer but Ross reached for the bottle again and Tony didn't even look at him, just raised it higher beyond his reach. He kept looking at her. She'd felt her drunken face smile and shook out a wobbly "no," but she was spinning into those hazel depths.

"You sure?"

That time, she'd nodded, and Tony turned back to Ross.

"Doesn't seem like she wants your drink."

Then Tony, always the cocky one, let the bottle slip out of his hand. It shattered on the gravel. *"Whoops."*

Ross looked Tony in the eyes. *"Screw you!"* But he'd known he was outmatched and walked away.

"Well, that was close," Tony had said. *"I would seriously have hated to break a nail."*

The two of them had just clicked and they spent the rest of the night side-by-side near the fire, watching the drunken antics of their friends. Near dawn, he'd driven her home and said good night, but hadn't tried anything.

She'd been a little stunned.

After that, they texted back and forth. Their conversations were fun but brief, and she never thought he was going anywhere with his flirting—since they went to different schools, it wasn't like they saw each other often.

Until things unexpectedly heated up. She had gone to a post-game backyard party and saw him playing the guitar, commanding an audience as Tony so often did. He was singing a parody of Taylor Swift's "22," changing it to be about teachers and their apparent love of shaved genitals. When he was done, he had moved out of the crowd toward her and taken her hand.

They were sitting on some lawn chairs by the pool when a shooting star fell across the sky.

"Should we make a wish?" Cliché, but why not?

"Why? It's only space garbage burning up in the atmosphere." Tony's response had made her regret the suggestion.

"Well, aren't you romantic?" was the only comeback she could think of.

"Oh, I have my ways."

He'd leaned close and raised a hand to her cheek. She had felt his warmth against her skin and thought he was going to kiss her. He hadn't.

When she opened her eyes, he was holding an eyelash on the tip of his finger. *"Wish on this."* He leaned closer, whispering in her ear, *"Wish for something special."*

She shook her head at the mushiness of it all, but closed her eyes anyway and blew. She figured he must be going to kiss her now, so she waited for a long time, but when she opened her eyes, he was gone. Vanished. WTF?

She'd asked around the party, but her friends Katie and Jessica hadn't seen him. She was feeling mighty pissed off when she'd turned around and suddenly there he was.

"Where the hell did you go?"

He'd wrapped an arm around her waist, pulled her close, and kissed her in front of all those people. It was bold and confident, and he seemed so sure that she'd let him.

And he'd been right.

"What? Wasn't that what you wished for?"

She grinned, completely pleased by his game, but unwilling to let him know—wouldn't do to make things too easy for him. *"You're such a weird asshole."*

He'd smiled. She'd smiled. And she knew he was the boy for her. That had been eight months ago.

He kept her guessing and always on her toes. He challenged her to be her best. He came to every one of her meets but gave her space to be her own person. Now, the only real issue they faced was that they planned to attend different colleges after grad. Oh, couples did it all the time, but long-distance is never easy—unless it's a run.

Sheri shakes the thought away. She's let her focus slide. Time enough later to think of the drama in her life—at the moment she needs to concentrate on her goal.

She starts to sweat just as a slight breeze picks up. Perfect. Maybe a good run has as much to do with luck as training. She follows the road to the path that takes her to the old tracks, pushing herself up the small incline. The next mile is the part she likes most. It's a series of gentle rolling slopes—a challenge that pushes her hard—and on the last rise she gets to really dig in.

She moves easily through each dip toward the picnic area by the pines. In summer, people come here to get out of the city and relax in the grass while their kids climb on the play structure. But at this time of year, even in the warm after-noon, the place is quiet, abandoned.

She glances at her watch. She's making excellent time—better than expected. If she continues without stopping, she'll crush her best time, but she only needs to prepare for the upcoming meet, not the Boston qualifier. She's done well and there's only a mile left before she can turn back. She recalculates. Even if she stops for a quick bathroom break, she'll still finish strong.

She jogs across the grass to the tree-shaded washroom near the playground. Winding down, she takes a breath, rolls her neck, and stretches her legs. "The Kids Aren't Alright" by The Offspring starts up and she can just hear Tony getting riled up by it. It makes her laugh. After her run, she'll take a long shower and drop by his house to see him.

She pushes open the door to the public washroom and goes in.

chapter 6

He first spotted her three weeks ago.

He'd started when he was young with cats and small dogs. When the attempt in Grade 8 had failed, he'd scaled back his efforts but his training had been interrupted. Once the family had settled in this new city—a move brought on by his idiot brother—he had rededicated himself to his practice, learning to suffocate larger and larger dogs. It was while burying a neighbourhood dog by some pines outside the city, that he'd seen her running. She was strong and lithe—a solid challenge. If he were to finally be successful, he needed to take his time and prepare.

She had the agile glide of someone confident in the steady movement of her body; he admired her determination. He had returned the next day at the same time, sitting by the edge of the play structure, but she didn't appear. Although disheartened, he vowed to return. He could be persistent too.

When he arrived at the play structure a few days later, he'd seen a figure far in the distance, already well on her way back to the city. He decided to repeat his watch and arrive a bit earlier. His diligence paid off when he saw her round the curve toward him. She ran past without seeming to notice him in the shadow of the pines.

He had arrived early again the next day, eager to see her, a thermos of tea and F. Scott Fitzgerald's *Tender is the Night* on the picnic table where he waited. He enjoyed the hunt, the focus it took to unwrap the mystery of how best to take her down. He worked it through in his mind, careful not to put anything on paper or leave any digital footprint of the plot. Imagining his performance, crafting it in his mind, made him sharper, honed his control.

Except he couldn't envision the circumstance of their meeting, the moment when he'd happen to her.

The thermos retained its heat well and he had drunk the tea slowly, considering. The picnic area sat on a plain beyond the undulating hills and he'd be conspicuous even in the knee-high grass along her route. Besides, it was too open, too public. And the pines were too far from the path—any attempt to come at her from among them would likely alert her, and he knew how fast she was. She would elude him.

Perhaps there was a better spot somewhere closer to the start of the path.

These musings were interrupted by the steady tick-tock rhythm of her soles against the asphalt running path.

He looked up to find her already in sight, moving toward him. So consumed had he been by his thoughts, he barely felt the trail of hot tea when it spilled across his slackened hand.

She turned her head to meet his gaze—her blue eyes on him—and he forced a smile. She looked right through him and crossed to the bathroom.

He stayed still, unsure of his next move. He set the tea down, wiped off his hand, and picked up the book he didn't plan to read. He kept an eye on his watch. 5:37. The second hand ticked slowly. One minute. Two. After four minutes, she exited the building. He didn't even glance up when the door banged against the stop and her feet picked up their steady rhythm, the sound fading into the distance.

He had his answer.

Now, three weeks later, he's waiting. He got here early, slipped inside the farthest stall, and locked the door. His shoes are already off and in his bag, and he sits on the toilet seat, legs crossed over the hole beneath him. There must be no indication of his presence. The possibility of germs, of bodily fluids, doesn't even enter his mind. He's focused. Ready. He's rehearsed his moves repeatedly, hitting all the right marks and making sure to remove any hint of noise. All his polishing, all his perfectionism, will pay off.

He leans back against the wall. There is no electric light but a skylight creates soft shadows in the gloom. The metal mirrors reflect distorted shapes like figures in a fog. It will helps disguise his approach, but he dislikes that he won't be able to see the show.

He wraps the bag around his hands. It's a white garbage bag this time—it makes less noise and, after being bitten by a particularly vicious canine, he had decided that the cheap plastic shopping bags tore too easily. He doesn't check his watch; she never runs on a tight schedule. Her timing varies so much that he knows he might need to wait for nearly an hour. In the past, he'd almost been caught more than once, but he's grown patient. He closes his eyes, calming his mind, absorbing the silence around him.

When the door opens, the noise surprises him. He can't tell if he'd fallen asleep. Footsteps cross to an open stall and the stall door clicks shut. He hears rapid breathing. It's her, he's certain. He lowers his feet to the ground and rises off the seat. Even this motion, the fundamental act of standing, he has trained for. Reaching over, he unlatches the door, holding it slightly ajar.

The toilet flushes. There are only seconds left. His stall door pivots slowly open on its hinges as she crosses to the sink and turns on the tap. He rushes toward her. She doesn't even have time to see his distorted image in the mirror before the bag is over her face. She drops to the floor.

All the rehearsal, all the contemplation, have prepared him. He throws the entirety of his weight on top of her, keeping his body low and his legs out of range. Her fingers grasp and claw at his arms, but his jacket protects him and she cannot get a good grip. She tries to leverage herself into a different position, but he predicts her every move.

He's ready this time. Ready for it all. Practice has made him perfect.

He leans against her and the tight lip of plastic digs into the flesh of her neck. Her defenses aren't working and she realizes it. She needs air. She claws at the bag and he knows that the struggle is tipping in his favour. He twists the bag in his fist, the white plastic wrapping around his hand, and he yanks hard, his forearm hard against her neck, pressing against her windpipe. She coughs and gasps again and again.

He leans in further, all his upper body strength pouring into his forearm, and pulls her hands away from the bag. She can't see and she's choking and crying and the fight has gone out of her. Her arms are weakening, the strained breaths between each gasp grow longer, her whole body heaves as it chokes on what's left, all her world contained in the white plastic bag.

She is slipping away. Her legs stop first, and he feels death move up through her body. Her hands slide from the bag, and he waits a moment until her chest no longer moves. He lifts his arm off her throat, then tugs off the bag.

Her eyes are open, her tongue out. Vomit and spit are on her cheeks and in her hair. Her skin is mottled blue—no, gun-metal grey—and he stares into her bloodshot eyes. All the little spasms and twitches are gone, and he wants to keep staring—but he can't because there is still work to do.

chapter 7

Dad has this great way of feeding us healthy food without it looking like a hospital tray. I'm not sure if it's a "stay-at-home dad" thing or a "being married to a doctor" thing, but either way, he does some pretty badass tricks with greens and quinoa. He knows he has to make us healthy food or listen to Mom's lecture on what happens to your insides when you don't take care of your body. I guess looking at sick people all day long does that to a person.

I'm at the bottom of the stairs when Dad yells, "Last one here can grab the milk and the glasses."

Heather appears out of nowhere, pushing me against the wall, racing to get to the table first.

"You stepped on my foot."

"Sorry, little brother, but I beat you."

I head toward the kitchen and open the fridge. Seeing nothing, I yell out, "Where's—?"

"Don't yell," Mom says over my shoulder, "It's the soy milk."

I wrinkle my face. "Making changes without asking? Not cool, Mom."

She reaches in and hands it to me. "Deal with it."

I take it to the table and plop the carton down in front of Heather.

"Soy? That stuff tastes like chalk."

Now I *have* to try it. I grab another glass from the cupboard and pour myself a glass of water. I feel my family's eyes on me. "Just in case."

Heather raises her empty glass in a mock toast. "To your health."

"It's better for both of you." Mom looks over at Dad. "For all of us."

"Sorry, hon. Tonight, I partake in the wine."

I shake my head. "Cheater."

"Now, son. Studies show—"

I grunt my disapproval, but he cuts me off.

"—a glass of red wine is very good—"

Mom tries to interrupt him too, but he doesn't stop.

"—when that person is an adult—"

Heather reaches for the bottle, but he pulls it away.

"—and living on their own."

"Fine, old man, you win this one, but only because you made the meal." I dig into the salad, put a billy goat's worth on my plate, and pass the bowl to him. "But make sure to eat your veggies."

Mom nudges her glass Dad's way and he pours her a glass of vino too. She savours it, then says, "Jodi called. She and Bryan are thinking about selling their place."

Jodi is my oldest sister and Bryan is her husband.

I take a slug of the soy milk, hoping for the best, expecting the worst. Yup, chalk. I put the glass down and take a long gulp of water to wash the taste away.

Conversation moves around the table. Ollie, our golden retriever, lies under the table, his butt on my toes. Dad talks about a contract he's working on. I have no idea what he actually does, but I know he does it at home in between the cooking and the cleaning. Mom wants to fire the receptionist at her clinic—apparently this one isn't very good with paperwork. Heather loves college. Everyone shares their day.

I try to appreciate this moment, to savour it all. It won't last forever because, like Coach said, you never know what's coming up from behind.

chapter 8

After supper, Heather and I clean up and give Mom and Dad some quiet time. The everyday business of the family is a lot like a good basketball game. It's not the whole game that matters but all the small plays that lead up to the win. Playing sports is a good analogy for a family: you always have to be on the same team.

As I put the dishes on the counter, Heather gets containers out of the drawer for the leftovers. Ollie sits in a corner, close but not underfoot, ready to catch any scraps we send his way.

"Some of us are going out tonight. Do you want to join us?"

She snaps the lid on the salad and chicken, and I'm already thinking they'll make a good lunch for tomorrow.

"Nah," I shake my head. "I'm beat and I still need to get homework done."

She grabs the food and heads to the fridge. I help her with the door.

"You just want to hang out with Sheri."

"I wish."

Fact is, I'm exhausted. It's been a long week and knowing when to hit the pause button to regain your focus is important. I open the dishwasher and Heather stacks dishes on the racks.

"What about you? Is what's-his-name going to be there?"

Some boy has been calling her lately but she's being secretive about him. She's still getting over her old boyfriend, so she may be thinking this new guy isn't worth her time.

"Isaac."

"Right. Isaac..." I swig down the last of my soy milk and cringe, glad it's finished. The empty glass is the last thing to go in and I close the dishwasher.

Heather hands me a wet cloth, and I go to the dining room to wipe the table.

"No. He's busy, which is fine. He's just not—"

I step back into the room. "Outstanding?"

She leans on the counter, shakes her head, and laughs. "I'm only here for another year and then it's law school. I don't know where he's going or where I'll be, so what's the point? Besides, he's a bit wishy-washy."

I toss the cloth in the sink and lean on the counter beside her.

"Hey, no judgments here. This is all between you, me, and Ollie."

My sister looks around at the kitchen and nods just like Mom. "Baby brother, you're getting really good at this cleaning up thing. Who'd have thought?" She heads for the living room. "I'm leaving in ten to meet Hayley, Lindsay, and Chad at McLarens, if you change your mind."

"Thanks." I won't be going and Heather knows it, but I'm grateful she asked.

Back in my room, I'm not in the mood for schoolwork, but I grab a seat at the desk and drag out my biology text anyway. There's a test coming up in Mr. Harriet's class next week and I need to memorize the biological classifications of fifty plants and animals from kingdom to species. I stare at the page. The words meld into an ugly mass of *-phyla* and *-zoa*. My eyes glaze over, and I move over to the bed and grab my phone.

Mike's text pops up first, something about him killing 200 lbs on the weights. I shake my head. He always thinks about size and never about speed. I move on to Sheri's text. It's her response to my question about the weekend.

yes.
visit tonight?

It kills me, but I text back:

can't.

I don't want to leave it at that, so I add:

text me when you're done.

I won't hear from her until after her run, so I go back to my studies. Somewhere between the family and genus of a mountain lion, my head hits the pillow, and I don't lift it until morning.

chapter 9

I wake up Thursday morning and wipe the little bit of drool off the book I fell asleep reading. Out of habit, I reach for my phone. The screen is too bright and I squint to see who's texted. There's one from Jessica, Sheri's best friend, and one from Katie—it's too early for girl drama so I ignore those. One from a number I don't recognize. And two from Mike. Nothing from Sheri yet. She's been working hard for competition lately, but it's strange. She must have been as knock-out tired as I was. I tap on her name.

Morning babe

And that's all I manage. It's painfully early and I fall head-first back into the pillow.

"You're going to be late for practice!" Mom hollers from the kitchen what seems like only seconds later.

My phone says half an hour has passed.

I groan quietly and drag myself out of bed. I know that as soon as my feet hit the ground the rush will begin.

I shower and quickly pull on my Adidas sweats. I toss socks, a tee-shirt, a pair of shorts, and a towel into my bag. I double-check for deodorant. Got it. Don't want to be late, because Coach will make us do extra laps.

Damn—I still need a shirt to wear.

Bzzz.

I grab my phone off the dresser. It's Mike.

Hey man. On my way. Picking up breakfast. Order?

I text back a delicious and thoroughly unhealthy choice from Mike's favourite fast food place. I'm hoping it'll get me through the grueling basketball practice that Coach has planned for us.

"Anthony!"

I pull the shirt over my head as I grab my gym bag off the bed. I text one last message to Sheri:

Heading to practice babe. Talk later.

I stuff the phone into my front pocket and go downstairs.

Mom's on me. "Practice starts in twenty minutes." Along with being magic, Mom's also a precise time-keeper. Although I act annoyed, I'm secretly grateful.

"You better get going or you'll be late for practice. Don't need to hear you whining about Coach Davies being hard on you again." She puts my water bottle on the counter.

"Thanks." I toss it in my bag.

"You have enough gas?"

I smile, knowing there's an offer of money coming. It's one of the advantages of being the youngest, the only boy, and the last teenager in the house.

"Mike's driving." I hesitate. "But if you want, you can give me a little extra cash... maybe a ten?"

She laughs and looks over at Dad, who's deep into the newspaper at the breakfast table. "Ben, the boy needs ten dollars."

Dad looks up from his paper, smirking. "I'm a bank now?"

"You know what I like about you, Dad," I nod at the paper, "You always keep it old school."

He hands me a little pocket cash. "Spend it on Sheri. Women like that."

I take it, always grateful for whatever they give.

"What's practice today?"

"Passing and handling."

Mom moves in with a refill for Dad's coffee. "It's good that Davies makes you sweat."

Bzzz—I take my phone out of my pocket. Mike again, right on schedule. He honks the horn outside for good measure.

"When's the next game?"

I love having my parents in the stands. "Friday. Seven. Against Cornwall High."

Dad nods and I know he's listening. Sheri says I'm the same way. It's like they say—apples and trees, chips and blocks.

A longer honk from Mike. He's in no mood to run laps.

Mom kicks the dishwasher door shut with her heel. "Tony, get moving. Ben, quit wasting his time."

Mike and Mom would get along great.

I move to the kitchen and grab my lunch.

"Nice shirt. Teal looks good on you."

I stare at her. "Really? You can't just call it green?"

She shakes her head. "What time will you be home?"

"Supper."

Honk.

"Go."

"Kay. Love you." The door shuts on her reminder to walk the dog when I get home.

At the bottom of the driveway, I toss my bag into the back of Mike's truck, and barely plop myself onto the passenger seat before he's moving. He has the radio station on some Top 40 garbage.

"What the hell are you listening to?" I change the channel to an indie station that plays some pretty sick hip-hop.

Mike just shakes his head and hands me my breakfast.

I unwrap the breakfast sandwich. The bacon is missing.

"Did you mess up the order?"

He keeps his eyes on the road. "No. I ordered it right."

I bite into the sandwich. "Well, where's the bacon?"

"I ate it."

"You took out my sandwich, opened it, ate the bacon, and then rewrapped it and gave it to me?" I really need to hear the logic behind Mike's thinking.

"Yup. Fair trade. You get to listen to hip-hop. I eat your bacon."

I shake my head. The guy's a great power forward but he really thinks in unusual ways.

A few moments later, we pull up to the school and hustle to the gym to get changed for practice. If all goes well, we'll finish by eight, right before first class.

We get our uniforms on, cram our bags in our lockers, and rush to the gym. Yet as we step out onto the court, we move like we're cool and composed, dropping our water bottles by the team bench.

Coach shakes his head. "Nice of you two to join us."

I glance over at the clock. Just in time.

"Well, Coach, we do what we can."

chapter 10

The next hour is a blur. Coach works us hard with drills, plays, and strategy. There are a lot of do-overs, yelling, and whistle blowing on his part. His expectations are high. At the moment, it's hard and I'm exhausted, but I know it's worth it in the long run.

Finally, Coach blows the final whistle and we all nearly collapse.

"All right, team—huddle up."

I walk over to him along with the rest of the players. We're dripping sweat and barely able to breathe. I savour the fact that I don't have to use my legs anymore. I might collapse.

Coach goes over his notes. "Solid effort. James, you need to focus a little more on defense, and Leo, you've really got to stick on your man."

Leo nods. We all start to relax. It looks like Coach is letting us off easy today.

"Good work, boys. Practice is over... after you do your lines."

We groan and drag our asses to the far end of the gym. Coach blows the whistle and I push myself to the first line.

Touch. Run back. Next line. Touch. Run back.

By the time I finish, I'm sure I've lost ten pounds in sweat. I head for the shower and quickly rinse off before first class.

I dress, exit the change room, and head toward my locker where I grab my binder for first period history and my psychology textbook for second. I check my phone.

Still nothing from Sheri. She must really be running late this morning. I send off a quick text:

Have a good day babe. I'll text you at lunch

and slam the locker door shut. I spin the combination lock and put the phone in my pocket. I still have a few minutes before class.

Mike walks up. "Man, that was a tough one today." Sarah, a girl from my English class, goes past, and he pulls himself up a few inches. "Tough but good, right?"

She ignores his obvious stare and continues down the hall. He leans back against the locker, sighing.

I try to change the subject. "Are we training after school?"

"Yeah," he mumbles, still staring in Sarah's direction.

"What about that girl from the movie theatre?"

He looks at me. "Who? Chrissy?"

I nod.

"Oh, you know. Trying to keep my options open."

"You even talk to her?"

Mike nods, but I can tell by his face he isn't even listening to me.

"Stay focused, Mike!" I yell, but it doesn't matter—his groin is already leading him down the hallway toward Sarah. I shake my head. Why does he even bother to carry a backpack? I'd better get to class myself, I realize.

The rest of the morning passes and I don't hear back from Sheri. Deep in my gut, a small, uncomfortable feeling settles in, but I bury it. I don't need to be insecure—I know she wants to be with me. Besides, it's something I'm going to have to get used to once we start college. She's way too driven and busy to have time for a clingy boyfriend.

The bell rings—time for psychology. I slip in and drop down in my assigned seat by the door. The teacher, Ms. Statten, stares at her computer. Her glasses are on top of her head, burrowed in her strawberry blond hair, and her long legs stretch out beside her desk, showing off whichever pair of heels she's decided to wear today. She's not old enough to be a mom but not young either—she's just in the neighbourhood of cougar. It's her second year here, and the entire male student body knows about her ever since Black Panty Friday, when some freshman claimed to have gotten a glimpse up her skirt. Since then all my buddies have had perfect attendance. Not one guy wants to miss a class, just in case.

All that aside, she's interesting because she hardly talks about anything other than school. She's down to business—unlike other teachers who tell us about their weekends, their kids, their spouses, dogs, whatever—but Statten? Nothing. Maybe she has boundaries or it's about respect, but for me, she's a secret—a riddle with really nice legs.

The bell goes and I'm pulled out of my short-lived little fantasy. The data projector is on, her notes are up, and she's ready to go. The first slide up—disorders. I write as Statten speaks: *Antisocial Personality Disorder, Avoidant Personality Disorder, Borderline Personality Disorder, Narcissistic Personality Disorder, Obsessive-Compulsive Personality Disorder,* and finally, *Schizotypal Personality Disorder.*

The subject is engrossing. I stare down at my notes. The chances of being what I would call a sociopath or psychopath are way higher than I would've guessed. In fact, odds are that I've already met one. I look around the classroom, considering all the people I know—friends, family, neighbours. Did any of them have one of these disorders? A thought struck me. Do I?

I shake the notion away when Ms. Statten tells us to read the first ten pages of Chapter 11. The class settles into silence.

Then the intercom pings. "Good morning, Ms. Statten. Is Tony Shepherd there?"

I look up from my textbook, surprised to hear my name. "Yes, he is."

"If it's convenient, could you send him down to the office?"

"I will." Ms. Statten looks at me and nods.

The intercom pings again. "Also, he's not likely to be back before the end of class."

That gets everyone's attention—including mine. A hushed, collective taunt rumbles through the room.

I grab my books and head for the door, not wanting to look back.

Ms. Statten calls after me, "Tony, questions one through eight—"

"For tomorrow. Got it, Ms. Statten."

chapter 11

I go straight to the office and enter. Mrs. Opal, the school secretary, sits at her desk on the phone. She looks up, sees me, and turns away, lowering her voice to a whisper. Constable Blake leans against the edge of the desk, listening to the call. He's jotting notes on a pad of paper. He's the school cop, our resource officer, and I rarely see him at the front desk in the main office.

Mrs. Opal ends the call and turns back to me. She smiles but it feels forced. "Hello, Tony. The principal wants to see you, but it will be a few more minutes."

I nod and stand there, feeling awkward.

She doesn't seem that comfortable herself. She points to a plastic chair against the wall. "Please, take a seat."

I sit. I can't think of anything that would get me called up to the office. This has to be about basketball or something, but no one's giving anything away, and the door to the principal's office is closed. Through the frosted glass I see several people moving inside.

Mrs. Opal and Constable Blake talk, low-voiced, between themselves, but they keep looking over at me and I start to worry. I've never been in serious trouble before, but I sure feel like I've somehow landed in the middle of it now.

"Do you know why I'm here?" I ask finally.

"Just a few more minutes," says Constable Blake. He tries to look relaxed, but he's got his arms crossed stiffly and he looks distinctly uncomfortable.

They probably don't have any more of an idea about why I'm here than I do, but *something* is going on. The worst I can come up with is that a low grade on a test might bench me from a game.

I decide to try and quit worrying and grab my phone. Two more messages from Jessica. She's the kind of girl who gets worked up over nothing. She should text Sheri or—here's a thought—even her boyfriend, and leave me out of it. I skip over her messages and see that Mom called—twice—which is weird. I go straight to my voicemail and listen: *Anthony, please call as soon as you get this message.*

This doesn't help me relax at all, so I keep pushing through my texts. Still nothing from Sheri, so I decide to send her another message:

> **Hope you're having a good day babe.**
> **What's on for lunch?**

This is the usual routine for the two us, since her noon hour break starts twenty minutes before mine. As long as she's not in class, she'll text back quickly.

As I hit send, the door to the principal's office opens and Mrs. Johnson steps out. She's a great principal. She always makes it to our games and knows us all by name when she walks the halls. But she doesn't smile when she sees me. That's when I notice the woman behind her. She's not a teacher but something tells me she isn't a parent either. She wears jeans and a black corduroy jacket and there is something about her posture that makes her look like someone off a show about hard-nosed New York cops.

Mrs. Johnson crosses the room to the secretary and lowers her voice—what's with everyone whispering around here? I hope she's only setting me up for a drive-along with the resource officer for law class, but I know it's doubtful.

Mrs. Johnson tells Mrs. Opal to hold her calls and my mind races. When was the last time I drove? Was I speeding? Did I blow through a light? Maybe it had to do with the last party I was at. Maybe I've been too friendly with the school dope dealer? I try to calm my spinning mind, but part of me feels like I've unknowingly slipped into a mess of trouble.

"Tony, I think we're ready. Can you come into my office please?"

chapter 12

I follow Mrs. Johnson into her office. She takes a seat behind her desk, and Constable Blake and the tough city cop follow us into the room. Constable Blake shuts the door and takes a seat, but the woman remains standing just behind my left shoulder. I want to turn and look at her but stand there feeling really uncomfortable.

"Have a seat, Tony." Mrs. Johnson motions to the chair.

I sit down.

"You know Constable Blake. And this is Detective Gekas."

I twist in my chair to look at them and force a smile.

"Hello, Tony." She puts out her hand and I shake it. She's tall and slender with dark, wavy hair. Although her face seems kind, she looks like she hasn't slept in several days.

"Tony?" Mrs. Johnson addresses me and I have to turn back to face her. "We've called your parents to let them know we'll be talking to you, but for now we have a couple of questions."

Detective Gekas starts. "Do you know why you're here?"

I shake my head. I don't have a clue.

"We understand that you have a girlfriend?"

As soon as I hear the words, my stomach drops. I twist back around to look at her and nod.

"Good. Her name is Sheri?"

"Sheri Beckman."

"And how long have you been dating?"

"A little under a year."

"It's serious?"

I nod. "Yeah, I love her."

Gekas pauses, her back straightening. "Would Sheri say it's serious?"

"I hope so."

Gekas moves around and sits on the edge of the desk across from me.

"When was the last time you spoke to her, Tony?"

I touch the phone where it sits in my front pocket. "Like ten minutes ago."

Detective Gekas, Constable Blake, and Mrs. Johnson look at each other.

"I sent her a text asking what she's having for lunch. I do it every day. It's normal."

Officer Blake leans in. "When was the last time you heard from her?"

I realize I've stopped breathing and inhale into my already full lungs. I haven't heard from her all morning.

I hear myself saying, "It's not weird. We're both busy—" My words are crystal clear in my head. I breathe out. "Um. Yesterday after school. I had practice. She had a run."

I look from Mrs. Johnson to Constable Blake to Detective Gekas.

Then I hear myself say the words that I've been holding back. "Why? Is everything okay?"

Mrs. Johnson's eye twitches and the corner of her mouth curls down. She's about to speak when my phone buzzes against my thigh. I look down and don't ask for permission. I reach in, take it out, and see the name.

"It's my mom."

Mrs. Johnson looks at Detective Gekas, who nods to me.

I answer it.

Mom's voice sounds calm but distant. "Tony, are you okay?"

"I think so."

"Mrs. Johnson called me."

"I'm in with her now."

There's a long pause. "When you need me, just say the word."

"Okay, Mom."

"Everything will be all right. I love you, Anthony."

I don't even say goodbye when I disconnect.

"Tony, we just have a few more questions to ask you."

I look over at the police detetective. A thick, dark feeling in the pit of my stomach slowly oozes to the surface.

"When did you last see her?"

"What's going on?"

"Tony—"

I realize I'm standing.

Gekas raises her hands, trying to usher me back into my seat. "Please stay for a few more minutes."

I look at Gekas and I'm no longer sure about her, but I sit down again.

"When was the last time you saw Sheri?"

"What's happened?"

"Tony, I need you to focus—"

"Night before last. I went over to her house after supper."

"For how long?"

"A couple of hours."

"And what did you do?"

I close my eyes and see Sheri before me. Her lips, her eyes. She's smiling. I look at Gekas and I know she isn't going to give me anything until I answer her questions.

"We hung out." Now it's my turn. "What happened to her?"

"Her parents filed a missing person's report last night when she didn't come home from her run."

My mind starts to spiral, "Have you talked to her friends? There's Katie and Paul and Jessica—"

"Yes, Tony—"

"And there's her ex, Dillon, who's a douchebag. And there's this guy who is always trying to get her drunk at parties—"

"Okay, Tony—"

"And, I could—"

Gekas raises her hands. "Tony!" She takes a breath and leans back. "Thank you. We're exploring all leads."

I glare at her, uncertain if I believe her.

"What I need from you is to help me answer a few more questions."

What I need is to get up and leave this office so that I can go start searching for her.

She leans forward again. "Tony? Okay?"

I agree.

"How was she the night you saw her? Did she seem distressed? Overly worried? Sad? Happy?"

"She was fine. Normal."

"Did she talk about going anywhere? Maybe she has a favourite place?"

"Running. She likes running—have you checked the trails?"

"We've got officers working out there now." She clasps her hands together, coming in close to my face.

"Tony—is there... anything she might have been keeping from her parents?"

I know I'm supposed to fill in the gaps, that she's asking for something underneath the question, but I can't think. Her perfume is too strong and I shrink back, trying to ignore the smell. My last texts to Sheri before she disappeared were duck faces and questions about the weekend. All that she was worried about was how to handle the long-distance relationship when we both went to college. Now, she was missing, running into a distance without end.

"Tony? Were there any secrets she—"

I feel the tears coming and I don't want to deal with any of this now. "No. Nothing. Can I go?"

Gekas sits up and looks away.

I quickly wipe my eyes with my sleeve and try to get myself under control.

She looks at Mrs. Johnson, who rises up from behind her desk. "It's all right, Tony. Thank you. You can go back to class now."

I get up and move toward the door.

Gekas opens it for me. "If you think of anything else, give me a call."

I take the card she hands me and get out of there fast. Yeah, I'm pretty sure I don't like her much at the moment.

chapter 13

On the way to my locker, I do my best to avoid anyone in the hallways. I get my backpack and go out a side door by the stairs. I feel like I'm going to vomit, and as soon as I hit the fresh air, I take a deep breath. I push around the corner and at some point realize that I've slid down the wall, my legs going out from under me, my knees bunched up in my face. I keep breathing deeply, trying not to be sick.

I don't need someone finding me here, freaking out. I've got to get myself up and moving, but I feel a frustration I've never felt before and want to hit something. I don't have time for this, and I stand and rush to the street and break for home.

I don't know where else to go but I know I can't stay behind the walls of this school any longer. I need to put distance between myself and this place. I could probably call Mom, but I need the walk, to surround myself with the noises of the city and drown out the buzzing in my head. I don't want to be asked questions about how I'm feeling, because frankly, I have no clue.

When they called me into that office, they had to be thinking that I might have had something to do with her disappearance. And that detective—Gekas—she was trying to get me to confess. She was hoping I would say something.

It's been almost twenty hours since Sheri and I texted. Man, almost an entire day has passed, and Gekas and her buddies haven't got any further than questioning me about what I know. Talk about a bunch of heads up the collective ass. It also means they have nothing. They have no clue what happened to her—whether she ran away or got taken or—

I push the thought out of my head and start running other scenarios.

Sheri isn't the type to take off. She was happy at home, happy at school. She had plans that required a sensible and stable family life. Also, she was strong. If there was a problem, she would face it head-on and deal with it.

Yet, Gekas kept asking me whether there was something going on or if she seemed in distress—

Still, she would have talked to me if something was bothering her. We were good together. She would have said something. I'm sure of it.

I want to clear the possibility of her running away off the table, but I don't have the energy to face the alternatives. She said she was hitting the trails and then helping Brody with his homework, but before all that she was at school. If I want to figure out where she's gone, I have to start there.

I go through the alley and open the gate into my yard. If Mom or Dad is home, they'll be waiting for me. I need to get in and out of the house with the least amount of confrontation, so I open the back door quietly and wait a moment before going in. Someone is moving around on the second floor and I sneak across the kitchen to the bowl of car keys. Whoever is in the house is coming down the stairs. I grab the set for Dad's car without asking. I'm pretty sure I hear my name before I shut the door, but I don't turn around. Quick as I can, I jump in the car, and pull away.

I don't look back in the rearview mirror.

chapter 14

Traffic is relatively quiet as I drive across the city to Sheri's school. I realize I've missed lunch entirely, what with the trip to the office and the walk home. I still have ten bucks from Dad in my pocket, but really, anything I try to eat isn't going to sit well in my stomach. Besides, if I have to sit in a line-up for a craptastic burger and salty fries, I might want to punch a plastic clown, and I just can't have that. I focus on the problem, forcing myself forward to find a solution and let nothing else in. It's all I can do right now.

Sheri's school is on the southeast end of the city, and as soon as I cross the freeway, I hit the soulless suburbs and the big box stores. Cookie cutter mini-mansions for the wannabe wealthy appear. The streets wind and twist around corners and cul-de-sacs and along the high walls that separate the neighbourhoods from the rest of the world. Sometimes I wonder if these man-made boundaries are meant to keep the riff-raff out or keep the inhabitants in—like an asylum.

The trees disappear and the road opens wide. It intersects the highway, and as I drive across, I see the paved asphalt stretch out of the city, slicing through the open prairie. If I needed to, I could turn right now and make a run for the border. I'd be there in only a couple of hours—if I needed to—if I were guilty—which I'm not.

I keep driving until I pull up to Sheri's school, Guthrie High. I hurry down the walkway to the double doors at the front of the school.

By now, it's fourth period; almost half an hour before the bell rings. If I'm careful enough, I should be able to get to Sheri's locker without anyone noticing. I grab the door handle and—dammit—it's locked. I pause for a moment and consider other options before moving along the building to find another entrance.

"They're all locked."

I look over. A guy about my age with shaggy blond hair kneels in the bushes, digging in the soil.

"What?"

He doesn't really acknowledge me, just keeps working the dirt with his hands. "All the doors are locked," he pauses, looking at the ground. "You'd think it's to keep out the troublemakers—" he looks over at me, "like you and me. But the wardens of this prison actually expect it to be protection for the students who give a shit."

I am pretty sure he must have just escaped from a psych ward. He rises, dusting off his jeans. He crosses over to the sidewalk that skirts the school and stops, looking back at me.

"You following me or what?"

"Uh, no."

"You don't want in?"

I size him up. He's shorter than me but he's built stocky and solid and likely enjoys getting into the occasional fight. I should be able to get away from him if he decides to take a swing—but if I get too close, I'm sure I'd be down for the count.

"You know how?"

"You think I just hang out, digging in the bushes of any old school?" He stares at me like I'm the idiot.

Since I'm considering following him, maybe I am.

"Yeah, what was that all about?"

He sighs, looking up at the sky, squinting in the sun.

"You coming or not?"

I walk toward him. He turns and heads for the corner of the school.

"Why were you digging?"

He doesn't answer, so I jog to catch up to him. He glances over his shoulder at me and goes around the corner. I stay close to him.

This side of the school is shaded and it's cool and windy.

"There's a side door used by the mechanics class so the grease monkeys can drive their cars into the workshop."

"Isn't it sort of dangerous to show strangers how to get in?"

"You know why they lock the doors?"

"Listen, I've had a real long day—"

He ignores me and goes on, "It's because our keepers expect students to want to be here. They think that when we're late and we can't get in, we'll seek redemption to ease our suffering. The sad thing is that most of us buy into that crap."

He walks up to the big shop entrance and peers through the window. "All clear." He moves to the regular-sized door beside it and tries the doorknob. It's locked, but he barely pauses before reaching into his pocket and pulling out a ring of keys. He thumbs through them and picks one. He slides it into the lock and opens the door.

He looks at me. "Anyway, I haven't seen you before. And no one goes into a school unless they're looking for answers or they've got a personal score to settle."

I think about all the students that must go to this school—hell, that go to *my* school. "How would you know? How could you possibly recognize everyone?"

He just smiles, and I know this guy's definitely got a few screws loose.

"Hope you figure out what happened to Sheri."

Before I can say anything, he shuts the door behind me and is gone.

chapter 15

Who the hell was that guy? And how the hell does he know who *I* am?

I shake away the thought—I don't have time—and cross the shop floor. Students are visible through the open door of the adjoining classroom. The day's events have knocked me so out of sync with the rest of the world that I've forgotten school is still on. The teacher is talking about the differences between two-stroke and four-stroke engines. I move past the door quickly and no one notices.

I've been to this school a couple of times to meet Sheri or for a game, but never in this area. The odours of oil, gas, and exhaust drift out into the hall, and although the walls are painted white, everything feels greasy. The smell of machinery blends into wood shavings and dust, and the high-pitched sound of a table saw tearing through boards screams somewhere nearby. The corridor tees off and I go toward a set of double doors that I hope leads to the main hall.

I come out a long passageway with lockers and classrooms on both sides. There's a set of stairs partway down and I head toward them. Sheri's locker is on the second floor, near the main staircase by the office. I'm hoping Detective Gekas hasn't found her way over here yet. I know that she will—but if I have enough time, and because I know Sheri, I think I might find something that Gekas won't.

I'm not quite halfway down the hall when a teacher steps out of his classroom. I move into the recess around a water fountain between the lockers and hope he doesn't see me. When I look up again, he's down at the far end of the hall, and I make for the stairs. As I duck through the door, he leaves the hallway, and now I can see where he's going: the open foyer by the front entrance where a huddle of adults stands in a circle.

I climb the stairs to the second floor and turn right.

The halls are empty. Sheri's locker is between the bio and chem labs, and I walk up to it, staring at the black "223" stenciled onto the small brass plate. Two sticky notes, *Come back Sheri* and *We <3 u*, hang on the outside of her locker. They're signed in colourful, glitter gel pens by a dozen or so names.

I feel a surge of frustration. These notes piss me off—it's probably some drama-seeking ninth grader who pounces on any opportunity to draw attention to themselves who put them up. I think about crumpling up the notes and throwing them on the ground but I don't. Gotta stay focused. I take the combination lock into my hand and realize I'm shaking.

Nineteen right, thirty-seven left, thirty-one right. I pull on the lock gently, not wanting to make a lot of noise, and it pops open. I glance left and right—still no one. I've only been here a moment, but it feels much longer. I open the locker and the faint smell of Sheri fills my head—*pang*—and my gut lurches. I close my eyes and breathe in. Enough. I have work to do. There's got to be something here that'll tell me where Sheri went.

On the top shelf there are only two textbooks and a novel. I reach up and feel toward the back, but there's nothing else. Of the three hooks below the shelf, the one where she'd usually put her jacket is empty, another has one of my old hoodies on it—*pang*—and the third holds a gym shirt and a small canvas bag. I quickly dig into its centre pocket and pull out some lip gloss, a hair brush, deodorant, and a small cosmetics bag. Inside are tampons and a bunch of hair elastics, like the ones she leaves everywhere that I end up putting in the glove box or my pocket or wherever, just in case she needs one. I put everything back where it was. I take her tee-shirt down, rub it between my fingers, and think.

What am I looking for? Is there something not right about her locker? Is anything out of place? If she was in trouble, she'd text me, wouldn't she?

I look down at the cross trainers snuggled in a nest of colourful, mismatched socks on the locker floor. Gym shoes. She has another pair she wears for outdoor training. I shift to the inside of her locker door and its magnetic notepad. Attached to it is the small map of routes she takes with her when she runs, with distances written in marker on each loop. A calendar hangs under the map. Each day is marked with times and distances and the type of run she plans to do:

THURS.
Race Strategy:
East Trails—6 miles

A photo of us, held by a heart-shaped magnet in each corner, overlaps the bottom of the map. She's laughing directly into the camera. I have my arm around her and I'm looking down at her with the biggest smile. I remember that moment. We were at the lake—we'd spent the day swimming and that evening, I'd asked her out officially.

pang—pang—pang

It's a wave I can't control. I close the locker and snap the lock shut. I rush to the nearest bathroom and straight into the stall, locking it. I lean my head against the door, eyes and fists squeezed tight. I'm breathing hard, chest pounding. I'm still holding Sheri's tee-shirt. I try my hardest to keep quiet, inhaling and exhaling, trying to find my composure.

I want to believe she's okay, but I can't explain why I haven't heard from her.

When my heart settles a bit, I take out my phone. Several missed texts and messages from my parents. One from Mike. I don't have time for them. I scroll to Sheri's name and see the long column of texts from me—and none from her. I type one more:

Babe, text me back. I'm worried. Where R U?

Send.

chapter 16

I want to punch something. The clock is ticking. The bell will go soon and I need to get back to Sheri's locker. I suck up my courage and stuff her tee-shirt into the pouch of my hoodie. I take a breath and step out of the stall, checking myself in the mirror before I leave the bathroom—and immediately slam on the brakes.

Two uniformed officers stand behind a maintenance person with bolt cutters beside Sheri's locker at the end of the hall. They break the lock and start photographing, removing, and cataloguing every item before ziplocking all of it away.

Dammit, Gekas, you got here too soon.

Before they see me, I duck downstairs and leg it to the closest back door. The last thing I need is to be found lurking around my missing girlfriend's school. No point in further confirming my prime suspect status.

In the car, I toss my phone on the seat beside me and glance at it frequently as I drive, praying that Sheri will get in touch before I get home.

Dad's at the window when I pull into the driveway. I haul my ass out of the car, ready for whatever he and Mom have to say. I don't expect it'll be fun—I spent the morning talking with a cop about my missing girlfriend and they likely know by now that I ditched school. On top of that, I took the car without permission and didn't return a single text. This isn't going to be good.

I walk in the front door and kick off my shoes. Dad comes around the corner and waves me into the kitchen. I don't argue. Mom's there but she's drinking tea at the counter. Dad takes a seat and fills a cup for me. I don't think I have a choice. I take a seat on a stool at the island but don't look up right away; all my attention is on the hot steam rising out of the cup, weaving tiny swirls in the air.

Until Mom's voice pulls me back.

"Anthony."

I look up at her.

"We love you."

I keep staring, waiting.

"Where did you go this afternoon? After the principal and the detective talked to you?"

I hold a long silence, or at least it feels that way.

"I went for a drive."

"Son..." Dad's voice is so gentle, it's like he's trying not to shake loose the reality that hangs above us like broken glass. I close my eyes, taking a deep breath as he continues, "It's fine that you took the car, but we wanted to make sure you were okay."

Mom leans on the counter across from me—she's not a very big woman but right now her presence looms. "We're asking because we want to help you. To keep you safe. To know there are no surprises."

I open my eyes, exhaling. "I went... to Sheri's school." I swallow. I really don't want either of them to get angry. "I wanted to see if there was anything in her locker that could help me understand why I haven't heard from her since her run. It just doesn't make sense."

My chin quivers and I look up at the ceiling, holding onto the tears. "I have this really bad feeling in my gut. I'm trying not to listen to it. I'm trying to believe that everything will be okay, that she'll turn up in some hospital with amnesia or something—"

Dad cuts me off. "You went to her school?"

I nod.

"Did you find anything?"

I shake my head and add, "Not before the police showed up."

"Did they see you?"

I know I shouldn't be angry but I am. "No! No one saw me. But what does it matter? What if someone *did* see me? Don't I have the right to find out what happened to her?"

I can see the strained look on Mom's face as she fills another cup of tea for herself. It reminds me to drink my own, and I wish for a split second that it was something alcoholic instead. I take a big gulp.

Dad thumbs the edge of his cup as he speaks. "We ask because you are our priority, Anthony. We want Sheri found, but we also want you to be safe and okay. This is hard on us, but we also know that it's a thousand times harder on you."

I nod slowly.

"So if we ask something that doesn't sit well with you, please try to understand why we're asking." Dad has an innate ability to settle me down. "So, let's figure some things out together."

In this moment, I know that I'm safe—and that I still feel like a kid in a lot of ways.

"You went to Sheri's school to look in her locker?" Dad asks.

"Yeah. To see if there was some clue to figure out where she went."

Mom pipes up, "You know her combination?"

"Of course, Mom." I roll my eyes a bit and as soon as I do I feel like an asshole.

"Did you find anything?"

"No. I wish I had but there's nothing. There's never anything unusual or different with Sheri, ever."

Dad leans back, looking up at the corner of the room as he thinks things through while Mom listens intently.

"Then, I went to the bathroom for a minute."

Dad gives me a look, and I can only shake my head and keep trying to explain myself.

"On the way back, I saw the cops, so I left." I push my empty teacup to the centre of the counter and Mom takes it.

"Good choice." She pours another cup to let me know we aren't done talking, which is fine by me. I could use my parents right now.

Dad asks when I saw Sheri last and what she was planning to do the night she went missing. I get it. They want information, and I try to answer them as fully as I can.

"We're going to call our lawyer to be safe. We know you didn't do anything wrong.

I'm relieved—they sound ready to fight for me.

"When her parents called last night after you fell asleep, we didn't think much of it. We suggested they try a couple of her friends."

"They called? Why didn't you wake me?" I'm stunned—I feel like a stack of wooden blocks is threatening to topple over inside me. Every minute counts and the minutes we had last night were lost.

Mom answers, her shoulder lifting slightly, "It seemed normal. They've called looking for her here before. It was probably before they even called the cops."

Dad leans forward. "People get mean, especially when they're scared and looking for reasons or explanations. You're going to be a target... you were Sheri's boyfriend—"

My emotions teeter and tip and crash down.

"Were?" I slam my hand on the counter and both my parents jump.

Dad rises. "Anthony, I'm sorry, that came out wrong—"

"I'm done." I push my teacup away and it spills. I go upstairs to my bedroom and shut the door with force. I toss myself on the bed and stare at the ceiling. I feel bad for yelling. I feel bad for spilling the tea. I know I should go back and clean it up, but right now, I don't care.

I stare at my phone. I want to pick it up, to look, to hope. It seems like it's been silent all day.

A few minutes later, I hear my parents come up the stairs and stand outside my door. I roll over and face the wall.

Dad knocks. "Son?"

Mom follows his lead. "We love you."

I close my eyes and wait for morning to come.

chapter 17

I wake Friday morning and don't even want to get out of bed. Although it's a game day, I couldn't really care less. Coach is tough, but I'm not sure he'll even want me there. I don't move. I just stare at the soft light on the ceiling.

The landline downstairs rings a few times then goes silent. I close my eyes even though the idea of sleep seems something that was lost with Sheri.

"Anthony. Phone!"

I'm guessing Coach has realized I'm not there. He might have to get used to it. I drag myself out of bed.

Mom stands in the kitchen clutching the phone in her hand. I go to reach for it and she pulls it back. I give her a look and realize she's upset.

"It's Sheri's mom."

My hand falls to my side. "I don't want to." It's a whisper.

"You can. You will." She hands me the phone.

I run through the decision in my mind—if I walk out of the room right now, I'll only make it upstairs before Mom and Dad are on me, telling me how deeply disappointed they are. But I know the moment I put the receiver to my ear, I'll hear the pain in Sheri's mom's voice, and I don't know if I can handle it.

I take the phone from Mom and suck in a lungful of air, maybe a little too loudly.

"Anthony?"

She sounds likes she's calling from Mars—isolated, far away—just like Sheri.

"Hello, Mrs. Beckman."

She gulps and takes a rattly breath. "I hope the police weren't too hard on you?" It feels like she's searching.

"I'm okay," I don't want to say it, but feel I must, "How are you?"

It takes her a moment to get it out, "We're just so worried..."

I imagine Mr. Beckman standing beside her, holding her close.

"The police will find her." I can hear the disbelief in my voice and hope she doesn't pick up on it.

"That's why I wanted to call."

Is she going to ask me details about my meeting with Gekas, or worse, tell me that someone saw me around Sheri's school? I didn't plan to make people doubt my innocence or make this any more complicated than it already is.

"The police say they've finished searching the running path and are going to explore other leads." She pauses, then, "They don't seem to think it's significant that her car was found at the head of the trail..." Her voice breaks, "we can't keep waiting... I can't wait for the phone to ring and—"

The phone drops with a clunk onto a distant counter and a low moan rises and cuts into my heart. There's a rustle and another clunk and the sound of a muffled receiver before Mr. Beckman comes on the line.

"Anthony? Sorry about that. Sheri's mother— It's hard, you know? We wanted to know—we've got some people together to walk the trails. See if we can find anything the police might have missed." For such a big guy, such a doer of things, it's hard to listen to the hesitation in his voice. "Would you be able to come out with us? To help us search?"

"Absolutely."

Anything is better than hanging around here, waiting for bad news to kick you in the ass while you're down.

chapter 18

An hour later, Mom, Dad, Heather, and I pull up to the crowd of people who have gathered to comb the area. The Beckmans stand beside a pickup handing out sunscreen, insect repellent, and water. Beside them on the tailgate are a couple of boxes of coffee and doughnuts. How they organized all this is beyond me. Sheri's parents see us and they give me huge hugs, thanking me for coming. The Beckmans, who sounded broken on the phone earlier, seem rejuvenated by this fight against fate.

Sheri's brother Brody hands us wire flags that we're supposed to use in case we find something that might be of interest to the police and send us across the path to the far side of the creek that stretches out into the prairie surrounding the city. The plan is to move east, away from the golf course, walking toward the first grid road outside of the city. Mrs. Beckman hands me a walkie-talkie, and it's clear she hopes we'll find something and need to report back.

We get in the car and travel back to Fleet Street, pulling to the side of the road after we cross the bridge. There are more people at this position, all waiting to begin. Yet, there seems to be no real order or plan, so Dad steps in to organize. He fans the crowd out into a straight line, asking us to separate ourselves by an arm's length. Once we are in place, Dad has me radio the Beckmans to be sure that no one else is coming.

We move at a slow, equal pace, sifting the deep grass. As the banks of the stream twist and turn, so do we. Sometimes we wrap around each other like a serpent's tail, stumbling into each other's lanes and, although it's frustrating, the mantra we start to spout is that twice the eyes on every patch of ground are better than none.

By noon, the clouds have passed over and a wind pushes in from the fields, bringing bits of straw and dust that gets into our eyes. When someone needs a rest or twists their foot stepping into a prairie dog hole, word comes down the line to halt and I radio the main staging area for a replacement. Food is brought out to us in the early afternoon, and we walk and eat, our eyes and free hands ferreting the land. There isn't much chatter on the walkie-talkies, so we don't know how it's going on the other side of the creek, but we know they're farther back because we hear the occasional indiscernible shout. It's late afternoon and everyone is exhausted. By the time we reach the grid divide, the foreboding notion that sticks like a nail in our guts is that we've come up empty.

We move along the gravel road back toward the gathering spot. The other group comes into view as we walk and we can see it on their faces—nothing. It's been an all-day thrashing of uneasiness and frustration, and when we reach the Beckmans, they no longer look like they have power over destiny. Actually, they seem to have resigned themselves to the worst.

"Anything?" Dad asks.

"We got a few flags we'll report to Detective Gekas, but..." Sheri's dad pauses for a long time. "We hoped... Even for the most dreadful... Just so this..." He sighs, holding a hand to his chest, "...could start to heal."

That's when Mrs. Beckman looks at me. "Anthony, if you knew where she was, you'd tell us, right? Right? You wouldn't lie to us, would you?"

She comes at me.

"Tell me what happened to my baby girl. *Tell* me! Tell me where she is."

People from the search party stare and Mr. Beckman puts an arm around her, pulling his wife and son back toward their truck before ushering her into the passenger seat and closing the door.

Her screaming and crying is audible outside.

Mr. Beckman doesn't look at my family or me and moves around to the other side. "She hasn't slept much the last two nights. Neither of us have."

I feel Dad's arm around my shoulder and he's pushing me toward our own vehicle as I watch Mr. Beckman slam the driver's side door shut.

"They need some time. There's nothing else we can do. Let's go home."

chapter 19

At night, I don't feel like sleeping but close my eyes anyway. Every time I start to drift off, I find myself standing in endless fields of grain. I sink into the long, yellow stalks; I can't rise above them. The grid road is in the distance and I try to wade toward it, but the wheat wraps around my feet and it's a struggle. I trip and fall into thick, black soil where worms and spiders creep. They crawl up my arms into my mouth and eyes. They choke me and blind me and I wake in a sweat.

I push the covers away and have to wait in the dark before my heart slows enough so I can move. I go to the bathroom and wash my face and neck with a washcloth.

When I see myself in the mirror, I know it's going to be a long night.

chapter 20

On Saturday, I wake up exhausted. I must really look like hell because when I head downstairs Dad sees me and says, "We're not going back out today."

I wave it off but he doesn't break. "We won't help. We'll only... get in the way."

I start to understand what he's telling me. Either he and Mom talked last night and decided that the best thing for me was to stay away—or the Beckmans called and suggested I shouldn't come back.

Either way, I don't like it.

"But I can help. The more eyes out there—"

"I know—the better. I get it. But we need to let things cool down."

"But I didn't *do* anything."

Dad comes over to me, placing his hand on my shoulder. "The Beckmans are trying to comprehend that their daughter is missing. The world they know isn't solid anymore and they need to concentrate on what's ahead, especially over these next few days. I appreciate that you want to do what you can, but right now, that means giving Sheri's parents time to handle the situation in their own way."

I hear what he's saying. I don't like it, but I get it.

"So what do I do then?"

"Well, first of all, you can do all the chores you've been skipping out on."

Chores are the last thing I want to do, but he gives me a look that tells me it's not an option. I head upstairs and get into sweatpants and grab an old University of Toronto tee-shirt of Dad's to wear. For the next four hours, Dad has me taking out garbage, raking leaves, cleaning the downstairs bathroom, cleaning my room, and sweeping out the garage. During all of it, my mind rolls over thoughts of Sheri, of my texts, of my meeting with Gekas and the principal, and of Mrs. Beckman yelling at me after I spent all day searching for the girl we both care about. When Mom calls me in for a bite of lunch, I am surprised how quickly half the day has gone.

I eat a chicken sandwich in the kitchen and check my phone. Mike texted:

We missed you yesterday buddy.

Down below are the results from yesterday's game. We lost.

I stare at the scores; I should care, but I don't. I'm too numb to feel much of anything. The numbers are just strange squiggles and twists divided by a thin line. On one side is a winning team and on the other is a loser. All that divides them are a few points. I push the phone aside.

"You okay?" Mom asks.

"Yeah..."

But she knows I'm not.

"I was just thinking..." I murmur. "What could be buried in a flower bed in front of a school?"

Mom scrutinizes me and I'm sure she wants me to talk to someone, one of her "professional" friends. And maybe—probably—it would do me some good. But now I'm thinking I might want to talk to another kind of professional—someone whose methods are a little more unorthodox.

Mom takes over for Dad in the afternoon, and I spend most of my time helping her organize the storage room in the basement. I take out three more big bags of garbage and take a trip to the recycling depot. Mom tells me I can keep the $16.85 that I get for returning the bottles—and that's when I know she must really be worried about me.

By the end of the day, I'm exhausted. My head hits the pillow and I surrender to sleep. Nightmares of barren prairie and scrambling creatures and dark, rotting earth don't invade my deep slumber.

chapter 21

When I wake the next day, Sunday, it's raining and I don't even try getting out of bed. I pull the pillow over my head and turn to face the wall. Mom, Dad, even Heather, all come into the room to check on me and I lie still with my eyes closed until they leave. By lunchtime, I decide it's time to face the world, so I drag myself out of bed and head downstairs. Everyone has left and the house is quiet.

Ollie runs over. He's attentive and happy and I open the cupboard and find his dog treats. He sits, tail wagging.

"Shake a paw."

Ollie puts his paw in my hand. I give him a treat.

"Good boy." I rub the top of his head as he swallows it whole. "Geez, chew it, would you?"

This time I get him up on his hind legs. I toss his next treat and he catches it in mid-air. I pat him again.

I grab a glass of orange juice and sit in the living room. I turn on the radio and some crap song is on, but it's good enough. I don't care—I just need some noise. My phone is on the counter and I send a text:

Hey mom where r u?

I drink my juice and my stomach gurgles in reply. I've barely eaten since Thursday.

The phone chimes. Mom? No. It's a Facebook notification. I click and it opens to a page: FIND SHERI BECKMAN. I don't know who started it, but it already has 400 followers. I feel sick and don't know what to do. If I join, all the drama will piss me off, but if I don't, it'll looks bad. I decide to join.

My phone chimes again—Mom.

We're out. Be home soon. Hungry?

I'm relieved.

Burger and fries?

Slim chance they'll get me junk.

Okay.

Whoa—not even an argument.

My phone buzzes again—a notification on the Facebook page: *we miss and love you sheri.* I put it down. Pretty soon, though, it's humming with every post and comment, and I already regret my decision. I can't leave the group without looking suspicious, so I turn off the sound and ignore it.

The dog looks up at me.

"I know, Ollie. It's annoying, isn't it?"

He gives a little whine.

It's been four days since she went missing and we've gotten nowhere. The police don't have anything and our search didn't turn up any clues. If they'd found something today, we would have heard. I don't get it. Sheri had no enemies and this place always felt safe—until now.

I hear a car in the driveway, and Mom walks in with groceries and fast food.

"What time did you get up?" She puts the food on the counter and sets a grease-soaked bag in front of me.

"Twenty minutes ago. Where are Dad and Heather?"

She ignores the question and starts pulling vegetables out of the grocery bag. "You must be starving."

"There's a Facebook page for Sheri, Mom."

She pauses as she pulls out a container of strawberries. "Did you join it?"

"I wasn't sure if I should, but I decided to in the end."

She nods, and I know she's weighing the pros and cons. She goes back to the groceries to hide this contemplation.

I dig into my very unhealthy breakfast and unwrap the burger, spilling fries onto the paper. I can't wait to sink my teeth in.

Extra bacon spills out the sides of the bun. She really went all out.

"Where's Dad and Heather?"

Mom's face tells me everything.

"Did you guys go back? Were you helping them search? Why didn't you wake me? What's wrong with you? I should've been there! I should've been there more than you or Dad or *anyone!* I loved—dammit!—I *love* her. I love her."

The tears come again and Mom comes around the island to hug me and I fall into her shoulder and she shushes me like when I was little.

I can't stop crying.

My head hurts, my muscles ache, and I'm so full of pain now that it won't stop spilling over.

chapter 22

It's Monday morning and I should be at school, but I'm not. I'm driving and even though I haven't put any thought into where I'm going, I know.

I park a block away from Sheri's school and get out and walk. I want to keep a low profile. The longer the search for her stretches out, the more people are going to start looking for someone to blame, and I'm quite certain that I'll be at the top of their list.

I head toward the student parking lot, hoping to stay unnoticed. Although I've played basketball here a few times and picked Sheri up after class occasionally, almost no one should recognize my face. I cut between the few cars parked in front of the student entrance and walk across the grass.

I'm sure security is tighter now, but it's early enough that the buses haven't dropped off their loads of students and it's nowhere close to the five-minute bell. It should be just me and a few teachers. If I steer clear of the office, I should be fine. My feet brush the dew on the grass along the backside of the school, and when I turn the corner toward the me-chanic shop, I'm hoping my gamble will pay off.

It does.

The guy with the shaggy blond hair stands by the roll-up door. He's beside another kid who wears a hoodie, and I see him handing over an empty baggie. They look at me and freeze. I feel like I just busted them. I slow to a halt.

The dirt-digger lifts his chin at me. "You're back."

I say nothing.

"No luck last time?"

I shake my head.

He reaches into his jacket and offers me a cigarette.

I shake my head.

"Suit yourself." He nods to the kid in the hoodie. "This is Robbie."

I nod and say, "I'm—"

"We know who you are, All Star. Everybody in this school knows who you are."

Shit. I never should've come.

"It's cool. I get it. I'd be here too if I were in your shoes."

I watch Robbie slowly pull a glass pipe out of his pocket. A thin crust of black residue coats the bottom of the bowl and he slides it into the plastic bag. He squeezes out all the air, rolls it up, and pulls the zip-top shut. He stares up at me.

"Problem?"

I feel tall next to the two of them. "Nope," I shrug, as non-chalantly as I can.

Robbie glares then turns to Dirt-Digger. "I've done my part. Now I need your help."

Dirt-Digger nods and I realize I still don't know his name.

"I got messed up this weekend," the druggie says, "and, well, I lost the car—the one my parents let us drive." He fishes a rolled cigarette out of his other pocket and turns to Dirt-Digger. "You got a light?"

Dirt-Digger pulls out a well-used Zippo from his jacket and hands it over. Robbie lights up. After a long inhale, he blows it in our direction. He's definitely not smoking a regular cigarette, and I definitely wouldn't normally hang out with this sort of crowd.

"So, did you crash it?"

"I don't think so, but that's not my problem. I can't remember where I left it."

Dirt-Digger watches Robbie, waiting for more information.

"I remember waking up in my bed. The car is missing. Everyone is pissed at me. Can you help me out?" He takes another drag.

Dirt-Digger shakes his head. "You smell like a Pink Floyd fan bus. Seriously. Stand downwind, man."

Robbie shrugs.

"What's the year and model?"

"2001 blue Civic."

"Any other distinguishing details?"

"I broke the driver's side taillight?"

Dirt-Digger nods but I can't help but laugh. "You sure it's worth it?" I realize immediately that I've crossed a line.

Robbie turns on me. "Go to hell."

"I'll see what I can do about your ride, but until then, get rid of the skunkified hoodie. You wear it to class and you'll be busted for sure. It's like you need a damn babysitter. Or maybe you want to get kicked out of this school too?"

Robbie just smiles.

The warning bell rings. Five minutes to class.

Dirt-Digger looks over at me. "Hear that? I think it's time for us to go."

"Where?"

Dirt-Digger gives me a look of annoyance but doesn't answer the question. "Follow me," is what he says.

And with reluctance, I do.

chapter 23

We leave Robbie at the door. He doesn't seem smart enough to clue into Dirt-Digger's good advice, and I feel sorry his family has such a dumb kid.

We move along the side of the school to another section of windowless wall at the back. Dirt-Digger pulls out his set of keys, selects one, and unlocks a door. We walk along a tight, dark corridor with pipes running overhead, pausing at a corner.

"The caretakers lock themselves in for coffee for about fifteen minutes every morning. They wait for the herds to flock to class before they come out and start their routine. If you don't want to be seen, this is the best way in now. You don't want to be seen, right?"

"Yeah, that's right."

We go around the corner. Sure enough, there's a door with MAINTENANCE on it, the faint smell of coffee mixed with garbage, and the sick, sweet odour of recycling bins.

We walk quietly past.

The door to the main hall is propped slightly ajar with a wooden doorstop.

"That's the only entrance without a camera. The head janitor, Mr. Hill, sits at the surveillance monitors every free minute."

I look at him. "Who *are* you?"

Dirt-Digger ignores me and pushes the door open without a sound. "Hill's so busy staring at screens that he doesn't see who's staring back. Sick bastard. I'm not sure if he's looking for trouble or if it'll find him."

When we're both in the hall, he taps the wooden doorstop away with the toe of his shoe. The door latches behind us.

"You've been to her locker?"

I nod. "I was thinking of checking her gym locker."

Dirt-Digger shakes his head. "What for? Just another dead-end the cops have likely covered."

"What else am I supposed to do?"

"If you don't know what you're doing here, why'd you come?"

I stare at him, lost.

He sighs, then points. "Second door on the left is the gym. Ms. Francis has prep in the morning. There's a room with a washer and dryer just beside the girls' change room if you need to duck out. No one goes in there. Consider yourself helped." He walks away.

I look down the hall at the double doors to the gym then back to him. "Wait."

He ignores me.

"Dude?" I don't want to shout, but he doesn't stop.

I chase after him and grab his shoulder. "Come on, man."

He turns and I think he might swing a punch.

"Listen, All Star, I'm gonna be late for class."

This guy doesn't care about class. He's here for something else.

"Where's your binder?"

I stand in front of him and he looks up at me, but I know he's not the least bit intimidated.

"I can't do this alone. I need your help. You've stepped up twice and you didn't have to."

"I don't need any trouble, All Star, and I sure as hell don't need any attention. You're headed for both. You go down this path, your mommy and daddy will get you a really expensive lawyer and bail your ass out. My mom might—just might—come see me once a month in juvie."

He turns and walks away again.

"I want to find Sheri." My words are quiet but intense. "Don't you?"

He stops.

I'm angry but I don't have any fight left. Sheri is missing. The thought that I'll most likely never see her again hits me, and I know I'm about to cry. I choke it all back as I say, "She meant something to you, too, didn't she?"

He stands there, back turned, unmoving. Suddenly, he turns and walks right up to my face.

"Here's the deal, All Star. First, stop with the bitch tears. Second, if anything happens, I don't know you." He looks up and down the hallway, then moves away quickly.

I have to sprint to catch up.

"And third, it's not *dude* or *man*." He looks over at me, shaking his head and offering his hand.

"It's Charlie. Charlie Wolfe."

part 2

chapter 24

He wakes in a sweat.

He's been sleeping well and dreaming deep and last night was almost no exception. The dream was the same one he'd been having for the past few nights. He walks in fields of yellow with blue skies above and the bright sun against his face. A warm wind blows, shaking the long stalks of grain. None of the nagging, twisting, wanting thoughts that have gripped him over the past few months have disturbed his rest. Almost none, except—

Over the past few days, the news has been covering the missing girl. At first, he tried not to notice the television, to feign disinterest, but he noticed that others had become invested in what the reporter called "a tragedy," so he began to pay attention, to slip amongst the sheep, and follow the script. The time spent has earned results—the lead detective, Gekas, is struggling with the problem he left her, leading the others further away from him and the answers she's seeking. He watches with particular interest as the parents gather friends and family to search the running trails. He's certain that he's taken the proper precautions but he needs to be sure. The police won't reveal what they know and the reporters are too stupid to pick up on the important details that lie in front of them, but he watches nonetheless, scanning the background of every shot.

What wasn't on the news, what was repeated again and again in the many rumours spoken in hushed tones in school hallways, was that the most serious suspect was the girl's boyfriend. His alibi seemed tight, but it didn't stop people from trying to bend reality to fit their own preconceived prejudices. He was the scapegoat, the sacrifice to appease the angry gods, the answer to the question: "Who did it?"

He knew that if he waited long enough, people would make the boyfriend pay. He knew no one suspected him.

Except—last night's dream. He had walked in the fields and felt the sun and the wind and he was alone. Then he opened his eyes and it was night and the moon was high and still he felt safe. Until, somewhere in the distance, somewhere across the plain, prowling beneath the surface of the fields, an animal howled.

And he knew he needed to hurt someone again.

chapter 25

I follow Charlie Wolfe through the school into the library and watch as he takes a red binder from a pile off the counter. We move through the stacks and he quickly grabs a couple of books off the shelves. We go to a table at the back. All his actions seem arbitrary.

I can't stand it anymore. "What are we doing here?"

He points at a chair. "Reconnaissance. Now, sit."

I take a seat, my back to the entrance of the library, and he sits across from me.

"Open them." I look at him, and he nods at the binder. "Open."

I flip the front cover and find neat, colourfully penned notes on Shakespeare. All the i's have perfect circles over them. I'm definitely thinking it's a girl's writing.

"The textbooks too."

I stare at him.

"For an all star, you are really slow on the uptake."

It takes me a moment, but I finally get that I'm supposed to look like I belong here. I shrug and comply.

Charlie looks over my shoulder, studying the space. "The librarian teaches English this period. The assistant doesn't get here until 9:00." He leans and looks past me to the front desk. "We're good. Give me your phone?"

"Why?"

"Just give me your damn phone!"

"Why, don't you have one?"

Charlie looks directly at me. "Give. Me. Your. Phone."

"All right." I take it out of my pocket, unlock it, and put it on the table.

Charlie takes it, scrolling through my messages.

I'm staring at him when he looks up.

"What? Do your homework. I'll be right back." He tosses my phone back at me as he leaves.

I stare at the wall and twist around, but Charlie is gone. I look down at the books he's grabbed from the library stacks: a collection of Edgar Allan Poe stories, a book about building the national railroad, and an atlas. I push them aside and flip through a few pages of my brand-new red binder to discover it belongs to a Jenny. The pocket at the back unzips to reveal a red pen, a blue highlighter, and a pencil with a broken end. Whoever Jenny is, she came very unprepared. I try to make the pencil look usable and hold my hand against my head, hoping to conceal my identity while appearing to study.

It feels like an hour before Charlie returns but my phone barely shows five minutes have passed. He's brought Jessica,

Sheri's best friend, along with her boyfriend, Paul, and a girl named Katie. They all grab a seat at the table.

I haven't seen anyone since Sheri disappeared, so it feels good that they came. Although Jessica is way more girlie than Sheri, she's always been there for her, so we've spent lots of time around each other. Paul is okay but rarely tags along with his girlfriend, so I barely know him. Katie is friends with Sheri, too, but pretty low key, and I only know her from the occasional party.

"Hey, Tony." I hear the strain in Jessica's voice—she's barely keeping it together. "Any word?"

I shake my head.

Charlie plops himself down across from me. "Why do you think you're here? For a chit-chat with long-lost friends?" His interrogation begins. "Who here's talked to the cops?"

We look at each other. Jessica raises her hand. Paul and Katie do too. I follow.

"Cool." We all look at him. "Figure out if they asked you all the same things. I'll be right back."

He's off again and I realize I need to get used to his style.

The four of us are quiet for only a moment before Katie starts. "They asked about the last time I saw her. Or if I knew about any fights she had with anyone." She pauses and I know everyone wants to look over at me. Thankfully, she doesn't linger too long and pushes through. "They gave me a card and asked to call if I thought of anything else."

We all share similar stories. Cookie-cutter questions that no one can provide answers to. It seems like no one is being accused of anything based on how they've questioned us, but I can't help but feel that I'm their best lead. I'd like to think that we're all being treated equally, but as her boyfriend the finger is pointed straight at me, and I hate it. Oh, sure, we're all sad about her disappearance, but I can't help but think I feel it deeper than the rest.

Charlie returns, this time with Sheri's ex, Dillon. I'm instantly uncomfortable.

Dillon nods in my direction. "What's he doing here?"

Anger bubbles up inside, but Charlie stares at him like he's an idiot—which he is.

Jessica comes to my defense. "Shut up, Dillon. Tony is Sheri's boyfriend—he's got more right than you to be here."

"Yeah, Sheri's boyfriend who fell off the radar the minute Sheri never made it home." His accusation is a punch in the face. Any sense of unease is gone—now I'm just pissed.

"And where were *you* the night she disappeared, you jealous prick?" I'm on my feet and he's standing and my fists are up and bunched tight.

Before I get a chance to swing, Charlie steps between us and pushes me back, knocking me hard against a bookshelf. "Calm down."

Every muscle in my body is tense and Charlie restrains Dillon like a referee in a boxing ring. "You calm?"

Paul stands now too and his arm holds me back, but his body is turned toward Dillon, ready to fight.

I size Charlie up—he's small and strong—and I'm still not sure whose side he's on yet, so I decide not to carry this any further. I relax to let Paul know the moment has passed, and he sits down again, slowly.

Charlie turns to Dillon. "Stop being a dick. We're not here to fight."

Dillon's fists drop and the rest of us sit back down.

Charlie leans in. "I want you guys to think about what the cop asked you. All the normal stuff right?"

We all nod.

"Now, think—is there anything else? All the things that seem weird or don't seem normal. All the things an adult or a cop might overlook. Texts? Snapchats? People? Things at school? Things out of school?"

We sit in silence and I run through every single day, minute and hour right up to Thursday when Sheri went missing, but nothing comes to me. I look over at Charlie and he stares back at me, stone-faced. He's not judging, only waiting for answers. I'm not sure where he's going with all of this, but I feel like he's the best shot I have.

He breaks his stare and looks to the others. "Another thing—you're going to stop texting—"

Katie cuts in, "Are you kidding?"

He glances at her impatiently. "Don't interrupt. You're going to stop texting anything about Sheri's disappearance. But if you stop cold turkey, it's going to look suspicious, so you can say some basic stuff about her. You've got to assume people are watching. Make sense?"

No one seems to like the idea, but they nod.

Charlie checks his watch. "It's almost 9:00. Get back to the routine."

Everyone gets up and leaves except for the two of us.

I look over at Charlie. He's smiling.

"That went well!"

"What are you talking about?"

"I told you—reconnaissance." Charlie's phone buzzes in his pocket but he silences it. "Jessica is definitely on your side and Paul seems like he'll go wherever she follows. Obviously, Dillon thinks you're guilty, but the interesting one is Katie. She's our ordinary Joe Public. Knows you but doesn't know you. She tells me that most people are still on the fence, so we're going to have to keep an eye on that."

"It was a test?"

"Well, no. It's good to get everyone to quit using their phones. Who gives a teenager a phone, anyway?"

"What are you talking about? All that stuff about the cops listening—?"

"What do you think this is? CSI?"

"Then why did you do all this?"

"I needed to know if people thought you were guilty. So I could decide."

I stare at him.

"I think I'm at a solid 99%."

"You were only deciding—?"

"If I could trust you? Yes. Among other things."

"Like what?"

"I also needed to figure out Dillon. He's definitely up to something."

The librarian comes into the library.

"Time for us to go." He stands. "Come on."

"Where?"

"You're taking me to the scene of the crime."

When I stand, I can still feel where the bookshelf hit me. What have I gotten myself into?

chapter 26

We step out of the student entrance.

Charlie's got his phone out but he seems to be struggling with the password. "Where's your car?"

"You know there's no real proven crime yet. She's only missing—"

"Keep telling yourself that, Junior. Where are we going?"

I point and he moves across the parking lot. Students are still driving in, kicking up gravel as they pull to a stop.

Charlie continues, "Not everyone around the school thinks you're innocent. Katie was waiting to see Dillon knock you down, so having you lurk around Guthrie High won't help our cause."

Charlie cuts toward the nearest yard and goes through the back. Across the lawn is a big patio door, with the curtains open. An animated raccoon is on TV.

I freeze at the gate.

Charlie looks back and sighs. "If we're going to work together, you're going to have to quit this bullshit. Grow a pair and let's move."

I follow, scooting up behind him. He goes between the garage and fence and I am tight on his heels. A dog barks inside the house and someone yells at it to shut up. We walk down the driveway and onto the street, only a few houses away from my car.

He's still wrestling with his phone and gets out his wallet.

"Is that why you hate teens with phones? Because you're technically inept?"

He doesn't even look at me as he pilfers through the billfold. A second later, he goes back to the phone.

Charlie shakes his head. "What an idiot! His own birthday!" He swipes the screen a few times and hands it over to me. "Ah, see, look at that. The day she disappeared, Sheri got three texts from Dillon."

I look down at the phone, "What are you talking about?"

"It looks like he's been trying to rekindle things with your girlfriend. I knew he was a sneaky bastard—"

I stop beside my car.

"What—? Whose—? Is this Dillon's?" I reach for the phone but Charlie pulls it away.

Charlie smiles. "Yeah, while you provided that great distraction trying to fight him, I grabbed his phone and wallet."

"What the hell—?"

"I'm guessing he's already figured out they're missing, so it won't be long before he locks it down. Or tracks it on GPS," Charlie scoffs as he continues to scroll through Dillon's texts. "Looks like Dillon is a busy, busy boy. He got texts to and from 'the X'—that'd be your girlfriend—but there's also texts to 'gf4now.' Man, this guy's a piece of work."

I'm not sure what to do. A part of me wants to know what Dillon and my girlfriend were texting about. Yet it doesn't feel right, the whole invasion of privacy thing. But most of me is willing to do almost anything to find Sheri.

"Should you be reading those?"

"Who's 'Mia-ow'? Sounds interesting," says Charlie without looking up.

I'm curious to know what he's reading but it feels like poison. I convince myself that I have to trust him, to trust his process. I need to be objective and focus on the bigger goal of finding Sheri, so I let it go, deciding not to ask questions.

He taps the text stream. "Dirty, dirty Dillon."

Damn, he's not making this easy.

"Mia-ow is definitely the tease.

I'm full of all sorts of surprises.
You want to know what? Then you'll
just have to come and find out yourself.

"Now I know why he calls her Mia-ow!" He holds up the phone. "Whoa, check this out!"

Ugh. It's sensational and terrible. Charlie's found a selfie of Dillon smirking in his bathroom mirror, sans shirt, pants pulled down to the low V cut of his obliques. It's one of those things I can't unsee.

"I wonder if there are any selfies of Mia-ow."

"Are you insane?"

"Hey, it's all useful information. It's either Dillon or it's not."

"Right? And when he tracks us down with the GPS, it'll be all of us."

"Aww, quit whining. We'll toss it long before and he'll never know. Speaking of which, let me take a couple of photos with your phone for reference later."

Every move he makes seems to come with such ease. No nerves, just actions. Maybe he's done this all his life. Maybe he just doesn't care.

But for me, it's all new territory.

chapter 27

We jump in my car and drive away from the school.

Charlie immediately opens the glove box. He doesn't ask, just starts rummaging.

"Dude?"

He doesn't look over. "What did I say? My name's not dude."

He rifles through the registration, flips through the owner's manual, and pulls out every information pamphlet the car dealership has jammed inside.

"Your dad's got an oil change coming up."

He lowers the visor and flips open the mirror a couple of times. The last time he holds his gaze longer than necessary, and the expression of mischief on his face slips away. He slams the mirror on the visor shut and looks around some more.

He goes through the console and checks the slot under the radio, jingling through the spare change. Leaning back in his seat, he tilts the back down, then up again, then down. He sits forward and wipes the dash with the flat of his hand

and studies the thin coat of dust on his fingers. I feel defensive and turn on the music to distract us both. Tom Petty sings "You Don't Know How It Feels." It's my dad's guilty pleasure and I'm embarrassed.

He looks at me.

"What?"

"The music. It's a classic. Nice!"

I stare at him, waiting for him to reveal the sarcasm beneath his words but he's already moved on, relaxing in the passenger seat, grinning. He opens the window and hangs his head out just enough to let the wind mess up his already unkempt hair. It's like I'm taking Ollie out to the country for a run.

"Where exactly should we go? On the trails, I mean? Everyone's searched there—the cops, her family, friends."

The window rolls up and he reaches into the side pocket of his baggy cargo pants and pulls out a piece of paper. I glance over as he unfolds it. It's the running map from Sheri's locker.

I grab Charlie's jacket in my fist. "Where the hell did you get that?"

"Pay attention to the road."

I squeeze my fist tighter.

He leans in. "You are a serious snapcase, man. You need to gear down."

I let him go and he sits back. "Sheri's locker. The day you came by the school. Remember? You pussied out and went to the bathroom, so I stepped in and took what was needed before the cops got there."

I'm dumbfounded. This guy's either got balls or is seriously stupid.

"You saw me?"

He nods slowly. "And you should thank me because I was able to finish what you never could."

My lips tighten. I know I should be grateful for this—and I am—but I'm also pissed.

He smiles. "Besides, what's a freakout gonna get you? Answers? Nope. You asked for my help and here we are."

Damn, I wish he wasn't speaking the truth.

"Now, if you can cool your shit long enough for me to explain, I think we can get somewhere. Think you can do that?"

I lean back in my seat and try to shake it off. I'm frustrated with myself and my inability to keep calm. It's not like me, I've always been able to do this. On the court. At parties. But now I'm slipping and Charlie is the only one holding it together. Or he's the one messing me up. I'm still trying to figure it out.

He holds Sheri's map between us.

"Looks like Sheri was doing a longer run that day, according to this. We'll start there and check things out."

He folds the map and hands it to me and it feels like a peace offering of sorts.

I take it and put it in my pocket.

I drive on and Charlie opens Dillon's wallet again, leafing through the contents. He pulls out a twenty-dollar bill. "Can we stop for an iced cappuccino?" He waves the money near my face. "Dillon's buying."

This guy is too much, but I laugh and find myself turning into the nearest coffee shop. At this point, I figure we both deserve it.

chapter 28

We arrive at the trails and I pull into the parking lot. The place is empty and all signs of the search are gone. The few wire flags have been removed and the litter has been cleared away. It's like the place has been abandoned for weeks.

It's unnerving.

I wait while Charlie works away at his beverage.

"Are we just going to sit here?"

He doesn't answer and peers at the entrance to the trail, past the barricade that keeps motorized vehicles off the footpath. The path runs east-west, and his eyes trace the flat horizon of prairie fields.

I try to figure out what he's looking at.

"Is this where Sheri parked that day?'

"I don't know. The car was gone when I showed up—"

"Right. For the search." He rolls his eyes. "But when you two ran, this is where you parked?"

"I, uh—"

"You ran this trail before, right?"

"Yeah."

"With Sheri?"

"Uh, no."

"You've never gone running with your girlfriend?"

"I have, just not this trail."

He looks at me, shaking his head. "You are so weird." He looks back out at the path. "Have you done the whole loop?"

"Yes."

"It's good, huh?"

I look at him, trying to understand his meaning. Charlie Wolfe seems like the furthest thing from a person who would go for a fun run out here.

"What? You think running is for rich people?"

"I'm not—"

"Don't. Let's not even start that game."

I stop trying to defend myself. "Why do you run?" I ask.

"To know."

"To know what?"

"To know what's out there. To know where I live. To know that I can outrun someone if I need to. Why did you run out here?"

I hear all of it in my head. To see if I was better than others. To keep my body fit. To prove something to myself.

"'Cuz."

His eyes are on me and I feel the sting of judgment, but I'm not sure if it's his or my own.

He slurps at the bottom of his drink until the last of it rattles up his straw.

"Do you have a napkin?"

I'm not sure why he asks—he hasn't made a mess. I shrug and look through the console and hand him one. He pulls out the straw, taps it on the side of the cup, then jams it in his mouth.

"All right, then. Let's get to work."

chapter 29

He climbs out of the car and walks over to the garbage can at the head of the trail. It's empty and has likely been searched and cleaned for clues by Gekas and her team. Charlie wipes the sides of his plastic cup with the napkin before dropping it in.

I follow him, locking the car behind me. It's a beautiful day, but the prairie wind pushes against us a bit. He looks out at the trail, the drink straw hanging out of his mouth as he flicks it up and down. The wind keeps tossing his messy hair into his eyes, so he raises his sunglasses to keep it out of his face.

He looks back at me, his hand out. "Map?"

I reach into my pocket and pull it out. I hadn't noticed the condition it was in until now, folded and wrinkled—not from Sheri, but from Charlie. It's one of the few things I have left of her, so I open it carefully. I catch Charlie watching me before he takes a step closer to look at it.

He digs in his pocket and pulls out another piece of paper. It's the calendar that was stuck underneath it.

I look at him. "Really?"

"When are the things I do going to quit surprising you?" He points at the date she disappeared. "She went for a long one that day. So that means..." he traces his finger along the map before continuing, "it means that we have a run ahead of us."

Before I know it, he's trotting down the path at a slow pace. I take off after him, following a step behind. He speeds up. I'm pretty sure he's doing it to challenge me but I keep up easily. After a while, he eases back beside me, pulling the half-chewed straw out of his mouth.

"Ah, look at that. We ran this trail together. Something even you didn't do with her."

"Are you just naturally a dick or does it take practice?"

"At last!"

"What?"

"You quit whining and had a bit of backbone there for a second."

"Screw off!"

"Excellent. You might be useful to me yet. But let's not over-do it."

He falls back into silence, looking left and right along the trails, and all I can do is shake my head. This guy enjoys pushing my buttons and although I know it's intentional, I can't figure out what his reason is.

He twists himself around and continues running in a sort of backwards shuffle, looking at where we've come from. I glance over my shoulder, trying to figure out what he's look-ing at.

He turns back around, sinking the straw back between his teeth. "A little bit farther."

He picks up his pace and I have to sprint again to catch up. I'm barely feeling it and know I've got energy to spare, but I can hear him trying to regulate his breath. After we run around a small hill and a bend, Charlie spins backwards again.

"Almost... almost... and there." He stops.

I turn, trying to find out what he's looking at.

"I don't... see it."

He pulls out the straw and points with it out past the hill.

Then I realize. The car is no longer in sight.

"Do you think...?" I don't finish.

Charlie pulls out a cell phone and takes a photo.

I can't figure out who he stole that one from.

"Whose is that?"

"It's mine."

"You have a cell phone?"

"Yeah. What'd you think? I'm Amish?"

"No." Just that you look like you can't afford one.

I catch him glaring at me. I hope mind-reading isn't one of his many mysterious skills.

chapter 30

"Everything after this point is fair game."

I stare at him, trying to catch his meaning.

"The hill provides cover. There's plenty of trees, shrubs, and low spots—all good places to hide. Another kilometre and the path crosses the end of a grid road." He indicates a spot ahead where we can see the glint of a truck travelling half a mile away. "Easy to avoid being seen by anyone in a vehicle, even if someone was looking."

"But the search parties covered this area."

"And they found nothing. Because...?"

At first, I wait for him to finish his thought, but when he leaves it for too long, I start to speak, "Because—"

He interrupts me, "Because it isn't the right place."

"What does *that* mean?"

"Whatever—no—*who*ever happened to Sheri chose somewhere..."

He trails off again. This time I wait, but he doesn't finish his thought and continues walking down the trail. We carry on in silence until we hit the end of the grid road where it stops at the creek.

"Did they search the entire trail?"

"Not on the day I went out."

"You didn't go the entire weekend?"

"No—"

"Why not?"

"There were... problems."

"What? You forgot your baby blanket to keep you warm?"

"No—!"

"Then what?"

"I—"

"What?"

"Forget it."

"No, don't. Don't forget it." He's in my face, fired up, and all of it's making me feel intimidated. "*Don't* forget. *Don't* forget her. *Don't* forget how all of this makes you feel. She's your girlfriend. We are the people going out of our way to make sure she doesn't just become—" He looks out past me, out past the horizon, searching. And then he's back. "Just don't. Let's keep looking. Okay?"

I know he's intense. I know he cares. Because he's here. And there are layers to him. I'm freaked that he's given me shit like someone who's lost something, but he's also lit a fire in me and I'm primed. I promise myself I won't stop until we catch whoever did this.

We jog past the grid road. Charlie asks for the map and I hand it to him. When I feel the paper slip from my fingers to his, I realize I'm letting go of this small piece of Sheri, but it's too late to grab it back without seeming crazy.

He looks at it, turning it around. It flaps in the breeze. He folds it and hands it back.

"This second half is the longer part of the loop. Four miles. There are two farms at each end," he points first to the east, then to the southeast, "but still plenty of cover to do something discreetly."

There's a small makeshift footbridge that's been assembled out of 2x4s and wood planks. He crosses to the south side of the creek and walks slow, scanning the landscape, tilting his head, studying the ground. I don't know what he's looking for, what hint he expects to come across. We wind along the creek, a play structure coming into view in the distance.

Even though the breeze keeps me cool, the sun is shining and my mouth is dry.

"You guys got along well." It's a statement, not a question.

"Yeah, we did. We do." I latch onto the word. It gives me hope.

"Girls can be such drama queens. They look for shit to make them sad. They overreact to everything." He looks back at me. "Sheri wasn't like that. And she was even less like that when you started dating. Wasn't sure if I was a fan of you at first." He stops and looks at his phone for a moment. "I'm getting to be, though."

"Look, man, I'm not looking for a fan or a friend. I just want to find Sheri."

Charlie looks up from his phone.

"Yeah, I definitely think you're all right now."

chapter 31

We carry on down the trail toward the playground, and now I can see the hunched concrete structure of the washroom ahead. Even though we aren't far from civilization, it feels like we're in the middle of nowhere—eerie and isolated.

Charlie stares at the washroom for a moment, then climbs to the top of the monkey bars and scans the horizon. I secretly hope he starts verbalizing what he's doing. I peer in the same direction but stop because I don't know what I'm looking for. He hops down, landing softly like an athlete.

He makes for the side of the building marked WOMEN. I wonder if it's unlocked this late in the season. With a closed fist he pushes the door open.

I step in behind him. The door's hydraulic hinge exhales shut. It's cool and gloomy in here. Sunshine, dulled by the dirty, frosted skylight above us, struggles to reach the depths of the space; shadows soften the edges of everything in here. There are two stalls with working doors, a hand dryer that looks like someone's beaten it with a hammer, and a mirror of polished metal. Small bathroom tiles line the walls and form a sink. Drawings, swear words, and the phone number of someone named Chelene are graffitied around the bathroom.

Charlie steps into the first stall and closes the door.

"You gotta go?" I joke.

He comes out quickly and walks over to the sink without saying a word. It looks like he's counting steps but who knows. He turns around and moves to the other stall. This time he shuts the door and locks it. There is a faint echo. He stays in there for a moment.

Click—he steps out.

I'm starting to feel useless. I don't know what he's doing and I don't know what we're looking for. I'm absolutely lost.

"Charlie?" My voice echoes and breaks the silence. It's louder than I expected and it startles me, but it doesn't seem to faze him.

He stands there for a moment. "What's in the garbage can?"

I lean in to look. "Nothing. Not even a garbage bag."

"Can I see your phone?"

"Why? You have your own."

"Come on. Quit arguing. It's lunchtime and I'm hungry."

I sigh and give it to him.

"What do you listen to? Hip-hop, no doubt." I shoot him a look but I see him scrolling through my playlist. "Ha, knew it. Nothing Top 40 and nothing old, right?"

I need to learn to ignore him but not just yet. "Right, because I listen to *good* music."

Charlie snorts with derision, then asks, "You got headphones with you?"

"Yeah?"

"Hand 'em over."

"Charlie—?"

His look speaks volumes. I dig into my pocket, pull out my earbuds and put them on his palm. Maybe this was all just an elaborate plan to get me to the middle of nowhere and shake me down. Except, I asked him to do it.

He unravels the cord and plugs them in. He hands me the earbuds. "Put them on."

Once I'm wearing them, he hits play.

"Can you hear me?"

I nod.

He turns it up. "How about now?"

Yup.

He cranks it a little louder. I see him say something and I pull out one bud. "What?"

"Nothing."

He motions me to put it back in my ear. As I do, he turns me so that I'm facing the mirror. His hazy, distorted reflection moves behind me like a creeping ghost.

He steps up beside me and pushes the tap on. The water runs and he walks back into the stall.

"Do you think she was in here?" I yell.

I don't see him and I turn. "Hey assh—!"

Suddenly, he's right beside me and it scares the crap out of me. I pull out the earbuds. "What the hell are we *doing* here?"

"Lay down."

"What's wrong with you? I'm not lying down."

He stares at me, chewing on the corner of his lip. The beat of the music pumps through my headphones but it's distant and far away.

"What are we doing here?"

He shushes me. "Lay down."

"Are you trying to help or is this you messing with me?"

"Down."

"No."

He sighs and flips on his phone flashlight and shines it on the ground beneath the sink. He crouches, looking under the bulkhead that holds the long trough, illuminating all the dark nooks and crannies of the space. He stands and aims the light at the mirror, then turns it so it shines beneath his face, illuminating him like a ghoul. He stares at himself for a moment and I watch.

"Spooky." He turns and smiles. "I think this is good for now." He shuts the phone light off and walks past me.

I take a long look around, trying to figure out what the hell we just did.

"Shepherd?"

I turn and Charlie's standing at the door, holding it open with a sleeve-covered hand. "Let's go."

chapter 32

Charlie's already heading back down the path to the car.

"What now?" I ask, following him. "Shouldn't we go that way?" I point out toward the distant fields.

"Nope."

"Why?"

"Because we're done."

I look at him.

He sighs and comes back toward me. "Take out Sheri's map."

I take it out, unfolding it carefully.

He points to the map and then down the path behind us. "This leads to the railroad. Then there's a farm and then another farm over there. After that, nothing. Just the path."

I nod.

"We're just wasting time going that way. If I was going to do something to Sheri, this would be the place."

"What do you mean if you were going to 'do something' to Sheri?"

"Stay calm, man. Quit thinking with your heart. I'm just saying that if someone was going to do something, it would have to be secluded or else they'd be seen or heard. This place is sheltered, it's concealed, and it gives whoever a place to do it."

I stare at him and feel the next question rolling out of my brain and hanging deep down, lodged in my throat before I can finally say the words. "Do what?"

He looks at me and he shakes his head. "I don't know, man. I really don't." He hands back the map, and looks across the fields to the south. "But whatever it is, I don't think it's good."

chapter 33

We're almost back at the car when I hear *bzzz... bzzz.*

Charlie pulls Dillon's phone out of his back pocket.

"Hey, I thought you were going to dump it?"

Charlie shrugs like it's no big deal. "You recognize the number?" he asks, turning the phone to me.

Dillon's phone vibrates again in Charlie's hand as I rack my brain. The *bzzz* seems so loud in this quiet place. I've seen the number before but my heart is beating too hard to recall who it belongs to.

"Wait." I reach into my pocket and pull out Detective Gekas's card.

"It's the same number? The cop?"

I nod.

"Cool."

Cool? I'm thinking none of this is cool.

"I guess they'll be talking to Dillon again, huh?"

He's as casual as can be. He walks to the garbage bin where he dumped his iced coffee cup and wipes the phone down with his shirt before tossing it inside. It rattles against the metal for two more rings before finally going silent.

He saunters over to the car and I wonder if I maybe need a little of his "who gives a shit" attitude.

He knocks on the hood with his palm. "Come on, time's a-wastin'!"

I shake my head, digging the car keys out of my pocket. "You sound like a middle-aged white guy."

He smiles. "Let's move along now, hear?"

I laugh and unlock the door and we both climb in.

As I pull back onto the road, Charlie spends a ridiculous amount of time adjusting the seat. He checks himself in the vanity mirror, drawing back his lips, running his tongue across his teeth, flicking his hair to ensure appropriate shagginess. He catches me staring.

"What?"

"Why are you so happy?"

"Why shouldn't we be?" he responds. "We're getting somewhere. We know where Sheri—" He pauses before settling on, "We know where Sheri disappeared from and we have the profile of the suspect, which, I think, is a hell of a lot more than Gekas has."

"Wait—? We have a profile? When—? How did we come up with that?"

Charlie smiles. "When they called Dillon."

"They think Dillon is responsible for all of this?"

"No, not him. But he fits their profile, just like *you* fit their profile."

"What? What are you saying?"

"When we had everyone meet this morning. All the stories were the same. Except yours."

"How was mine different?"

"You're not from her school."

"So?"

"That made you the anomaly. Until now."

"The phone call?"

"Yeah. No one else has been called on twice, that we know of. Something has made him a suspect."

"But what?"

"I don't know and I don't really care because that isn't part of our investigation."

"If he's a suspect though—?"

"We can't go chasing Gekas's lead. It's counter-productive. Let her do her own work."

"So, what then? Do we ignore Dillon? "

"Well, he's still a suspect. But he's not the only one."

"Who else do we have?"

"Based on what the cops are looking for? A teenager. Most likely a male. Relatively decent home life." He rolls his eyes at me. "Seems to have some connection to Sheri, maybe goes to her school or knows her from parties or some other activity." He stares out the window thinking until I interrupt.

"Earlier, you said *is*."

"Huh?"

"When you were talking about Sheri and our suspect, you said whatever it *is*."

"So?"

"You don't think this is done, do you? You don't think Sheri is the last."

"No, I don't. She may not even be the first. But there's something else..." He gets quiet for a moment.

I stare at him. "What?"

He sighs and shakes his hair out of his face and relaxes back in his seat. "Don't know." He points to the car stereo. "May I?"

"Go ahead."

He twists the dials and Dad's Tom Petty compilation comes on. Charlie joins Petty at the top of his lungs, "I'm freeeee fallllling!"

He sings all the way back to the school. He knows every word.

It's actually impressive.

chapter 34

Back at Guthrie, classes are still on and there's no one outside. Charlie sings out the last note of "Don't Do Me Like That," then turns down the music.

"That was awesome! An in-the-moment moment, you know?"

He's right. Despite the fact that Sheri's missing, at this precise moment things feel light and sort of right. It's been too long since I've felt this way.

Charlie digs into his back pocket, pulling out Dillon's wallet. He rips it open. "Pfft. Velcro? Grow up," he says to himself, and it makes me smile again.

Charlie removes the last of the paper bills. At a glance, it looks like about fifty bucks—a twenty, couple of tens, some fives. I know it's not right but I don't stop him.

He stuffs the cash in his front pocket and nonchalantly tosses the wallet out the window.

Two uniformed constables come out of the main entrance, talking to a man Charlie says is Guthrie's resource officer.

I straighten in my seat.

"Easy," Charlie whispers, not taking his eyes off them.

They walk across the grass toward a patrol car parked down the street. The resource officer stands on the curb, waiting for them to drive away.

"See, nothing to worry about. My guess? They're looking for Dillon Ross."

Charlie and I watch the resource officer go back into the school. We exchange glances. It's the first moment I actually feel connected to him. I look down the street—the police cruiser is waiting at the stop light.

Charlie gets out of the car and shuts the door, but bends down to the open window when he hears me say his name.

"Charlie? We're going to find her, right?

He straightens up, tapping the roof of my car. "Go home, Shepherd. We'll talk later."

He turns and walks away from the school.

chapter 35

At home, I park the car in the driveway. It's almost the end of the school day. Although I haven't been to school, I'm exhausted. My body, my brain—I want to close myself in my room and shut the world out. I need some time to process everything Charlie and I did today. Mom's probably still at work but Dad's likely home. I'm hoping if I walk in quietly enough, he won't notice.

In the house, I slide off my shoes and set the keys on the counter. The house is quiet, so I'm relieved. I head straight up to my room.

"Anthony."

It's Dad. I freeze halfway on the stairs.

"We need to talk to you."

We? Mom shouldn't be back from work this soon. Gekas? Is she in the kitchen?

I don't want to do this. I exhale in annoyance.

"Your mother and I are waiting. Come on now."

I'm not in the mood for a conversation, or an argument, or anything. I walk into the kitchen.

The counter is bare, no tea like a few days ago.

Mom's standing and her arms are crossed.

I try for lightness. "Aren't you supposed to be at work?"

"Weren't *you* supposed to be at school?"

I make one last attempt to save my ass. "Uh. School's done?"

"I cancelled my appointments because we need to have a talk."

I cringe.

"We got a call from the school that you weren't in class—at all—today. Can you explain to your father and me where you went and who you were with?"

I quickly run through my day. Taking the car without asking. Going to Sheri's school without permission. Almost getting into a fight with her ex, Dillon. Taking off with Charlie Wolfe—who picked Dillon's pocket, btw—then going to the last place Sheri was seen.

None of this is gonna fly.

"I drove around."

"You drove around. By yourself?"

"Yes."

"All day?"

"Yes."

"You expect us to believe that?"

"Yes."

I roll my head in a gesture of total irritation and I'm not apologetic about it either. I'm getting fed up and tired and it's making it difficult to edit my thoughts.

"Anthony, it's not like you to disappear for a day and not check in, not return texts, not tell us where you're going. It's just—"

"Get off my back!"

I never raise my voice but I need to do something. There's no way I can get into all the messy details with them. They won't understand and they'll get in the way of my search for Sheri.

"Anthony! Don't raise your voice to your mother."

"Look," I say, trying not to raise my voice and failing, "I'm tired and I don't need to tell you anything!"

I know I'm out of line. This isn't typical for me, but I also know this has nothing to do with them.

"Yes, you *do* have to tell us—"

"No, I don't. Just send me to my room."

Ollie barks and I can see my parents are speechless.

Silence hovers between us.

"What? Are you going to ground me?"

They never have—there was never a need to—and I know they won't.

"So I skipped. Big deal! So you didn't know where I was for a few hours—you don't need to know my every move."

Dad doesn't raise his voice, "Yes, we do. We're your parents." He's so calm right now it only makes me angrier.

"What do you think I could possibly be doing?"

Mom isn't as composed. "You weren't at school, where you were supposed to be. You weren't with your friends. You're not at the gym. You need to be responsible."

I'm offended because they know I *am*—or at least, I was.

"You need to let us know where you are at all times."

"What for?"

My parents look at each other, then Dad says, "Since Sheri—"

I don't need to hear another word.

"Things aren't safe for you—"

"I'm done here!" I turn and this time I make it upstairs.

"Anthony!" Mom tries one last time, but I ignore her and slam the door to my bedroom.

chapter 36

Practice makes perfect.

He had worked hard to prepare for the runner. He had considered the details, rehearsed the steps, and when the time came, he had performed perfectly. He hadn't left a thing to chance. The police hadn't found her yet, hadn't figured out what he'd done, and he was quite certain they hadn't even begun to figure out who he was.

But the first girl was a misstep. And that failure now marred the perfection of his premiere. He needed to remedy the mistake.

If at first you don't succeed...

With the runner, he had planned ahead and didn't act as rashly. When the idea first came to him and he imagined its execution, he had chosen a setting where things were familiar and safe. He had wandered the halls and moved among the students. He knew the layout, had visited the bathroom prior to the act and thought he'd known what to expect. Yet, all his knowledge, his anticipations, had failed him.

This time he's chosen a different school.

He had rehearsed so much the movements were smooth and easy; he no longer had to think it through, his body flowed with the rhythm of his victim. They could exist together in the moment, adjusting to each step, each action leading to a new and exciting reaction, until they reached the catharsis together, where they could go no higher, and their moment together would come to its resolution.

After the runner, he knew he had to re-stage the first act and rectify his mistake. His chosen setting was a school that had been built in the city's southwest to accommodate the influx of families that had moved into the new subdivision in recent years.

He arrives in the afternoon to get his bearings, but not early enough to attract attention. He had scouted the location the morning before, watched as the students went inside, and took notes on how they dressed. Jeans and a tee-shirt, and he would be set for the role. There were also a lot of baseball caps at this school, but it felt like they drew attention to his desire to be inconspicuous. He opted for a hoodie instead, which worked as camouflage for his body type. He had copied a schedule of his brother's and altered it with names and classes from the school's website in case a teacher asks why he is wandering the halls.

He slips into the library, going to the stacks to grab a book by Cormac McCarthy before sitting down at a cubicle in the corner to wait. When the bell finally rings, he's read through a couple of chapters and reminds himself to pick it up after he's finished here. Outside the library, he finds his way to the gymnasium. Boys' basketball occupies both courts, so he moves on. There's likely someone in the girl's change room too, so he proceeds down the hall.

The main office is at the end of the hallway he's in, two teachers stand outside. He's running out of options if he wants to remain inconspicuous. Turning down the next corridor, he sees a brunette—most likely a senior—come out of a classroom, backpack slung over her shoulder. She turns off the light, locks the door, and looks over at him with a brief smile before turning away to leave.

That suits him just fine. His pulse kicks up a notch.

He saunters to a water fountain and takes a long, slow drink, waiting for her to disappear from view. When she turns a corner, he goes after her.

But the next hallway appears empty and silent, and he is surprised by the depth of his disappointment. Then he spots her at the far end, half hidden by an open locker door.

He watches, hoping she'll be the one, and his heartbeat steadies at its new pace.

She closes her locker, crossing the hallway to go into the bathroom.

He smiles and follows.

chapter 37

It's late and the hard work is done. He waits in the darkness of the bathroom because the janitors clock out at 11:00. When he's certain they're in another part of the school, he opens the door and peers down the darkened hallway in both directions. The exit signs glow like beacons. He holds himself motionless, making sure that he is alone, that he has all the time in the world.

In the girl's bag is a set of car keys.

When he scouted the school the previous day, he had noticed the shop doors on the east side, so he heads in that direction now. He should be able to find something he can use to move the body.

He's still cautious. There is always the chance that a teacher has come back late to work. He doubts it but if he is wrong, if his luck turns bad, then he'll have to make a choice. If they're strong—a coach or gym teacher, say—he'll have to run and hope to hell he can get away. An art or science teacher, he could probably overpower. Either way, a confrontation is not part of the story he's imagined and the possibility of an unpremeditated moment is worrying.

It's best to be careful.

But he encounters no one on his way to the industrial arts area. The door is locked and he doesn't want to leave any trace of his presence, so he decides not to break the glass window to get inside. He checks the garage next and finds it shut tight as well. He considers the options. The maintenance rooms will likely be secure, as well as the gym. He moves stealthily back down the hall toward the library. There's a set of double doors with a wide gap between them and he pulls out his jackknife and slides it in and against the latch. By wiggling it back and forth, he slowly pushes the bolt past the strike plate. The door swings open and he walks inside.

Behind the checkout desk is a back room. Its door is unlocked. In the back corner, a projector squats on a cart. Perfect. He lifts it off and pulls the cart out of the library, wheeling it down the halls back to the bathroom.

The girl's heels drag on the tiles as he pulls her out from the back stall. Lifting and shoving, he manoeuvres her onto the cart, careful to tuck her hair under her so that it won't catch in the wheels. Rigor mortis makes her easier to load but unwieldy to move on the projector cart, and he makes a mental note to give the cart lots of room going around corners and through doors. Tugging a thin bedsheet out of his backpack, he covers her. As he pushes the cart around and out of the room, he catches sight of his reflection in the mirror and smiles to himself. He wheels the cart and its burden steadily toward the student entrance on high alert.

He looks out the thick-paned glass doors, considering. If the doors close behind him, he won't be able to retreat to the safety of the school. He thinks a moment more, then reaches up to adjust the hinged arm at the top, forcing the door to stay open. Across the street, light fills the windows of houses that look like they've been cloned. Down the street, though, construction is still in its early stages, the bare framework of new homes caught in the cold, clean radiance of the streetlamps.

He presses a button on the car keys. Parking lights flare in the near distance. There is no one out there but him.

And her.

He moves carefully and quickly across the student parking lot. At her car, he opens the back door and hauls her body inside.

A quick glance around—still no one—and he takes the cart back into the building, wiping it down with his sleeve before making sure the door shuts firmly behind him.

He drives to a row of unfinished houses where he can take his time and make things right, turning off the headlights to glide through the concrete and wood skeletons.

It feels like he's travelling into the past. Soon that first performance—a bad audition, really—will vanish from view. Vanish as if it never existed.

chapter 38

I wake up every hour on the hour through the night. I'm off my game. I'm tired. I'm anxious. Thoughts spiral in my head: images of the trails, of that echoing bathroom, of Sheri. I miss her so much. I finally give in to the morning before my alarm clock sounds.

I sit up, rubbing my face, and grab my phone. Just a couple of texts from Mike, checking in. I figure I should go through the motions of a regular day, get everyone off my back. And maybe I need a break from the drama of all of this garbage, too. I'm conflicted.

I get dressed and make my way downstairs. Ollie is lying on a mat in the kitchen. No sign of anyone else. Heather's at school, but Mom and Dad are usually around in the mornings. I guess not today. I'm curious about where they are but more grateful for the silence.

I open the fridge and get out the soy milk. It feels like a punishment but I pour it on my cereal anyhow. Dad's left a note on the counter, which I read while silently crunching my breakfast. *Taking Mom's car for an oil change. Here's $10 for the day.* The money's underneath and I realize it's a peace offering of sorts. There's nothing from Mom. I feel bad, but I'll have to make amends with her later. I stuff the money in my pocket and head for the door, hoping for an ordinary day at school.

When I open it, Detective Gekas is standing there.

Shit.

"Hello, Anthony."

I smile and it's awkward.

"Your parents gone for the day?"

"They'll be back later."

She nods in acceptance. "You don't have to answer now, but what were you up to last night?"

"Why? Did something happen?" I feel a twist in my gut, a defensiveness.

"There's—"

"Another girl gone missing?"

"No—"

"Then why are you coming to me?"

"They found a body, Tony."

My stomach twists up sideways and I grab hold of the door frame.

"No, it's not Sheri. Someone else."

I look at Gekas. "Another?"

She nods.

My head swirls. Charlie said he didn't think Sheri was the first—or the last. And if they found *one* body...

I shut my mind to the thought.

"I don't think you're the one doing this, Tony. But I do think there's something you're not telling me. Something that might be important to the case." She stands there, leaving a big canyon of silence for me to fall into.

I stare back, holding my ground, waiting for her to continue.

"All right…" she says finally. "If you think of anything, can you give me a call?"

"I have your card."

She nods and is halfway down the steps before she turns back. "Now that this body's shown up, there'll be a lot more rumours floating around. Don't let them get to you, okay?"

I nod. Maybe she's trying to be nice and I've been completely resistant to her up to this point.

She nods again, looking down at her hand where it rests on the railing before turning to leave.

For the first time, I consider that she's struggling to find some way forward in the investigation.

She's at her car when I call out, "Detective Gekas? If I hear about anything, I'll let you know."

Gekas turns back and smiles.

Now, I only hope I can help.

chapter 39

School this morning hits all new levels of crap.

I arrive early to talk to Coach about my absence. He says the team needs me but I can get back to practice when I'm ready. I tell him I'll start fresh on Monday and he's cool, but the truth is I don't want him to be nice. I want him to be hard on me, to push me, to be the coach and not let me be lazy or, worse, scared.

Mike shows up at my locker and encourages me to party with him on Friday. Jessica sends me a text:

Paul thinks u should come out.
We're heading to the Coffee House.
Maybe the dunes after.

I appreciate the support my friends are offering but I'd far rather stick my head under my pillow and stay there until everything blows over—or the end of the school year rolls around—whichever comes first.

That's when it happens.

A couple of Grade 10 girls are looking at me, whispering, and I know the story of Gekas's dead girl has gotten out. Everyone's talking, looking at their phones, and it moves at a supersonic pace through the hallways. Radio and TV news crews are on the scene, streaming live. Social websites drone with speculation as the few details filter out.

Maggie Phelps was a senior at Ashworth Comp, the new school in the southwest of the city. A blue-collar type found her in a ditch at a construction site early this morning. Not much else is being said and a makeshift tent was erected to shield the girl's body from the cameras.

It doesn't take long for the questions to start: *Is there a connection between Maggie Phelps's death and the missing girl, Sheri Beckman?* The police spokeswoman offers no comment. The next question skirts what's on everyone's mind: *Does this indicate foul play in Sheri's disappearance?*

No one says it, but I can just about see the thought bubbling up out of everyone's brain. The thing I've been avoiding for so long, even when Charlie and I walked the trails yesterday. The thing I don't want to believe, the thing Sheri's parents don't want to hear.

Her parents. In no time, I'm sure, news crews will be dispatched to their home, asking more uncomfortable questions. All the pain and anguish they'd tried to tuck away during the search will now spill over.

Everyone seems to have one of two reactions when they see me in the halls: steer clear or get right in my face. I avoid some people, but others collide into me, knocking me into the lockers.

I'm pissed and I want to fight, but there's judgment in enough eyes—the odds are against me. I'd lose.

By afternoon, grief counselors are set up in the office for people dealing with the unexpressed emotions created by Sheri's disappearance and Maggie's death. I come back from psychology—even Ms. Statten couldn't get me out of my funk—I find that somebody has taken a Sharpie and written on my locker: KILLER.

Everyone's looking but I don't care anymore. I stare at it, shocked that someone would be bold enough in all this tragedy to be such a dick. And, like that, I'm done for the day. I toss my bag inside my locker and slam the door.

I'm halfway down the hall when I hear, "Shepherd!"

I turn, ready for a fight, but Charlie's standing there, holding a box from the local doughnut shop.

"What are you doing here?"

His eyebrows shoot up behind his hair and he mocks my tone. "What am I doing here? Are you serious? We got a new lead."

"What? When?"

"The girl. Come on."

"Where?"

"Scene of the crime."

chapter 40

Charlie and I drive across town. He's opened his box of deep-fried, gooey goodness and is already digging into a Boston cream. He hasn't offered me one, not that I'd take it, but they sure smell good.

"Ashworth Comp? Why the hell do we need to go there?"

"Far as I can tell, the cops haven't considered that Maggie may have been killed at the school."

"But the news didn't say anything about Ashworth. Why would you even think that?"

"Because that's our guy's MO."

"What is?"

"The news says the last anybody saw her was when she was working after school in the student council office. They also found her car not too far from where her body was discovered. The assumption is that she left, our guy saw her and attacked her or took her out to the construction site, then killed her."

Again, that word.

"But you don't think that?"

"My sources—"

"Your sources?"

"Yes," he says impatiently. "My *sources* say that a janitor said he saw her leaving—"

"But you don't believe that?"

"Hell, no! People suck at remembering stuff like that. Eyewitness accounts are, like, fifty per cent accurate."

"And you get this statistic from where?"

He ignores my question and goes on. "The janitors are out of there by 10:00 or 11:00 at the latest. That means our killer"—I feel myself wince—"needed maybe four or five hours to lay low."

"So what are you looking for?"

"Proof of the pattern, man!"

I stare at him. I'm not really sure I know what he's talking about.

"And why am I here?"

"Because we're a team!"

News to me.

chapter 41

I stop the car a block away from the school. The street is swarming with news vans, worried parents, and cops. Lots and lots of cops.

Charlie stares at the activity. "Shit."

"What?"

"They might mess up our crime scene."

"What? This isn't ours—this is theirs. We should let them do their job."

"And how's that working so far? For Sheri."

"This isn't a game."

"No, it isn't. We're trying to stop a killer."

I can't deal with this anymore. "Stop."

"What?"

"Stop using that word."

"What? Killer?" He stares at me for a second, then, "Okay, I pussyfooted around it yesterday, but it's time we face this. Whoever did this to Maggie is likely the same guy that killed Sheri."

There it is. The two words, side by side.

I've known it all this time but haven't wanted to say it. I chew my lip, staring past Charlie to the chaos at the front of the school. There'd been a similar scene at Sheri's school only a few days ago. It had been broadcast all over the news, Facebook, and Twitter.

Charlie keeps at me. "The sooner you quit deluding yourself and face that truth, the sooner we can find whoever did it. That *is* what you want?"

I'm nodding without thinking. "Yes."

"Good. So let's go in—"

"Whoa." I'm upset but not crazy. "I can't go waltzing into that school on a day like today."

"Why not?"

"Gekas may not think I... May not connect me to what happened with Sheri or Maggie, but every angry parent and teenager will be looking for someone to blame."

"Good point."

He looks out at the school, mulling it over. "Okay, you stay here and run recon. You see or hear anything that might be valuable, let me know." He shakes his phone.

"What's your number?" I ask.

"Programmed it into your phone yesterday. It's under 'Hot Diggity.'"

I must be getting used to him because I'm a little less fazed by this today.

He grabs another doughnut, a honey dip, and opens the door of the car, swinging his feet onto the pavement.

"Okay, gimme fifteen, twenty minutes to get in and out."

I nod.

"And don't touch my doughnuts, okay? You want some, you buy your own—got it?"

I can't help but laugh at his manners; he doesn't seem to notice or care.

He stares out at the school, mulling something over in his head. He looks back at me. "You talk to Gekas today?"

"Yeah. Why?"

"Just that you didn't tell me. If we're gonna be partners, you gotta keep me in the loop."

Then he's gone and I'm left wondering when we became partners—or accomplices.

The wait for Charlie is excruciating.

It's already been ten minutes and even though I'm supposed to give him another five, I'm ready to call and tell him to get back here. I'm certain he won't listen to me, though, so I don't know what good it would do. Might even make things worse by drawing attention to him. But if I do, then at least I can say that I was against his actions when the authorities track us down and take us in.

I watch the crowds outside the school. Parents keep swooping in and airlifting their kids out of harm's way. Fear has set in and rational thought is out. Nothing has happened to anyone while they were in class; everything has occurred after school. If anything, these crazy adults should be locking their kids up once they get home from their daily education.

Reporters keep questioning everyone, desperate for a sound bite they can play at 6:00. Moms and dads aren't having it, so every socially needy teen crowds around the cameras hoping to be interviewed. I like being a part of our connected generation, but for every interesting person or story out there, there are a dozen duck-faces and angry rants from someone desperate for attention.

I'm watching the action out there, but my mind keeps drifting to what Charlie said. *Sheri was murdered.* The thought is like a spike driven deep down in my brain. I keep having this memory of her smiling at me—I don't know where we are—all I know is it's sunny and warm—knowing that I won't—no, that I may not—see her again. I want to throw up. I want to cry. But I force it all back, roll down the window and suck down the fresh air that washes in.

A dark car pulls up to the school—I've seen it before. Gekas steps out and I sink lower in my seat. I'm sure I'm far enough away that she can't see me, but I don't want to take the risk.

I grab my phone and text Charlie:

Gekas is here. Get out.

I hold the phone, staring at it, waiting for a reply. Nothing. I peek over the window frame. Gekas is talking to a couple of officers at the front doors. She's facing my way and I'm hoping she doesn't see me. A guy sitting in a car by a school where one of the students has just been murdered is suspicious. A guy slunk down, trying not to be seen in front of that same school is a whole new level of wrong.

I look at my phone. A minute has passed and still nothing from Charlie.

Where the hell is he?

Gekas moves inside the school with one of the officers; the other remains stationed at the door.

I text again.

Gekas is inside.

I wait for a response but at this point I'm not expecting anything. I'm considering the possibility of sneaking inside to find him. Where would I even start? How quickly would someone realize I don't belong? When would Gekas come after me? What would happen if I showed up? I might not even make it across the front lawn before reporters and cops figure out who I am and swarm me.

Bzzz.

Finally. I look at my phone, but it's not Charlie—it's Jessica.

FYI - Dillon was dating murdrd girl

What? How do you know?

I wait, watching Jessica type, the little grey dots cycling over and over.

**Katie told me. She was interested
in him til she heard. Says he still
tried to make a move on her.**

Ah, classic Dillon. Playing as many girls as he can. Which also explains why Katie maybe didn't seem to be on my side at our little gathering. And Charlie stole Dillon's phone.

I go to my photos, scrolling through them until I find the screenshots he took. *Gf for now*—I am guessing that's Maggie. Damn. I look over the messages but really there's nothing there:

Want to come over?

Cant. Football

Later?

Maybe

The guy's as boring as '90s soft rock. I have no clue what Sheri ever saw in this idiot.

I text Jessica a **thx** and look at the time. Charlie's been in there for twenty minutes.

I'm stuck. I'd drive away but that would be a dick move and I've thoroughly convinced myself that I'm not going in. My mind tries to put the pieces together about Dillon. Two people he's been with have had... bad things happen to them. Plus, there's a third—Mia-ow, whoever that is—waiting on the sidelines. Right now, he's my number one suspect, and I want to figure out what the hell he's up to.

"Didja touch my doughnuts?"

I nearly crap myself. Charlie's kneeling beside my driver's side window.

"Where the hell did you come from?"

"Ah—I had to take the long way back. Seriously, did you?"

"What?"

"Touch my doughnuts."

"No!"

"Cool. Did you know Gekas is here?"

"What do you think I've been texting you about?"

Charlie looks at his phone. "Oh yeah, I forgot I turned it off."

"What? Why?"

"I figured you'd get panicky and start texting me every second."

"Then why'd you tell me to keep an eye out?"

"To keep you out of trouble." He circles around to the passenger side and jumps in. "Let's go."

I start the car and pull around the first corner I can. Once we're a little way down the block, I hit the gas and put as much distance between us and the school as I can.

chapter 43

Charlie opens the box and starts munching on an apple fritter. I'm not a fan but I guess someone's gotta eat them.

"Can we stop at a gas station?"

"Sure. You need a coffee to wash that down?"

He pulls his doughnuts farther away from me. "That's just gross."

"So what did you go looking for in there?"

Charlie chews for a bit, pondering the question. "Yesterday, out at the trails, I kept wondering if the place he chose maybe wasn't for convenience."

"What do you mean?"

"I wondered if it had significance in itself." He points at a gas station on the left and I pull up to the store.

He runs in quickly and comes back with a map.

"There's an app for that, you know," I say.

He ignores me, motioning me to start driving again, then continues with his thought, "I wondered if he attacked Sheri in the bathroom for a reason."

He looks at me, waiting.

"What?"

"You going to act up every time I say her name?"

"I didn't say anything!"

"You don't have to. You just get all weird and edgy."

I could argue but I know he's right; I've lost all ability to put on a game face. I resign myself to the inevitable, "Go on."

He watches me for a moment, assessing. "I don't think it's simply the convenience of the attack, you know? You could hang out in a stall, wait until someone comes, then attack."

"But how could he expect—" I pause, then push through, "Sheri to show up there?"

"I don't know. Unless he was stalking her. Or he knew her and this was the end of something."

I hate him saying any of this but I also think of Jessica's text about Dillon. I'm about to tell him but he's talking again.

"I don't think it's just a perve thing, like wanting to watch them pee. It's something more..." He trails off, thinking and I don't interrupt. "Anyway, I wanted to see if there was a pattern there, if the bathroom had significance."

"And?"

He gets this big grin on his face and pulls out his phone to show me a picture. It's white and grey and has some writing on it, but with all the bumps and potholes on the street and my desire to not make us crash, I give up. "What is it?"

"It says, 'A stitch in time.'"

"That's it? No, 'saves nine'?"

"Nope."

"What's it mean?"

"I don't know. But you wanna know where I found it?"

I shake my head because he's on a roll.

"On the floor behind a toilet in the last stall of the first floor girls' bathroom on the west side. "

"You think it's from Maggie's killer?"

"You know how many bathrooms I checked in that school? All of them. At least, I *think* I found all of them. And this was the only one with writing."

"So, a threat? Like, nine people to die?"

Charlie shakes his head. "Nah. My thought is the guy had four or five hours to wait around, pre- or post-attack."

"So, he either got bored and started doodling or he's getting cocky and leaving a signature."

Charlie nods, excited by the idea. "Better still, do you know what else is on the west side of Ashworth Comp?"

I try and think about the school and how it's laid out, but I barely remember anything except for the reporters, the students, the cops, and Gekas.

"The parking lot!" Charlie exclaims. "The west entrance opens right onto the student parking lot, which is in direct line of sight to the new subdivision where they found her body."

It's all circumstantial, but I wonder if he might be onto something. "Did you just say you went into every girls' bathroom? And no one saw you? In a school pretty much on lockdown you never once got caught?"

"What can I say? I'm the magic man."

"I thought you were Hot Diggity?"

"That too!" He finishes off his apple fritter and opens up the map.

I still don't know what he's looking for.

chapter 44

Now it's my turn. "While you were sneaking around toilet stalls, I connected with my own sources."

"It's about time. I can't do all the work."

I try to ignore the shot, but it's true. I'm not really sure what I've been doing to help. "Turns out, Maggie was dating Dillon."

He pulls out a jam-filled doughnut caked with sugar. "Oh, that?"

"Wait? What? You knew?"

"Of course I did." He pauses, realizing. "Did I forget to tell you?"

I nod. So much for being partners and sharing all the info.

"Shoot. Sorry about that. After you dropped me off, I decided to follow up on Dillon. He works over at that burger place on Quance—"

He looks at me, as if I should know the place he's talking about.

"You know, Romeo's Burgers—"

"No clue."

"Anyway, he works the drive-thru on weekends." He pauses, taking a big bite of doughnut.

Sugar sprinkles are everywhere. I watch with dismay as it falls around him—and all over my dad's tidy car.

Charlie's oblivious. "I could really go for one of their Sloppy Chew specials..." he adds.

"Dude?"

He looks and I nod to the mess he's making on the seat.

"Oh, sorry." He grabs a napkin from the glove box and begins dusting off his lap and the car seat.

His revelations aren't over. "So this morning after I heard about Maggie, I went and looked through their employee records—"

"How do you even do that?"

He looks at me and I realize who I'm talking to.

"And sure enough, Maggie Phelps worked there, too. I did a bit more digging around, and guess what? Never mind, I'll tell you. They were dating." He looks at me as he licks off a glop of raspberry jam from his hand. "I don't suppose we could stop for a burger—"

"No."

I drive in silence.

"What's up your ass?"

"What about all your 'we're a team' or 'yeah, we're partners' or 'keeping each other in the loop'?"

"You're mad because I didn't tell you about Dillon?"

"Yeah!"

"Ah. I, uh, see how you could be upset about that."

"You could, could you?"

"Yeah, I think so."

His ability to be this much of a dumbass astounds me. I laugh.

He stares down at the last doughnut in the box—chocolate covered with sprinkles. "You know, Dillon's at a football game this afternoon."

I look over at him.

"We could go check him out. Of course, Gekas and her homies will make the connection soon enough and likely be on their way."

"Sounds good."

He closes the lid on the last doughnut, saving it for later. "Sweet."

chapter 45

School buses sit at the players' entrance of the city stadium, a handful of cars edged around them. Even though schools play in the stadium of our national league team, turnout is minimal.

Charlie hops out of the car, taking his map and doughnut box with him.

I follow him to the main entrance. "Are you ever going to share?"

"Let it go," he says over his shoulder, then realizes I'm talking about his food. "Why should I? You're rich. Get your own."

I jog a bit to catch up. "I'm not rich."

"So says the guy who lives in snob central."

"Whatever."

"What do your parents do for fun? Art gallery openings? Night at the symphony?"

I laugh but their last date was for a hospital foundation fundraiser. I decide not to comment.

"My mom's idea of a good night is watching reality TV drunk on the couch."

I'm guessing it's not a lie and have no idea how to respond.

"You and I are night and day."

He shifts the doughnut box to the side away from me.

"So why are you hanging around?" I get up the courage to ask.

He looks over at me.

"I mean, if we're so different, if who I am pisses you off, why are you even bothering?"

He glares at me for a second, then a sly smile comes across his face. "You know, trying to make me feel like a jerk isn't going to get you anywhere near my doughnut box."

I smile and let it go. But somewhere beneath all the attitude is more to the story of Charlie than a kid from a broken home and a mother who doesn't care. At least, that's my best guess. His indifference makes me think that if she's around, she's an irrelevant feature of his life.

He keeps poking at my so-called "rich kid" status too, and it's annoying. I'm not the stereotype he thinks I am, but then Charlie definitely doesn't act like a poor kid from the wrong side of the tracks, either. He's full of surprises. He pulled that cell phone out of his pocket when I didn't even think he owned one, and for all I know he could drive around the corner one day in some souped-up muscle car. If he keeps going the way he has been, nothing will surprise me in the end.

Inside the stadium we take the ramp up to the second level; the seats above the few spectators there will give us a good view. We come out to the bleachers on the shady side of the stadium. The sun is out but a fall breeze keeps things cool.

Charlie zips up his sweater, pulling it tight. "Maybe I shoulda bought us some shitty gas station coffee."

I smile. "Would have been good for a stakeout."

The players are on the field. The game is in its second quarter. Dillon's team has the ball and it's third and one, but I can't see where he is.

Charlie points toward centrefield, "Our boy's the running back."

I see his name, ROSS, number 27, to the left of the quarterback, number 48, waiting for the snap. He circles around as 48 takes the ball and cuts quick across the back. The quarterback twists and pitches the ball under his left arm into Dillon's waiting grasp. Dillon digs down and runs and I can see the speed in his legs. He's quick but not observant and he's rushed by the safety, who slams him hard to the ground.

I admit I enjoy seeing him taken down.

The offensive line moves off the field and Dillon takes a seat on the bench. He pulls off his helmet and pours some sugary electrolytes down his throat. The whole action seems posed, like he thinks he's in a commercial and everyone's watching.

Unfolding the map, Charlie scoffs, "He's always announcing how he's an elite athlete in the halls."

"What a douche."

"Couldn't agree more."

I lean forward. "What if it's all a show for someone... special."

The stands are filled with adults, mostly parents, and a few students. Cheerleaders hang out on the sidelines, mingling during plays, occasionally smiling over at the guys on the bench. Yet, Dillon doesn't seem to be one of the smiled-upon. He appears focused on the game, until suddenly he looks over his shoulder at someone down low in the stands to the left of us. He shoots whoever it is a quick, dazzling grin before turning back to the play.

"Did you see that?" I ask and realize Charlie isn't even looking, his eyes focused on the map. I *still* don't know what it's for.

For once, I've seen something Charlie hasn't, and I point in the direction Dillon was looking.

"No one I can see—oh, wait..." he pauses, holding his hand out toward me.

"What?"

"Your phone."

"You have your own."

"Yeah, but I can't use it for this!"

"For what?"

"Just give me your damn phone."

I stare at him.

"Please!"

"Fine," I say with disgust, but inside I'm laughing. I guess I *can* teach a stubborn dog new tricks.

He takes it, tapping in my passcode without even asking. I'm guessing it took him only seconds being around me to figure it out. He opens the browser.

"Why can't you use your own?"

"They always figure out it's me."

"Quit with the pronoun game. Who?"

"School officials."

I react, grabbing the phone to find he's on an admin page for his school. A spreadsheet of teachers' contact information lists names, addresses, and phone numbers. He steals it back and scrolls down the page.

"Oh, snap." He hands back the phone, pointing. "See down there? Second row, fifth from the end?"

I scour the crowd and see a pretty, tall, blond woman, maybe in her late twenties, her hair pulled back in a ponytail.

"That's Miss Turner." He taps at my phone.

I search the list and don't see it.

He points. "Mia Turner."

I look at him. "Miss Mia-ow Turner?"

"Double snap!"

That's when Gekas walks into the stadium, flanked by cops, headed straight for Dillon.

chapter 46

As soon as Gekas hits the field, it's chaos. Refs blow whistles, coaches run out, parents in the stands yell.

Dillon sees it all happening but doesn't seem to register that they're here for him. He stands in position, waiting for the next play, and it isn't until Gekas beelines past the quarterback that what's going on finally dawns on him.

He backpedals a little, but she yells, "Don't do it, Dillon," and he freezes on the spot.

She's talking quietly now, and the coach is shouting and the refs are trying to figure out why the hell this woman has interrupted the game.

I look over at Charlie but he's gone. I search the crowd and see him ducking into the nearest exit. I follow.

"Where are we going?" I ask as I reach him.

"As soon as Gekas showed up, Mia-ow took off."

"You think they're in this together."

"Oh, they're into something, all right."

We see her walking briskly down the ramp toward the parking lot and sprint to catch up. By the time we're outside, she's rushing to her car.

"Miss Turner—"

She doesn't turn. "I don't know anything—"

"Miss—"

"Please, just leave me alone." She struggles to get her keys out of her purse, battling to get the door open.

"Mia-ow."

She pauses and turns, finally looking at us. "Charlie?"

He slows to a halt, hands raised. "I just want to talk."

"About what?" The sight of him has thrown her off and her keys slip out of her hand.

"Dillon."

Her face drops and she begins to cry.

chapter 47

When Mia's tears don't stop, I suggest we sit in her car, at least until Charlie and I figure out exactly what's going on.

She unlocks the door and Charlie looks at me.

"Shotgun," he whispers, and moves quickly into the front seat on the passenger side.

I shake my head at his lack of decorum and climb into the back. It's packed full of papers, makeup, and dusty mixtape CDS.

Charlie ferrets out a tissue—I don't know where he got it from—and hands it to her.

She wipes away the tears and snot and groans as she looks at herself in the visor mirror. "God, I've had better days."

Charlie opens up his doughnut box. "Have the last one."

She looks at it, shaking her head.

"Come on, Miss Turner. It'll make you feel better."

"I think we're a little past the 'Miss' part," she says as she gives in to the temptation of the chocolate-covered treat.

I lean forward, wedging myself between the seats. "Can you tell us what happened?"

She takes a big bite of the doughnut and sprinkles shower onto her lap. She stares out the window, running the side of her pinkie along the corners of her mouth to catch any chocolate.

"At the start, it was innocent. Nothing but him hanging around, asking questions. I didn't think anything of it. He was a student and there are some lines you simply don't cross. Then the guy I was dating cheated on me and it hurt.

"One day, after school, I was feeling like crap and he hung around and I started talking about my ex and he listened. It felt good. He said nice things to me. He said I deserved better. That I was pretty."

"And then it kept happening. He'd visit and we'd talk. It was always about things he'd done or things he wanted me to do and it was never about school or other girls. It was interesting and I knew what I was thinking and how I was starting to feel, but I kept saying to myself 'as long as nothing happens, it's all right.' All I had to do was make sure we didn't cross that line."

She's chewing meditatively, and I already know what she's going to say next.

"But Dillon was persistent and kept gently pushing that line. He gave me his number 'just to talk' and I took it and left it for the longest time. Then I had one long, bad week, and I went home that Friday feeling miserable and I had a drink and saw his number and..."

She holds the last few bites of doughnut hovering in front of her mouth and looks like she's about to cry again. She shakes it off, though her face crumples like she's maybe mentally berating herself. Finally she adds, "We never did anything."

"Mia, we read some of those texts—"

"It never meant anything. It was all talk, all flirting, all..."

Charlie finishes her thought. "Foreplay."

She looks at him, shocked by the accusation. She wants to get mad, play the teacher, but knows it's useless—and all too true. "Now, he's in trouble, and soon they'll figure out it's me. I'll lose my job and—"

"Wait, you think this is about you two?"

She looks at Charlie, confused, then turns to me. "Isn't it—?"

Charlie shuts the lid on the empty doughnut box.

"Oh, Mia, this is so much worse."

chapter 48

The last of the parents pull out of the parking lot and only a few buses and cop cars remain. Mia isn't handling the new facts very well.

"But that's impossible."

"I promise you, it is."

Mia protests. "No, he couldn't have."

"Why not?"

"Because—" She's not making this very easy.

"You said you two didn't do anything."

"No, but—"

The nature of their relationship dawns on me. "It didn't stop you from hanging out together."

The pained expression returns to her face. "He showed up at my house one night. We visited. Then we did it again, watching movies. I'd sit on one side of the couch, he'd sit on the other."

Charlie laughs. "Like that's a buffer."

Mia really hasn't figured out much about life even though she's likely ten years older than me.

Charlie pushes the questions forward. "Was he with you last night?"

She nods.

"What about last Wednesday?" I ask.

She thinks back. "Yes. I think we watched the new Matthew McConaughey movie that night."

I lean back in the seat and ponder the mess Mia has made for herself. "You need to tell the cops."

"What do you mean?"

I'm shocked by her naiveté but I persist, "Dillon is the main suspect in a murder case."

"But if I tell them, I might lose my job."

"And he might go to jail."

I can see the gears grinding in her head and I can't believe she isn't even considering helping him. "I like him. He's so sweet. But I've wanted to be a teacher for so long—"

Charlie interrupts, "You know what, Mia. Don't."

I turn on him. "What?"

"He'll spend a few nights in jail, but there isn't enough evidence to hold him."

"You don't know that for sure."

He ignores me, turning back to Mia. "Wait it out. Go home and think about it. Don't rush your decision."

"Charlie—?"

"I'm sure it's going to work itself out." He puts a hand on the door handle and I know he's about to leave.

I lean forward. "Mia, don't listen—"

Charlie's already getting ready to go. "Thanks for your help. We'll let you go."

"Charlie! Mia—"

But he's popped open the door and is gone.

I want to convince Mia to talk to the cops but I also need to catch up to Charlie.

"Go tell them the truth. Ask for Detective Gekas. She'll be able to help you keep it anonymous. I'm sure of it."

Charlie's gone and I can't wait any longer.

I open the door and look back at her. "Mia, please, do what's right."

I get out of the car, feeling certain she's not going to listen to me.

Charlie's standing by my car, his hand on the roof, waiting for me to let him in.

"What the hell was that about?"

"You said it yourself. Dillon's a douche. Just let him spend a few nights in jail," he says.

"You can't be serious."

"What's it matter to you?"

"It's wrong."

"So?"

"We don't let innocent people go to jail!"

"Why not? It buys us some time to sort out this case without spending every second trying to stay ahead of Gekas."

"Are you for real?"

Charlie's hand slips from the car. "You know what? *You* go do what's right. *You* go talk to Gekas and tell her everything. Tell her about everything we've been up to and see what she thinks. Maybe she'll say, 'Oh, thank you *so* much for all this wonderful information, Mr. Shepherd,' right before she throws your ass in jail for tampering with evidence, obstructing justice, or maybe because you've made yourself seem like a pretty good suspect again. Yeah, that's right, go on, have fun."

He walks away and I let him.

I can't believe Gekas would really think any of what Charlie's said. She said I wasn't a suspect. But I also know that she'll likely be pissed about Charlie and me snooping around the investigation.

Except, there's no need to get him involved. Nobody really knows about the two us working together, so I could keep the focus on me. And I haven't contaminated any crime scenes, so it gives me deniability. Can't say the same for Charlie. Also, Gekas is headed for a dead-end with Dillon. Letting her know the truth will get her back on track, or at least searching for the right person.

Still, Dillon's an ass and he wouldn't help me if he had a chance. I know that's not the point, and I dismiss the thought as soon it pops in my head.

When I see Gekas and the officers come out of the stadium with Dillon, his hands cuffed behind his back, I know what I've got to do.

Charlie's nowhere to be seen. He's already disappeared somewhere across the railroad tracks that border the south end of the parking lot.

chapter 49

Gekas sits behind her desk, staring at me in disbelief.

She didn't want to listen to me outside the stadium. Dillon was already in custody and had been read his rights. She wasn't going to release him because of hearsay from some kid. She told me to come down to her office at the station in an hour, but I ignored her and drove to the station immediately, determined to sit on the benches at the front until she would see me.

When the officer behind the front desk called to let her know I was there, I could tell by his face that she wasn't impressed. She let me sit there for almost two hours. My gut just couldn't deal with letting an innocent person be stuck in jail if I knew there was something I could do about it—even a douche like Dillon.

"I told you to come talk to me if you had something, but this isn't what I had in mind."

I try to relax in the chair but the dying sun streams in brightly through the window behind her right into my eyes. "Dillon's got an alibi."

She pulls a cup of coffee toward her and by the rings around the inner edge I can tell it hasn't been washed in forever. She takes a sip, cringes, and pushes it away.

"I know. He told me."

I didn't think this through enough. Of course he did. He doesn't care about Mia's job when it means his life.

"Except, I can't seem to track down the person he was with."

I'm not sure how much to say. "She was at the stadium."

Gekas leans forward, smiling. "Really, Anthony?"

Shit, how much have I already screwed up?

"And how do you know Miss Turner, since you don't even go to her school?"

"I..."

Gekas doesn't say anything, just leans back in her chair, and waits for me to put my foot in my mouth.

"Sheri told me."

"Oh, she did." Gekas smiles again. She knows I'm full of crap. "She told you about her ex-boyfriend's relationship with his teacher."

"Yes." When all else fails, just keep shovelling the bullshit.

"Even when he was trying to get back with your girlfriend at the same time?"

I know she's digging at my emotions, hoping to crack my lie. "Yeah. That's why she told me. I saw a text from him and was pissed. She told me not to worry, that he's just playing everyone. She told me about her, and Mia—Miss Turner, and Maggie."

By now, all I can see is Gekas' silhouette. The heat of the sunset bleeds into the room. Or at least I hope it's the sun, because I know I'm starting to sweat.

"Well, she seems to have told you everything. Why didn't you tell me any of this when I came to your house this morning?"

"Because I didn't know it was relevant." At least, I hope I didn't. "You never told me the girl's—Maggie's—name."

I can't remember anything about this morning, so I open my mouth and my brain pours out whatever it invents.

Gekas looks at me, still smiling, shaking her head. She rises and leaves the room, taking her cup with her.

I'm not sure if we're done, so I look out the door behind me and see her down the hall, in a break room, dumping her coffee and filling it fresh from the pot. She comes back in and sits down.

"This is all really nice of you, Anthony, helping out a guy who hits on your girlfriend, dated your girlfriend, who you got into a fight with the other day at the school of your missing girlfriend."

Shit.

"Oh yeah, I know. You and—" she opens a folder on her desk "—Charles Wolfe had a little visit with some of Sheri's friends, including Dillon, with whom you had an altercation."

She closes the folder. "Nothing serious. A little pushing. A few threats. Nothing a person could go to jail for." She pauses for a moment, building up to her pitch. "My question is, what are you and Charles up to?"

"Nothing." Swing and a miss.

"Anthony? You can do better than that."

"I was only asking what you asked the others, to figure out if I was a suspect."

"And you enlisted Charles to help you with this?"

Ugh—strike two. I keep going, "Yeah, he knows the place, the people—"

"Anthony, cut the crap."

Gekas is ahead of me and we both know it. The only question is how soon I admit it.

I come clean. "I want to know what happened—who did this—who..." I look out the window above Gekas at the long shadows of the city's skyline. "I want to know who killed Sheri."

"Do you know the kind of person Charles is?"

I've got a pretty good idea, but I'm sure she's going to tell me anyway.

She turns in her chair and grabs a second folder. This one's thicker than the other. A lot thicker. She slaps it down on the desk and opens it.

"Seems like Charles is a busy boy. The times we've caught him, he's been arrested for invasion of privacy, gambling, possession of prohibited weapons, public nuisance, public mischief, vandalism, disorderly conduct, theft, breaking and entering, trespassing, arson, criminal negligence, bodily harm, dangerous use of a motor vehicle, identity theft, and attempted escape. He was too young to get tried as an adult for half of those. He's also suspected of corruption, misleading justice, possession and trafficking, false pretenses, forgery... Do you get the idea?"

My head spins. I knew he was trouble—I *knew* it—but I don't think I expected this much.

Gekas wheels her chair close to her desk out of the bright sun. She's not smiling now.

Still, I can see her eyes and I know she cares.

"Anthony, I'm going to find out what happened to Sheri. I promise. But you need to let me do my job. You and Charles need to quit doing what you're doing so that there are no mistakes. We don't know that Sheri and Maggie are connected. At the moment, these are two separate incidents and need to be treated as such. But when we find out what happened to Sheri and we find the person or persons responsible, they go to jail. You've got to do this for us, okay? For you, me... and Sheri."

I nod. I know she's right. But in the back of my head, I'd really like it if she'd send the person responsible to the morgue.

chapter 50

After I'm done with Gekas, I go home. I'm wiped. All I want to do is to lie down and sleep the night away. I'm not sure if I'm ready for Mom and Dad, so I hope I can sneak inside.

Ollie greets me, giving me all the unconditional love I need. I toss my bag on the floor by the shoes at the kitchen door and give him a good rubdown.

The house is quiet. I'm sure Dad is here somewhere and Mom is too, but I don't want to get into anything. I'm dreaming of the old days when I could make it through a day with only good old uncomplicated teen angst to be concerned about. The normal stuff. Not the parent-fighting-cop-questioning-girlfriend-missing stuff.

Yet, I don't even get a hello and it stings. Sheri's disappearance opened a hole in my life and it keeps getting wider and I feel like I'm going to tumble in and never return.

Maybe it's time to allow some small semblance of normalcy back into my life. Since there's no supper cooking, I leash the dog and put a plastic bag in my pocket. But before I get outside, Dad calls from somewhere in the house.

"Son?"

"Yeah..." I wait for a moment.

"Where are you headed?" He can be so casual, so passive-aggressive sometimes. I bet what he means is "don't even think about leaving without saying where you're going before dinner."

I try not to sound defensive as I call back, "It's still a bit early. I was taking Ollie for a walk."

Silence. Ollie looks impatient and I feel it too.

"Your mom's picking up Thai on the way home from the clinic. She'll be home about 7:00."

"Got it, Dad." I look down at Ollie. "Come on, boy. Let's get the hell out of here before he says anything else."

We head for the creek and walk along the path. The sun has sunk still further and it's cool out. I pull my hood over my head and settle one hand into a pocket. Ollie walks without pulling and sniffs at everything. He doesn't leave a tree trunk, bush, or leaf unturned.

I mull over these past few days with Charlie.

Damn, he's different. Not someone I'd hang out with. He doesn't think like anyone else I know and some of the things he does—the way his brain works—he doesn't care or give a crap about what's right or wrong, or what should or shouldn't be done. I worry that one day he's going to cross a line and end up in a whole heap of trouble and I might be around when it happens.

He's led us—where exactly? He assumes Sheri was attacked in the bathroom on the trails and that Maggie died in the bathroom at the school. But there's no hard evidence to back up either of these suppositions. All we have for it—no, all *I* have for it—is a huge fight with my parents, skipping school and practice, and dealing with Gekas while we mess up her investigation. He was wrong about her, and every step forward I make with Charlie wrecks everything else in my life.

And I don't think we're any closer to finding out what happened to Sheri.

Still, my gut says that I should pay attention and keep him around. And that scares the crap out of me. That seems unstable. Everything in Gekas's file makes him a straight-up sociopath, if Ms. Statten's psych class has taught me anything.

But if Charlie is right, maybe it'll take someone like him to find this killer. Psychopath, sociopath—aren't they all the same disorder, one's just a little further off the rails?

Charlie's got something on his mind, something going on in his head, and I need to trust him. And now that Gekas knows about us, I wonder if I should warn him. Would it even matter? Would it slow him down? Or stop him? Or would it just push him to do more?

I open my phone, and bring up Hot Diggity.

Gekas knows about you.

I'm sure there's more I should say but I leave it at that.

Ollie finally does what he came out for. I pull a bag out of my pocket and do the good pet-owner thing.

"All done, buddy? Should we go a little further?"

I'm not in a rush. The only thing waiting for me is take-out and an awkward supper with the parents, followed by a huge, heaping load of homework.

I walk a little further, enjoying the cool wind, the last of the sun, and the auburn trees. I take a deep breath in and close my eyes, the smells of walnut and rich spice spinning in my head.

I open my eyes. A leaf falls from a tree and lands on the path and Ollie pulls me ahead to greet it.

chapter 51

My prediction for an awkward supper is a hundred per cent on the money.

Mom and Dad talk about their day. Dad's wrapped up the contract he's working on and Mom's made some calls to hiring agencies for a new receptionist. It's all small talk—nothing with real meaning—and dead air fills the room.

I miss Heather. She's out tonight, but if she were here, she could at least share tales of university and make it a little less uncomfortable. It hasn't occurred to me until this moment that maybe she's skipped this family meal on purpose.

I know *I* would have.

None of us bring up yesterday. By now they likely know I've missed most of the afternoon at school again. They probably haven't asked how my day went, fearing I might lie—or worse, tell the truth.

I'm guessing that if they ever met Charlie, I'd be grounded for sure.

The Thai food is tasty and since there are no dishes, clean-up goes faster than normal. Which is good, since all I want is to get out of here as fast as possible.

In the safety of my room, I shut the door. I sink heavily into my desk chair and stare at my bag of homework. It feels like forever since I cracked a book or did anything school-related. I've got assignments from every class.

The right thing to do is to cut ties with Charlie, let Gekas do her job. I can go back to my ordinary life of school, practice, and regular meals with my folks. In a week or two, life will go back to normal, and maybe with Charlie and me out of the way, Gekas will find Sheri's killer.

I pause on that thought. Somewhere along the way, I've come to terms with the worst possible scenario. I've accepted that Sheri isn't coming home, and sadly, it's almost a relief.

I sway in my chair, looking at the books stacked high on my desk and sigh. I pick up my phone and see a message from Mike and another from Jessica. Both are asking me to come to the party this weekend.

I'm not in the mood to socialize.

I'm not in the mood to do much of anything.

I turn off my desk lamp and my room slips into darkness. I lie back on my bed, headphones on, and go to my playlist. I cue up some music and open a mindless first-person shooter app. I'm in my own little bubble, listening to Run the Jewels, defending the Earth from an alien invasion, letting everything else fall away.

chapter 52

"Anthony!"

I'm jolted out of sleep. My earbuds lie somewhere beneath me, and my phone is nowhere to be found. I look at the clock. It's almost 9:00 p.m.

"Anthony!" Dad yells at me from downstairs.

I go to the door, unwilling to leave the safety of my room. "Yeah?"

"There's someone here to see you."

I run through the list of who it could be, and although I wish it were Mike, or even Gekas, I'm sure I know who it is. "Be right down."

At the bottom of the stairs, I take a quick peek around the corner.

Damn.

Charlie Wolfe is standing in my front hall and Dad is right there, talking to him.

"I read *The Spy Who Came in From the Cold* and thought, 'Whoa, this is great. I need more of this.'"

"You should read *Tinker, Tailor, Soldier, Spy*. I found it most satisfying."

"I hated that one. I kept waiting for something to happen. It's like Le Carré was being obstinately obtuse."

Dad's quite a bit taller than him, but Charlie holds his own, not seeming intimidated at all.

"What about craft and subtlety?"

Charlie laughs. "What about a good story? And the mole? I knew it was him all along."

I can't believe my ears. Or my eyes. He's here, standing in my house, arguing with my dad. I want to ask how he knows where I live but it might be better if I don't.

I need to cut in. "Hey."

They both stop and look at me.

"Oh, Anthony. Charlie here dropped by to check on you."

"I see that."

"Hey," he says, nonchalantly.

I think I want to punch him.

I nod back, and the most silent moment of silence follows.

Dad stands between us, waiting, and finally he can't take it. "Well, I'll let you two chat. Charlie, it was nice to meet you. If you get a chance, try *The Secret Pilgrim*."

"Thank you, Mr. Shepherd. I will."

Dad goes back into the family room. I watch him go.

Once he's out of earshot, I close the distance between me and Charlie. "What the hell was that?"

"What the hell was what?"

I don't have time for his bullshit. "What are you doing here?

"Maybe we should go outside."

chapter 53

Charlie and I stand on the front step. Getting him out of the house makes me feel a little better, but it's dark out and I shiver in the cold.

Charlie nods at me. "You should have put a jacket on."

"Why are you here? What's going on?"

"Your dad seems nice."

"I know he is, Charlie. Answer the question."

"I never knew mine." He looks up at the porch light and I think he's genuinely sad.

I soften. "What's going on?"

"I think you should stay in for the next couple of nights."

"What are you talking about?"

"Don't hang around me. Get back to your usual schedule. Go back to practice. Hang out with your friends. Then come home, do your homework."

"Where is this coming from? Is this because of the text?"

He's distracted, his mind struggling to catch up to the conversation we're having. "Oh, yeah, the text. I figured as much."

"Gekas knows everything we've been up to so far," I say, debating whether or not to tell him everything.

He beats me to the punch. "Did she show you my file?"

I don't answer and he smiles. "It's thick, huh? Every cop likes to show that off when I go in, thinking it'll scare me straight." He shakes his head. "Everyone—school, cops, parents—expects us to want redemption. You know who doesn't care? The kooks out there hurting people who try to play it straight."

The look on his face reminds me of the first day I met him, but I'm exhausted and now I can't keep up with the conversation. "Charlie—?"

He pulls out the gas station map he bought earlier in the day. He unfolds it quickly and I see he's labelled it with a marker.

"Sheri disappeared here," he points. "We don't know what happened to her, but we don't think it's good."

I know he's avoiding the word "murdered" on purpose and I'm grateful for it.

"Our theory—" he looks at me, "okay, *my* theory, is that whoever attacked her did it in the bathroom on the trail."

He flips the map over to the other side. "Maggie was found here, dumped in a ditch behind the construction site in the new subdivision. Two young women attacked? Most likely the same guy. So, I go on the hunch that he'll stick to his MO and check the location where she was last seen," he indicates Ashworth Comp, "where I find some writing on a toilet in a bathroom near the student council room where she was working."

He looks up at me. "I know it's all pretty flimsy, but we don't have much else so far. It also seems that whoever our killer is, he's been focusing on high schools and, so far, has been trying to keep his distance from the centre of the city."

"But Sheri—"

"I know. There's an anomaly. Both are high school students. Both are female. Both final locations are on the edge of the city, but I feel certain that Maggie was attacked in the school. Sheri was nowhere near the school, but that isn't to say our guy didn't follow her *from* the school. All this goes with Gekas's profile that we're most likely dealing with a teenage boy.

"If he attacks again, I'm guessing it'll be up here." His finger brushes a wide arc across the upper portion of the map, then he taps the top right corner. "This is all industrial warehouses and factories. There's only one school and it's more east than north." He points to the top left. "There are three schools up here. One is a Catholic school, two are public. If he were to attack anywhere, it might be here. The area is twenty years old and the city has grown up around it quite a bit. It might put him off. But there's also a new mall and a lot of the students wander over there for the food court and the movie theatre."

I know his mind is buzzing now.

"So, what then, Charlie? You going to watch all of them?"

"Yes."

"How—?"

"All I need is for you to stay safe and out of trouble for the next while."

"And what are *you* planning on doing?"

"Keep yourself surrounded by people," he ignores me. "Friends are good. Your folks are better."

"Charlie—"

"I think I can catch him, but I need us not to mess it up."

"Catch him?"

"Gekas makes it harder, but we just need to keep out of her way."

"Charlie? What are you going to do?"

He looks at me and his eyes light up. "Me? I'm gonna get thrown in jail."

part 3

I wake the next morning facedown in my pillow. I'm beyond tired. It seems the events of the last two days—really, that's it, just two days?—have worn me out. All the conditioning Coach has put me through doesn't seem to protect me from the runaway train called Charlie Wolfe.

He didn't explain much to me afterwards, taking off into the night to supposedly get arrested. He seems to enjoy crossing the boundaries that lead to trouble. He's just plain crazy. That's the only explanation for his choices. I don't know how his plans will catch the killer but I don't think his math adds up. Once again I am left with questions.

Yesterday, I thought he might be a sociopath—and what with his impulsive decisions and total disregard for the law, it's probably a fair assessment. He just doesn't care and he'll keep sliding downhill until one day he takes out everyone in his path. The farther I am from him, the safer my family, my friends, and I will be.

I drag myself out of bed and head downstairs. Mom is drinking a cup of coffee at the breakfast table. There's no avoiding it: if I want to eat, I'm going to have to sit across from her. I grab some bran and raisins, skip the soy milk in favour of the real stuff, and take a seat.

She starts us off. "Good morning."

"Morning." I chew away at the cereal, not sure what to say next, hoping it stops at a short greeting, but knowing it won't. And it doesn't.

"Your friend, Charlie—"

"Not my friend—" I'm short about it but the less I associate with him the better. Besides, those were his orders.

"Okay, the boy that stopped by yesterday—" She looks to make sure I approve.

I nod.

"Your dad had a nice visit with him."

"Yeah."

I should be more responsive but I don't know what to say. Charlie seems like the kind of guy who would say or do anything to get what he wants. Was he actually interested in what Dad had to say? My brain decides to blurt out what I'm thinking, "I'm not even sure he's read those books."

"Maybe not, but sometimes we have to give people the benefit of the doubt."

Is Mom defending *Charlie*? What the hell is going on around here?

"Is he in a class of yours...?"

I quickly slurp up some cereal and make a show of chewing the raisins, shaking my head, hoping that if I wait long enough she'll move on.

She doesn't, though, so I finally say, "He's from Sheri's school."

"Oh, so you met him through Sheri?"

She's digging.

I wonder if Gekas has already talked to her and Dad. "I think he might've been a friend of hers."

Mom catches my use of the past tense as quickly as I do. We stare at each other across the table, each seeing in the other's face the understanding that Sheri is likely gone forever.

She clears her throat and swallows. "So, he's pretty upset as well?"

I nod. "He just wants to know what happened."

She reaches across the table and takes my hand, giving it a gentle squeeze. "We just need to be patient. Okay, son?"

I look at her. She loves me. I nod again.

It feels good to kick the door open and let Mom back into my bubble after the past few days.

chapter 55

I walk to school, setting my phone on vibrate and stuffing it deep in my bag. I want some silence to prepare myself for what's ahead. After the media got hold of Maggie's death yesterday, the school turned on me, even though there was no evidence to back it up. The only way to survive is to ride it out and stay off the radar. Whether Charlie intended it or not, his recommended recipe of family, friends, homework, and practice was probably the best I could do right now.

At school, though, it feels like a wave has swept yesterday away. As soon as I'm through the doors, people are already coming up and giving me nods or an acknowledging "s'up." I'm still getting sad puppy-dog eyes from some of the younger girls, but in general, the whole mood is different. Even my locker door has been scrubbed clean, with not even a hint of marker left on it.

Mike greets me with a solid bro hug. "Good to finally see you back on your feet."

"I was here yesterday—"

"Yeah, but you looked like crap."

"Thanks. What's going on around here?"

"Haven't you heard?"

Apparently, Mike tells me, Gekas had a one-on-one interview with the local paper about Maggie's murder and Sheri's disappearance. She said that despite the many similarities, no evidence of a connection has yet been uncovered. Dillon's arrest was shortly followed by news of his release, and Gekas statement that "confirmation of his innocence has been substantiated by two witnesses." So it would seem that Gekas has finally tracked Mia down.

She also announced that another team, headed by Detective Ben Waters, would be investigating the circumstances of Maggie's death while she continued to focus on Sheri's disappearance. She expressed her gratitude to "the family and friends of Miss Beckman for their tireless patience and support," and promised that these separate incidents would each be "given the Homicide Department's foremost attention."

This information is supposed to put me at ease, but I'm not sure if it does.

I go to my first class, history, and grab a seat. I expect the whispers, the looks, but there's nothing. Everyone looks either bored or half asleep. No one is looking at me. I look up at the board. Maybe the only thing I should be caring about is that King John of England signed something on June 15, 1215 and it seems pretty important.

I grab my pen and take notes, trying to figure out what's going on and what was so significant about the Magna Carta. I'm finally making the connections between it and the Thirteen Colonies when the bell rings. The last hour has zipped by.

By noon, I'm back in the groove of things. Whatever notions of vigilante justice swept through school yesterday seem to have been settled by Gekas's news interview. I sit with Mike and some of the other guys from the basketball team and listen to their take on last week's game. Again, I'm told I was missed and they hound me to get back to practice this afternoon. I push them off until tomorrow, knowing I need to carve out a chunk of time to deal with homework. Catching up will suck but it's necessary. Who knows? A few hours of running drills tomorrow morning with Coach yelling at me the whole time might make things feel like they're *really* back to normal.

It isn't until the 1:00 p.m. bell rings that I recognize the painful ache in the pit of my stomach for what it is. I miss the familiar *bzzz* of Sheri's lunchtime texts. I have to force myself to think of other things. Afternoon classes fill the emptiness. I discover we've started George Orwell's *Animal Farm* in English. In chemistry, I'm completely lost trying to understand mole conversion calculations. The last bell rings and I'm absolutely grateful to drag myself out of class.

People fill the halls, talking, laughing, pushing, yelling, making out, breaking up, running ahead, and falling behind. I move among them, with them, between them. Yet, I feel different. There's a space between those of us who've only known the ease of life and those who've felt the thorniness of death.

Charlie would know what I mean.

I push the thought away, forcing it into a deep, dark hole. It's time I get back to living—Sheri would want it that way.

chapter 56

When I get home, Dad's on the couch reading—this time it's *Better* by Atul Gawande. The aroma of fresh baked bread fills the room.

"You've been baking?"

He doesn't look up from the book. "I needed the right sort of something to go with my chicken green chili."

It's all for effect. When Dad makes his chili, he starts in the morning and it simmers all day. A meal that Dad puts this much effort into usually means something good has happened.

He must know that Mom and I have made peace.

"How was school?"

"Good." The word comes out without thinking.

"Hope they're not taking it easy on you with homework."

"Nope. I'll be at it until I'm your age—" I drop my heavy backpack.

"Don't say it—"

"What? 'Old man'?"

"I can still throw you over my knee."

"Come on, bring it."

We look at each other and smile. I've missed this back-and-forth with Dad.

"Get cleaned up before your mom gets home."

"Sure thing, Pops."

He grunts in acknowledgment of the insult as I head up the stairs. I toss my bag on my bed and am surprised to hear Heather behind me.

"Ah, the prodigal son returns."

I know things are getting back to normal when I turn around and see her.

"You must mean the prodigal daughter."

"I wasn't about to stick around while the three of you fight. You were kind of a dinkus."

I shrug. I kind of was.

She comes over and hugs me. "But seriously, are you okay?"

"I was until you got all PDA on me."

I'm joking, but it really does feel good to know she cares about me.

She doesn't let go and squeezes tighter, scrunching up her face. "But you're my widdy-biddy baby brudder!"

I feign a violent attack of vomit, then decide to play along, clutching her tight and swaying her side to side.

"Oh, thank you, my big sissy-wissy."

She shrieks with laughter, trying to get out of my bear hug. We bump into my desk and almost fall over with our shenanigans. When we turn, Mom's standing in the doorway.

"You two are so very weird."

That's all it takes and we're on her, pulling her into the mix, and she can't help but giggle as she tries to push us away.

"Stop it, you two," she shouts between hysteric breaths.

I let them go and Heather and I crack up as Mom tries to gain her composure.

It feels good to laugh. I feel like I haven't laughed in forever.

chapter 57

Dad's chili is amazing.

I savour each mouthful and sop up the leftover sauce with fresh bread. I don't think I've ever enjoyed Dad's cooking so much and tell him so. I'm certain the unspoken truth at the table is that the events of the past week have given me a refreshed outlook on life. But I couldn't care less about coming through a tragedy—I'm not worrying what might happen or thinking about what horrible things people can do to each other—I'm enjoying the good things life offers in the present.

After we're finished, I volunteer to clean up the dishes, but Mom and Dad send me upstairs to do homework. Knowing the stack of assignments I've got to catch up on is waiting, I reluctantly oblige. I don't want to do any of it, but it's gotta get done and there's no way out of it. I drag myself up the stairs and sit down at my desk.

I flip through the assignments and choose biology, since I skipped Mr. Harriet's test on Monday. He's given me a take-home version that's twice as long, and I figure working on it might prompt some goodwill. It takes me until almost 7:30. When I'm done, I put it to the side and open up my psych text. There's six chapters of reading and questions to get through and I want to get it done before bed.

As I work, my phone vibrates. I check it quickly. All the usual faces, except for one—Charlie. For a moment, I wonder what's happened to him. Did he really get himself thrown in jail—and if so, why? I dismiss it quickly and go back to reading about developmental psychology, working my way from childhood to old age.

I surprise myself and get done before 10:00. The house is dark but for the blue glow of the TV when I wander down to grab a glass of water. Mom and Dad are in the den, watching a movie. I say goodnight before going back upstairs.

I shut the door to my room and climb into bed. If I'm going to show up to practice tomorrow before school, I'll need my rest. I crack open *Animal Farm* and read, but can barely keep my eyes open after the first few pages. Setting the book down, I turn the light off, and fall asleep.

chapter 58

The next morning, I get to practice early. The doors are open, but the gym is empty. I grab a ball from the supply closet and bounce it, listening to the *thunk-thunk-thunk* echo in the cavernous room, building my willingness to give in to the energy of the space. I pass the ball between my left and right hands, shifting back and forth, building speed, my shoes digging into the court, the rubber squeaking each time I alter course. My eyes are on the hoop and I dig in, knees bending, muscles tightening, until I power into a jump and feel the ribbed leather surface of the ball solidly in my grip. I roll it off my fingers, ignoring the backdrop, slamming it home. I land rock-hard and it feels good. I feel like I'm me again. I've missed this.

That is, until Coach and the rest of the guys show up and drills begin. By the halfway point, I feel like I've been away for a month and I'm dragging behind everyone else.

Mike dashes past me, chuckling, "Too many bacon burgers on your time off?"

I wipe the sweat from my eyes, ready to argue, but choke on my breath, which only leads to further razzing. I let him gloat. I know myself—it won't take me long to get back in shape, then Mike'll be dodging me and *my* smart ass comments.

At the end of the hour and a half, I'm about ready to fall over. My muscles are worn out, I'm soaked with sweat, and I'm only now catching my breath. But I feel alive. The rush is comforting and familiar. I'm glad I got up early to be here. I'm even grateful for Mike's verbal abuse.

In the locker room, we get ready quickly then hustle to first period. Mike suggests plans for lunch. He wants to go to the new sandwich place because there's another girl, Haley, that he likes.

I roll my eyes. "Wingman extraordinaire. You'd never get anywhere without me."

"You wish." He raises his arm, flexing the bicep. "It has nothing to do with you. It's all this." He kisses the muscle. "Who can say no to *this*?"

I gag and he laughs as he starts to stride away down the hall. Somehow I find myself agreeing to tag along.

I reach biology class and sink into a desk just as the bell rings. My phone is off and tucked away—Mr. Harriet hates distractions. He was good enough to give me a break on the test, but he's all about order and things being done a certain way. He expects our notes to follow his rules and if they don't, we lose marks. Yet, I force myself to focus not only because I have to, but because I want to.

Ms. Statten's psychology class is next, and I'm actually kind of looking forward to it. I'm even there early, before the bell goes. The lights are dim, and the vibe in the room is quiet, though the projector isn't on yet.

I go up to her desk.

"Anthony?"

"Hi, Ms. Statten. Here's my missing assignments."

She smiles up at me, taking her glasses out of her hair to put them on—the guys in my class love this look. She glances down at the small stack of papers I'm holding.

"Thank you, but I'll be taking late marks."

I nod. "That's fair."

She always says she's preparing us for what's to come after high school, and her standards are high and rigid. I respect that. And I'm grateful that she doesn't feel sorry for me, that there are no favours here. She upholds her classroom principles no matter what and it makes me feel totally normal.

She takes the papers from me and I go back to my seat. The projector snaps on and note-taking begins. Before I know it, the bell is going again. It's been another productive hour and even the last class of the morning—chemistry—flashes by. By the end of it, Mr. James has helped me understand mole calculations and I'm feeling almost caught up. That swamp of work I had getting back into things is less consuming, and what I have left to do from these morning classes seems manageable.

chapter 59

As I exit the student parking lot doors, I go to reach for my phone out of habit but quickly tuck it back in my pocket without looking. I want disengagement from the digital world and let myself just be here, now, on this beautiful, warm fall day.

Honk! I look around. It's Mike and he's in a hurry. He's motioning me into the red rust bucket of a truck that is his pride and joy, the over-amped stereo pumping. This sandwich date's got him worked up, apparently. I make like I'm running in slow motion and he honks again, so I jog over.

"Sorry, man," I grin as I get close. "Just buggin' ya."

"Get in! I've got important things to do."

I hop in. "Like getting the number of this Haley girl?"

"Hell, yeah!"

He kicks up gravel as he peels out of the student parking lot. It's not possible to look more desperate than he does right now, but I like his enthusiasm. I laugh.

"Easy, tiger."

He looks at me, one eyebrow raised, and turns the stereo up even louder.

I shake my head and yell, "Man, you've got a *lot* of work to do on your style."

He reaches for the volume again and I swat his hand away, surrendering with laughter to his crappy choice in music.

chapter 60

We walk into the food court at the mall. I stand behind him while he looks for the new sandwich joint.

"There it is." He scans the crowd and smiles. "And there she is."

I look across from the sandwich shop and among all of the people is Mike's new dream girl, Haley, sitting with another girl.

Mike starts to make a beeline for her, but then stops abruptly to get some food. He orders two drinks, two sandwiches with the works, and two cookies. I hope he's buying.

"No sauce," I chime in as the sandwich is made.

I watch as Mike shifts his weight from foot to foot—he's nervous. It's pathetic and brave all at once. He has the tray in his hand but hesitates.

I look at him, then at Haley and grab the tray.

"Follow me." I meander through the crowd and plunk down beside the girls. "Ladies, two free cookies in exchange for two seats? Or a chance to meet two interesting guys?"

Haley looks at me only briefly. "You can just have the seats."

She doesn't want to talk but I'm feeling confident. "Thank God! Because my friend Mike here and I, well, we're really stunted in the conversation department. Really, our goal is to try and speak in complete sentences."

Both girls laugh. The ice is broken.

I hold up a cookie. "You want a bite of my mocha chocolate chip cookie?"

Haley shakes her head no.

"Your loss." I take a bite, exaggerating its deliciousness, but not by much.

The girls laugh again and I know they're warming up to us.

Mike and I banter back and forth with the girls, laughing and being ridiculous. It feels good—real and distracting—that is until I realize the time. "Crap! We've got to go. Ladies, nice to meet you both. We'll have to do this again sometime."

As Mike and I head for the car, I ask, "Did you get her number?"

He shakes his head. "Negative."

"Why the hell not? I thought that was the point."

"Uh, *no*. The point was to work on my game—and I got it, game that is."

"Like how you got the movie theatre girl's number?"

He scowls. "Listen, I like Haley, but I need to make sure I *like* her like her before every other lady loses out on this fine piece of man."

A huge bellow of laughter bursts out of me in the parking lot. "*Every* other lady? There are that many?"

"Shut up," he glares.

I climb into the truck. It's a good day.

chapter 61

The afternoon goes as quickly as the morning, and before I know it, I'm sitting in fifth, the last period of the day. The intercom crackles and a heavy jolt kicks me in the stomach.

"This is a reminder from Mrs. Tavler to all students of the drivers ed program: tomorrow is the final chance to submit permission forms for in-car instruction. If you don't get them handed in, you will miss your session and not continue on."

The intercom clicks off. Relief floods through me and dissolves the weight in my gut.

The bell rings and I head for my locker. Tonight will be another night dedicated to homework and catching up, but it's a lot more under control. I pile the books I need into my bag and sling it—oof, too heavy—across my chest. Outside, the air is cool, so I pull my hoodie over my head and walk home.

Mom and Dad have supper figured out, as well as some of my time too. They get me to walk Ollie, take the garbage out, carry some donation boxes to the front step, and bag some leaves. I don't complain. It's their way of keeping things real, and keeping me busy and distracted.

Heather joins us for supper. Her mid-terms are done. She'll be relaxed only for a day or two.

Afterwards, I negotiate doing my homework in lieu of dishes, since I've already done a bunch of chores. Heather kindly volunteers.

Upstairs, I close my door, shutting out the clattering in the kitchen, and pull the heavy books and binders out of my bag. The stack of them is only slightly intimidating and I'm ready for another mini-marathon of homework. Being in top shape mentally is as important as it is physically. I stay up until 10:30 finishing the last of my homework, then crash into bed. I lie there, peaceful, eyes closed, the tension of schoolwork slipping away as I drift into the pleasant nothingness of sleep.

chapter 62

Friday. The end of a long week.

Dad's pouring coffee in the kitchen and Ollie barks a friendly hello when he sees me.

Dad shushes him. "Heather's still sleeping, Ollie. Be nice."

I grab a bowl of Raisin Os and take a seat.

Ollie moves over and sits on my foot for his morning pet.

"How'd you sleep?" Dad asks.

"Really good."

"You look rested."

"I feel rested. Where's Mom?"

"Already gone for the day. Big game coming up?"

"Not until next week."

"Think you'll win?"

I know what he's up to—reinforcing the routine—so I go with it. "Hope so."

He smiles and pats me on the back in a fatherly way before leaving for work. I take my bowl to the sink and go back upstairs.

My phone vibrates with plans for the weekend. Mike's found a party that Haley's going to be at. Paul and Jessica send separate texts letting me know what they're doing, and invite me to join them. A couple of guys from the basketball team check in to see if I want to go to a show. But I'm not ready to commit to anything, so I put the phone down.

The school day flies by. The last bell rings and we're released, rushing out the doors into the streets, escaping a week of drudgery. I am more or less caught up at this point. The weekend will be a breath of fresh air.

As I walk home, the phone buzzes in my pocket again. I'm sure some study somewhere says this is going to cause crotch cancer in the future, but I keep the phone in my pocket anyhow. I check—looks like plans are falling into place and people want me to make some decisions, but I feel no urgency.

Back in my freshman year, a teacher always said, "If you're cool, they'll wait for you," when we herded at the door at the end of his class. I've always thought it was a good mantra.

I ignore the messages for now.

First home, then supper.

chapter 63

When we're done eating, I get up and put my arms around Mom and Dad. "You two have a date night?"

Mom giggles. "Maybe. Why? You want us out of your hair?"

"No, just figured you deserve one. I'll do the dishes and then I'm going out, probably with Mike. I may meet up with Jessie and Paul. Not sure."

Mom looks at Dad, and I can see the relief in their faces. It feels like everything is back to normal for the most part, but she still gives me the look.

I laugh. "Yeah. Yeah. I'll let you know when I know for sure. Sound good?"

She pours another dollop of wine into her glass and salutes Dad with it, smiling. "So what *are* we going to do?"

Dad checks his watch, then looks at me, mouth twitching. "How long are you going to be gone?"

"Dad, seriously? Gross!" My reaction is just for show—I'm happy my parents love each other.

They leave the kitchen, wine in hand, laughing.

I quickly clear the dishes, jamming them into the dishwasher. By the time I'm wiping the table, I hear the familiar sound of Mike's arrival—*hooooooonk*. I pound up the stairs, give myself a shot of cologne, and rush out to his truck.

"What's your hurry? We got all night."

"You, maybe, but me? Not so much. Word is Haley's at PJ's Pizza with a couple others from Central, her school, then they're headed to a farm party."

I shoot a text to Paul and tell him what I'm doing and that he and Jess are welcome to join if they like.

We get to the restaurant and check the place out. A couple of Mike's friends from Mitchell Ross Collegiate are there and he questions them about Haley. She and her friends have already left, but they'll be at the farm party just west of town at around 10:00. That gives us some time to kill. Mike has a few drinks that he buys with a fake ID, no doubt trying to calm his nerves over seeing Haley. We eat pizza and play a game of pool. I let him kick my ass and he gloats, but I let him have that too. A couple of hours later it's time to get to the party.

I have Mike's keys and we climb into his truck. He turns on the radio to some crappy early-2000s rock and roll, and punches my arm. He loves it when his music bugs me.

I look over at him. "I'd say something—"

"But you're too much of a nice guy?"

Sometimes the wingman's job can be a drag, but tonight it feels worth it.

The DJ announces the next song. Tom Petty's "I Won't Back Down." My smile fades.

I haven't spared Charlie a single thought over these past few days of blissful normalcy. He just told me to be with my people and bounced. I haven't received one message from him—nothing—and it's unsettling, like I'm waiting for something. Mike's belting out the lyrics, keeping time on the dashboard, but it's not the same.

Where *is* Charlie? Is he in trouble? *Is* he in jail? I feel the urge to text him but talk myself out of it, shaking off the bad feeling, reassuring myself that there has to be some sort of an explanation.

If anyone can dodge a bullet, it's Charlie Wolfe.

But the reminder is too much in the meantime and I change the channel. Mike's annoyed until he realizes it's now Lynyrd Skynyrd's "Sweet Home Alabama," and he rolls with it, air-guitaring the licks as we drive down a country road.

We pull up to the farmhouse. The yard is full of cars and a bonfire burns high. Mike races off, looking for Haley, and by the time I'm mingling with the crowd of people, I've nearly forgotten about Charlie.

chapter 64

I'm face down in my pillow and my eyes are still closed because the light is too bright in my room. My head pounds ferociously, and I'm not a fan of the rhythm. I drag myself up and wipe drool—gross—off my cheek. I'm still wearing my clothes from last night. My phone's in my hand. I tap to turn it on, but the battery is dead.

I swing my legs off the edge of the bed. My ears start to ring and I'm dizzy. This is terrible. What happened last night? I reach into my jacket and take out my wallet. At least I wasn't robbed. That's something.

"So much for listening to my advice."

I look over. "Charlie?"

He sits at my desk chair, staring at me.

"What are you doing here?"

"Gekas wouldn't let me stay in her jail anymore."

"No, I mean, what are you doing *here*? In my bedroom?" Then I realize what he's just said.

"What? Wait! You *were* in jail? That's horrible."

He shrugs, like it's no big deal.

"Drunk tank or cells?"

"Temporary holding." He rifles idly at some papers on my desk, unconcerned.

I try to imagine what it was like. "Were you alone? Were you with criminals? Were you scared of getting the shit kicked out of you?"

He's ignoring me, still reading whatever it is on my desk.

"Charlie!"

He looks at me and sighs. "Fine. Your folks are off at the Farmer's Market and I let myself in."

"You *broke in*?"

"No, I figured out where you keep the spare key."

"We don't have one!"

"How can you not have a spare key? What happens if you get locked out?" He stares at me but I don't break. "Yeah, fine, I broke in. Happy?"

"You need to get out. Now."

He stands and pauses at the door. "Out of your room? Or your house?"

"Out," I point.

He tosses up his hands, as if *I'm* the one frustrating *him*, and goes out.

Now I'm awake—really awake—but I want to pull the pillow back over my head, worried by what I'll find out next. I drag myself out of bed and throw on some clothes. It's clear Charlie isn't done with me.

And sure enough, by the time I get downstairs, there's a bowl of cereal on the counter and he's finished brewing himself a pot of coffee.

"These are nice beans. Is this your Mom or Dad's thing?"

I assume there's no getting rid of him. "Dad's."

He sniffs the brew, a small frown of concentration on his face like some sort of coffee connoisseur. Which maybe he is—who knows? "Nice. We don't get this in the trailer park."

I'd never really considered where he lived, but it's hard to tell whether he's telling the truth or dramatizing for effect.

"Charlie," I finally ask again, "what are you doing here?"

"I told you—Gekas kicked me out of jail."

"Seriously?"

"Yeah. She questioned my motivation. Thought I was doing it on purpose. Can you believe that?"

"Yeah, I can believe that, because the last time I saw you, you said you were going to get yourself thrown in jail!"

"I did? Hmm..."

"How?"

"What? Get sent to lockup? After I saw you, I went to the closest convenience store, walked over to the chocolate bars, took one, made sure the clerk was watching, opened it and ate it. When he just threatened me, I walked out of the store and sat on the step. He still didn't call the cops on me, so I went back and got myself an energy drink, which was a bad choice for a night in jail, and went back outside."

I stare at him in disbelief. "Why?"

"For an alibi. Why else?"

"For what?"

"For the murders, man. Aren't you keeping up with our investigation at all?"

I don't usually have the urge to cuff someone in the head, but I sure feel like doing it now.

"Anyway, it's a minor offence. I admitted to it and they kept me for the night."

"But then that means you were out on Wednesday."

"Yeah, so I had to do it again, which really sucks, because I had to really commit myself the second time."

"Why?"

"Well, my buddies from lockup the night before couldn't figure out who'd be so stupid as to steal a chocolate bar and a drink, except someone planted by the cops. They thought they should stick a shiv in me and let me be an example."

"How'd you get out of it?"

Charlie digs his spoon into the very large bowl of cereal and crunches away.

I wait impatiently for him to swallow.

"Stayed awake for most of the night. Couldn't convince them I wasn't a rat. At some point, I started thinking I should let them cut me and if I survived, I'd be in the hospital. The thought of risking an infection or bleeding out kept running through my mind, though, so I decided to wait them out instead."

He seems to be really enjoying his granola crunch, and adds a healthy dose of soy milk to it.

I shake my head and try to remain expressionless. "And so you went back in?"

He nods. "I went back in, scared I wasn't going to sleep again but the third night was easier. Mostly drunks and druggies. There was a guy with some mental health issues coming off something bad, but he was in a cell at the far end." He shrugs. "By Friday night, Gekas was on to me and wouldn't let me stay. I found the nearest all-night restaurant and just waited the night out."

This is really unbelievable.

His spoon hits the bottom of the bowl—*clink*—and he moves to the cupboards, looking for a mug. I point and he pulls two down, pours us each a coffee, and hands one to me.

My head's still pounding but the first sip seems to ease the pain. "So, why are you here now, Charlie?"

"Haven't you heard?"

chapter 65

Charlie pulls out his phone and scrolls to a news site. On the front page: SECOND TEENAGER FOUND DEAD. ONE STILL MISSING.

"Shit."

He takes his phone back. "I know, right?" He doesn't seem sincere. "Look where they found her!"

He sounds excited and it bothers me, but before I can say anything, he grabs the map out of his back pocket and unfolds it. He lays it out on the kitchen counter and points. "Right here—Lone Pine Mall."

It's one of the places, along with the schools in the northwest part of the city, that he'd pointed out the other night. "You were—"

"Right? I know. Get used to it."

That cockiness again—

"I read this guy. Best of all, we've got him."

"What do you mean?"

A grin spreads across Charlie's face. "After I left you at the stadium, I kept building my map, figuring it out. I saw what looked like a pattern. I knew I could take a gamble and try and get there before him and set a trap."

I don't say anything—I don't want to encourage his enthusiasm.

"I pulled some trail cameras—you know, the type hunters use—and duct taped them in the bathrooms—"

"You what?"

"Chill, we're not being pervy peepers—"

"But that goes against all sorts of people's privacy—"

"Yeah, yeah. Moral, ethical, blah, blah…"

I get in his face. "Charlie, a girl died. You get that, right? Someone's daughter, sister, friend… and girlfriend. Not just once, but three times. So you cut this shit about it being a game and acting like we're the Hardy Boys. Because we're not. Nothing like that. Sheri died, then Maggie, and now this girl, whoever she is, because of some weirdo who has sick ideas about women. So, cut it out, okay?"

He's quiet. He's never quiet. He doesn't move, but he sinks a bit in his seat.

I wait until he says something.

"Okay."

That's all he's got to say? Okay. I don't move, inches from his nose.

"Tony—?"

"What?" I snap, realizing he's never used my first name before.

"Let's get this guy."

chapter 66

Charlie and I are in Dad's car, driving to the northwest end of the city. My head's still pounding from the bad choices I made the night before. Coffee and pain relievers haven't helped, so I've got the music on low. It's some vocal pop guy singing about love and loneliness and being far from his girl. I try not to latch on to it, but it's hard not to be affected.

This whole thing with Charlie is bad business, and I don't like digging up the dead for clues. The past three days of peace have been wiped out by his presence, and me yelling at him didn't help. But I don't feel bad about it—he was acting like a jerk.

"You don't think I care, but I do," says Charlie now as he stares out the window. "Sheri was a good person who didn't deserve to die. I didn't know Maggie or this other girl, but I'm sure they were decent people."

He's quiet for a moment and I think he's done. "But they're strangers," he continues after a moment. "I have absolutely no connection to them. Sheri was nice to me in school. She didn't whisper behind people's backs, she wasn't a snarky bitch. But we were from different worlds and we didn't mix. I don't know how to feel sad about people I don't know."

"Then why are you doing this?"

"Because you've got a problem that needs solving."

I look over at him. "That's it? Really?"

"For now, sure. That works for me."

It's not a good enough answer and it makes me wonder.

"Charlie, did something like this happen to someone you knew?"

He looks out the window for a bit, then opens his phone and flips through apps. He leans over to show me the screen. "This new girl's name is Bonnie McCallum. She lived in the northwest, went to the Catholic school there. She had a night shift at the Citrus Shack, which stays open late to catch the late-night movie crowd. She was supposed to close with another girl but disappeared at the end of the night. The other girl looked for her, thought she flaked out, and went home. She didn't think anything of it until Bonnie turned up in a dumpster behind the mall."

Nothing—that's all he gives me—something about the victim. Whatever's going on in that head of his, whatever past he's hiding, he's locked it away and shoved it way down deep. It's clear pushing him won't help, so I focus on what's ahead.

"What's your grand plan?"

"We go to the mall. I think Gekas will start cluing in to what's going on soon enough. Too much has been happening around bathrooms for her not to search them. We'll have to get there quick—get in and get out. The place'll be busy, but they'll be looking around the Citrus Shack, points of entry, and the path between the store and the dumpster. I'm hoping the place isn't totally closed, that some of the stores are still open. That way, you won't look conspicuous."

"Wait—me?"

"Yeah. If I'm spotted at the last place Bonnie was seen, it'll start looking weird. Almost thirty per cent of killers return to the scene of the crime."

"Where do you get this stuff?"

He ignores me. "If I show up again, they'll more than likely pick up on it. Crime scene photographers are documenting the crowd half the time, just in case they get a guy who likes to revisit his handiwork."

"Again, how do you know?"

"Come on. You do realize there is a thing called a com-pu-ter, right?

I shoot him a stop-messing-with-me look.

"Oh right, you're gonna get all up in my face again." He's got that shit-eating grin again, pleased to have gotten a reaction out of me. "It's good to see you growing."

He's edging toward being an asshole again. "Charlie—"

"No, I mean it. The sooner we face what the killer does, who he is, the sooner we quit fooling ourselves and stop him from doing it to someone else."

I stare at him in dismay. Of all the things I think he'll surprise me with, sincerity is the last I expected.

chapter 67

We pull up in front of the mall and, of course, it's surrounded by police cars and news vans.

"Here we go again," I say. I don't mean to be flippant; it just comes out.

Charlie knows what I mean, though. "Yup," he says, assessing the scene.

"So I just walk in there, and...?" It's like I'm mentally stunned; I can't keep up with Charlie's thought process.

"Yup."

I wait for more. I really think he's going to answer my question because I'm not sure what to do, yet the silence drags on a little longer than I'd like.

"*And...?*" I repeat, still staring at all the vehicles and officials and officers that stand in our way.

"Drive," he instructs.

I put the car into drive and pull away from the mall. "Where am I going?"

Charlie makes a "just go" gesture without saying a word.

I drive forward slowly. He points to a small street nearby and I turn.

"Park."

I pull over to the curb and park the car. The action is now all behind us. I glance in the rearview mirror. No one is racing around in a panic, but there's consistent movement of uniformed and plainclothes police between the store and the cruisers.

I don't feel as calm as they all look.

"When a burglar is about to break into your house, you know what he does?" Charlie finally speaks.

I look at him. "I've got no idea, Charlie."

"He finds a place he likes. One that looks nice. Curb appeal. Something worth entering. Then he parks a block or two away.

"Yeah?" I'm wondering what his point is but he always seems to have one, so I give him time.

"Then he walks right up to the front door and rings the bell. Just like that. He's all full of balls and rings the bell. And if someone comes to the door, he just makes something up like he's lost or looking for so-and-so, or selling something. Pretty good, huh?"

I glance up at the rearview mirror again.

"We can't ring the doorbell at this place. They'll know we're not selling cookies," I add.

Charlie's not fazed in the least. "If no one answers, then he goes around back and tries the back door, or the window or the garage. They don't care about alarms. Neighbours ignore those. Cops don't get there in enough time."

I look at him, hoping I'll be less confused in a moment or two.

"Ever locked yourself out of the house?"

I nod.

"Well, how many ways can you think of to get in without a key?"

He waits and I realize he actually expects me to come up with an answer, so I go through the options I've considered every time I've lost my key.

He asks again, "How many?"

"Three."

"Times three."

"Pardon?"

"If *you* know three ways to get into your house without using your key, then a burglar knows nine. Into your own house!"

He sounds impressed, but I don't want to know how he knows this information. I really hope it's from the internet.

"They walk in and do a sweep in around eight minutes. They get what they need and walk out calmly through the front door to their car. It's pretty seamless."

"Thank you, Charlie Wolfe, for that mini lesson on B&E's. What's your point?"

Charlie smiles. "You're in and out in eight minutes."

I cock my head trying to understand what he's just said. "Sorry. I'm what?"

"You're going into the mall, through the back door, getting what we need, and getting out."

My eyes widen and I realize what Charlie is telling me to do. He sees my expression. My brain flashes an uncontrollable fast-forward to a night in jail with some mentally ill druggie or one of Charlie's "ole" buddies with a shiv, then leaps to my parents paying bail. None are good outcomes.

"Don't panic. You've done this before."

I give him a look. Riiiiight.

"My school, remember? You're practically a pro. And you're better at it than you think, Uptown Boy." He pats me on the back. It's both patronizing and reassuring.

"Remember, there's more than one way into every single place."

Charlie unbuckles his seatbelt and gets out of the car. I shut the car off and follow. We walk a little farther down a side street, out of view of the scene at the mall.

"Doesn't look like the entire strip mall is shut down. I think they'll have police caution tape to keep people away unless they find something solid."

Charlie walks beside me. We turn a corner and head back toward the mall, but from this street I see we're coming up along the back where deliveries are made.

"We'll just hang out here for a bit. Something will come to us."

Charlie is so certain. I admire that about him. I don't know his life or what it looks like, but he puts such an optimistic spin on everything, even this—even jail. He thinks an opportunity will present itself. How does he know? Practice or is it simply patience? I'm not sure he'd be able to tell me even if I pressed him for an answer.

"When the time is right, go inside. Go in like you're supposed to be there. Like you work there or you own the place. Go to the bathroom, not the one near the food court but the one away from the main square, down the hall by the music store. Walk straight in."

I listen and then it dawns on me. "Wait—you want me to go into the *women's* bathroom?"

"Yes."

"Charlie, I'm not sure if you noticed, I'm a six-foot-tall dude."

Charlie lifts his sunglasses over his head to hold back his hair and looks me up and down. "Oh, I noticed." He puckers a kiss and smiles.

"Man, how can you be joking right now?"

"Look, if you act like you're supposed to be there, nobody actually pays attention. If you act nervous and out of place, and—well, like you—people see that kind of energy."

"What if someone catches me?"

Charlie tilts his head. I can feel his annoyance. "Wow, man, do we have work to do."

I know he's thinking that I'll never be part of his world, that he and I are in completely different time zones.

"If someone walks in on you, apologize and act embarrassed. Swear, act stupid—that'll be easy—and ask where the right washroom is, then leave. People make mistakes all the time."

It makes sense, but my brain panics, worrying about police asking me what I'm doing.

"Stop thinking. Go in and get out. Once you have what you need, you can stop by the deli and get me an Italian classic."

I look at him. "What?"

"Gives you an excuse. You're there buying a sandwich."

I give him a second look.

"Oh, and no sauce."

I shake my head. Besides wanting to figure out what happened to Sheri, no sauce might be the only other thing we have in common.

"You're something else, Charlie Wolfe."

I run through the scenario in my head, visualizing it like Coach gets us to do with plays, while we hang out, waiting. Sure enough, a back utility door swings open moments later.

I tap Charlie's shoulder. "There."

Charlie looks at the door.

"Should I go?"

"Wait."

A woman exits with a cart full of garbage. She props the door open so that it doesn't slam shut behind her.

"Nice. Business as usual. Some things keep going no matter what." He looks over at me. "When you think it's right, get up and walk in."

That's all he says. Nothing specific. It's all up to me now.

I feel my heartbeat speed up as I watch the woman pushing the cart over to the large bin. I get up and cross directly to the door.

She's almost done and I'm thinking I won't make it when I hear a phone ring. My breath catches for a second until I realize it's her phone. As she turns away to answer, I speed up and walk right behind her, through the back door into the mall.

chapter 68

The hallway stinks of the piled-up garbage that hasn't made it to the bin. I hold my breath and move swiftly to the end of the hall before gaining entry to the mall courtyard.

The police are all on the one side. The Citrus Shack has barriers around it, with an officer to keep people moving along. I risk a brief glimpse to see if Gekas is around, but I don't see her. I keep moving, putting space between me and the law. In the centre of the retail area, I slip behind a lottery kiosk to obscure my presence.

Charlie was right; the other stores are open. There are a few customers and I do my best to become one. I walk, trying to window shop, but it feels awkward and forced. I think about what I would normally do when I come to the mall and my mind goes blank. I decide that if I wanted something, I would go directly to it, so I make for the music store.

Inside, two employees are busy stacking shelves. I walk casually over to a bin of two-for-one movies and flip through them.

"Can I help you?"

Shit! One of the workers is looking at me. My head spins, trying to remember what I would normally say.

"Uh, nope. Good." I'm happy I almost got a complete sentence out.

"Well, let me know if you need anything."

I nod and force a smile and move around the bin so my back is to them. I work the next step through in my head, trying to imagine myself getting into the women's bathroom. Coach would be so proud that I'm using his visualization exercises.

Now I'm out of the music store, going around the corner to the short hallway that holds the mall's second set of washrooms, the ones away from the food court. I can no longer feel my head pounding—my heart is outdrumming it.

There's no one down here. The men's washroom is on the right; the women's on the left. It hasn't been taped off yet. Charlie is one step ahead of the cops. Again.

I walk up to the door on the left.

This is a really bad idea—no, dammit, this is a *good* idea—for Sheri. I listen for a split second. Nothing. Good.

I go inside.

chapter 69

There are eight stalls in a row and a very long counter with four sinks. Two hand dryers hang on the wall beside me. I'm frozen in place and have to force myself to move.

I kneel down under the first sink and look. Nothing.

The twists and turns of plumbing and the dark underbelly of the countertop offer plenty of places to hide the camera. I realize I'll have to check every sink.

Why didn't I ask Charlie where it would be?

I move over and look under the next sink. Nothing.

I hear a shuffle of feet behind me and my muscles lock up again. There's a pair of black-heeled feet at the end of the row of stalls. Dammit! What do I do if she comes out and finds me here? Now I'm shaking, but I breathe through it; I've got until she's done.

The motivational voice inside my head is on repeat, and I propel myself to finish what I came in here to do. I squat at the third sink, groping under the counter, then move to the last one.

There!

A piece of duct tape hangs down and I pull on it, but there's no camera. My heart speeds up even more. This is worse than the final minutes of a tied game.

I put my head under to take a better look. Nothing.

The toilet flushes behind me—shit!—and I'm moving. The stall door clicks open as I push open the washroom door and stride down the hall to blend in with the handful of shoppers.

chapter 70

The whole thing is a bust. Some cleaner or maintenance worker must have found the camera and yanked it out. Hell, they probably have a security camera of their own, waiting to find the sicko who taped it there. With everything going on around here, they'll see me going in and think I'm the perv. Or, worse, they'll make connections and think *I'm* the one who killed Bonnie McCallum.

I'm pissed off at Charlie for getting me into this mess. This was a bad idea from the beginning. These past few days it was so nice to get back to normal life—how quickly Charlie has turned it upside down all over again.

As I'm thinking this, I'm toying with the piece of duct tape in my pocket and suddenly feel something stuck in it. It's hard and thin, like a small MP3 player. I peel back the adhesive to find a small SD memory card embedded in it.

I let out a long breath and it feels like the first one I've taken since I walked into the mall.

Then my mind starts to race. Somebody left it for us.

No, the *killer* did.

My heart skips a beat—he knows about us. But also—Charlie found him.

No matter what I think of Charlie, no matter what sort of stuff he gets me into, he did it. He found the killer.

I yank the duct tape off the memory card and slip it into my jeans. I scope out the passersby—no one's really paying attention to me and my heartbeat falls back into something like a normal rhythm.

At the grocery store, I find the deli and order the Italian classic because today my man Charlie deserves a sub, no sauce.

The guy behind the counter assembles it as the radio behind him plays "The Kid's Aren't Alright."

I smile.

"Anything else you want today?"

"You have no idea, mister."

chapter 71

I've got the sub, a sports drink, and a couple of bananas when I leave the mall, aiming for the back alley, away from Detective Gekas and her buddies. I've actually stopped worrying about how I'm acting; I'm moving with my natural, easy swing. I still feel the rush of discovery, but the remnants of adrenaline that had me shaking have burned off the last of my hangover. I'm not sure if it was nearly getting caught or finding the SD drive—either way, I'm feeling something very new.

I walk around back. Charlie's nowhere in sight.

Where the hell is he? I feel a little kick in the gut.

I go to the edge of the parking lot and scan the entire area. Can't see him. What am I supposed to do now? What do I do with the memory card? I sigh and walk back to the car.

Traffic now fills the Saturday morning streets. The buzz I was rolling with is gone and my headache starts to seep back across my brain. It's clear to me that a few hours with Charlie equals one bad night of drinking.

He's sitting on the curb by the car.

"Hey," he says, all casual.

"Hey," I say. After all this, I'm not in the mood for any crap.

"What took you so long?"

I throw the bag with the sandwich at him as hard as I can.

He catches it. "Easy, man."

"Why'd you leave?"

"There was just too much action. It was better over here and I knew you'd find me."

His answer doesn't make me less angry, but we can't stay.

"Come on. Let's get out of here."

Charlie unrolls the paper from around his sandwich. "No sauce, right?"

I glare at him over the vehicle.

"Okay, okay. Gee whiz, dude." He takes a big bite and nods approvingly.

"You get the camera?"

"Sort of. It wasn't there."

"What?"

"The only thing was this." I hold up the memory card.

"Where was that?"

"Stuck to the tape under the sink."

Charlie gets that distant look on his face and a smile crosses it. "Looks like someone wants us to come out and play."

And I can't help but grin because for the first time since I've met him, we're on exactly the same page.

chapter 72

Charlie digs into his backpack, pulls out a card reader and plugs it into his smartphone. I wonder what other sorts of spy toys he's got hidden in there. I also wonder how much of it he actually paid for.

The card loads and thumbnails pop up. They're small and hard to see.

"Once it transfers over, we can view them either as stills or time-lapse video."

I realize what I'm about to see and the idea of watching something horrible happen to this girl is too much for me. The excitement of catching this guy melts away.

"Wait. If he knew about the camera, how do we know we'll see who he is?"

Charlie watches each image appear. "Yeah, he's probably onto us. And I'm sure if he was daring enough to leave these images for us, he was careful enough not to leave finger-prints. Still, I'm hoping he's screwed up and left *something* we can follow."

Our lead is slipping. Charlie's phone signals that loading is complete and he scrolls to the start and pushes play.

A view of the bathroom pops up, the top eighth of the screen cut off by the underside of the sink cabinet. At the bottom is a date-and-time stamp that begins on Tuesday evening after Charlie left me at the stadium. Nothing happens on the screen for a while. Legs zip back and forth across the bottom of the screen and the lights wink on and off, yet even in the dark, the stall and floors are illuminated.

"See that? Night vision. That feature costs extra."

"What store'd you buy it at?

"Pffft. Stuff like this begs to be liberated."

My suspicion is confirmed, but I have a feeling he might've said it just to mess with me.

The time-stamp skips forward a day. Women's feet shuffle across the screen and the lights flick off periodically. Nothing out of the ordinary. I know we should speed ahead to when the attack likely occurred, but I'm tense, keeping an eye on the time, waiting uncomfortably as it moves toward yesterday. Charlie's sandwich rests uneaten on his lap as he waits. When it jumps to Friday, we both sit intently, focused on the screen. The clock zips past noon, then three, then six.

"Soon," Charlie says quietly.

I look at him, expecting anticipation, but am surprised to see sadness. On the screen, there are more feet, then something on the floor, then the image freezes on an empty room.

I'm confused. "What happened?"

Charlie taps the rewind button frame by frame until he and I are staring at the swollen, red face of a girl that I assume is Bonnie McCallum. I don't know what I expected, but it wasn't this. Tears have run down her face, ruining her makeup; her eyes are wide but relaxed, her face calm.

Because she's already dead.

Charlie doesn't immediately go back to the previous frame and I have to look away. Out the window, a man rakes leaves across the street. A pink bike lies in the driveway. These ordinary things make me feel sick. Poor Bonnie.

"He's choking them."

I look back at Charlie.

"Looks like a piece of cloth or fabric. I can't tell from this." He's tapping the images backwards and forwards.

I'm not in the mood to watch. Our sensationalized world has apparently not desensitized me.

"Dammit, there's only a few pictures." He must realize what that sounds like because he adds, "It's hard to see him."

He turns the phone to me, but I refuse to watch.

"There's this one of her, post-mortem." Sometimes I wonder if he really thinks he's a crime scene investigator. "Then, this one, but her body's turned around and he's kneeling. Then here are her feet and his knees and hands. Then, him standing behind her. The last one is her feet, standing at the sink."

He goes quiet. I look over at him, and he's studying the image. Then suddenly he grabs my arm. "Wait. Look."

Reluctantly, I do. I see her feet—she's wearing jeans and running shoes, at the sink. "What?"

He points. I don't see it. "That's him."

Then it registers. Caught on the top edge of the still frame is a pair of feet in the stall behind the girl.

"What's he doing?"

"Waiting for his prey..."

chapter 73

I stare at the pair of sneakers in the corner stall. Charlie skips the image backwards and the feet disappear. He skips forward and they reappear, and then the killer is behind her before he pulls her down. I remember the day at the trails with Charlie and my mind fills in the blanks. He waited in the bathroom for Sheri, hiding in a stall until she arrived. He likely stood on the toilet seat with the door cracked open, and when she was at the sink, he lowered himself down and came up behind her. He wrapped something around her throat and choked her until—

I can see Sheri staring at me, smiling; I swear I can even smell her.

Charlie interrupts the memory, "Something doesn't make sense."

"What?"

"Well, he's here behind her and he pulls her down backwards. And she struggles against it."

"So?"

He clicks ahead to the image of her face in the camera. "How does she end up here?"

"What do you mean?"

"How does she get here? He's got her. She's on her back and he's got the full weight and force of his body on top of her. Unless..." He doesn't finish and starts skipping backwards through the frames again.

He might finish that sentence, but he'll do it in his own sweet time.

He keeps flipping backwards, then stops. "There."

The camera is in infrared mode and in the corner stall are the splayed-out feet of the killer.

"He waited in the corner like he did at the school. If he sat low enough, long enough, then maybe... maybe..."

He seems to have forgotten I'm here.

"Finish your thought!" I yell.

He jumps. "Geez, Shepherd, relax." He sighs and smiles. "Maybe he saw the camera. Maybe it made some sound and he heard it. Either way, he knew we were there. And he left the SD card for us to find."

"So?"

"He's performing for us."

chapter 74

I watch the footage again, frame by frame, watching the steps of the action. I've tuned Bonnie out of the image—it helps me deal with the horror of her death. "He did this on purpose?"

"Not the murder. He planned that long ago. But once he knew we were watching, he made sure we saw her."

"And him killing her?"

Charlie nods.

"We need to take this to Gekas."

He snatches it out of my hands. "What? No way. We're not going through that again."

"You have something that could directly help her case."

"That I did illegally and you helped to retrieve. Don't forget, you're an accomplice now."

"Wait, you did this on *purpose*?"

"No—well, maybe—but that's not the point. We show this and they'll toss us in jail. For real." He drops the phone into a pocket inside his jacket, but doesn't seem to notice that he's left the reader with the memory card on the console between us.

I set the bag with the energy drink and bananas on top of it.

"Besides, it wouldn't help with the case. The same reason we'd get tossed in jail is the same reason they couldn't use it. It's inadmissible evidence."

He's got a point, but it doesn't stop me from grabbing the energy drink and knocking the memory card into my other hand beside the console.

"The only good that comes out of this is we work through the other days and see if he makes an appearance and shows his face."

I think about it. "Wait. What about those time stamps? Are they accurate?"

"Yeah, of course. Why?"

"What if I call and tell Gekas to check surveillance cameras around the bathroom at those times?"

"She's gonna have questions. She's gonna want to know how you knew and why."

"Who cares? She knows we're snooping around. I'm sure she didn't think we'd stop. She might say we're obstructing justice, but in the end, we're only helping her. She can't get too mad about that."

"All right, Shepherd, let's go with your plan." I knew brazen disregard of the law would win him over. "Let's just hope you're right about her."

Yup, you and me both.

chapter 75

Charlie wants us to swing by the mall when I make the call. He hopes to see her outside and get a reaction. I think it's childish, but the fact that he's doing what's right and not serving his own pride makes me go along with it. I find a spot close to the entrance where the forensic truck is parked and pull in. Gekas's card is in my wallet and I pull it out and dial the number.

She picks up on the second ring. "Anthony?"

I'm a little surprised she knows it's me. "Detective Gekas."

"I wondered if you'd be calling."

"Uh, really…?"

"Every time there's another attack, either you or your new friend, Charles Wolfe, seem to turn up."

I glance over at Charlie, uneasy with all she knows. "Detective—"

"Anthony, relax. We know you aren't part of this. I've already talked to several people who were at the party with you, and I'm sure Charles has told you all about his escapades." She pauses, letting me process. "But I do have the distinct feeling you haven't been listening to my advice."

"Uh, no," I say, looking away from Charlie, "not really."

"You need to bring this to an end, or else I'm going to charge you with a felony—"

I take a leap of faith and close both eyes. "Detective Gekas, you need to check mall surveillance."

"Anthony, stop. We're doing—"

"Our guy, the one you're looking for, was in the women's bathroom by the music store last night, a couple of hours before the murder."

She's silent for a beat, then the questions start, "What do you mean 'our' guy? How do you—wait, do you know what he looks like? Have you *seen* him?"

"No." I want to tell her about the images we have of Bonnie but it will only make it worse.

"How did you get this information?"

I know it's time to get out of this conversation but I'm not sure how.

"Anthony?"

Charlie's gesturing at his phone.

"Anthony?!"

I muffle the speaker and look at him. "What?"

Charlie whispers, "It's my camera. The one the killer took."

"What about it?"

"The GPS just turned on."

That's when I hang up on Gekas.

chapter 76

"Are you kidding?"

Charlie shows me the indicator on his phone.

I feel a rush and I almost can't think. Charlie's got a GPS signal pointing to the killer's possible location and I've just hung up on the lead detective on the case.

"What do we do?"

I think Charlie is wondering the exact same thing—what *do* we do? Maybe it's not a dumb question.

My phone rings. Gekas again.

"No," Charlie says in a strong, non-negotiable way.

I play it out in my head. She's got the training and an entire force behind her. They could catch this guy, bring him down, take him to jail.

Or it could be a trap. And we don't even know if this *is* the killer.

What would I tell Gekas? How did we get here? How did we get to the point where Charlie's duct-taping stolen cameras in washrooms after finding a clue at the likely expense of contaminating two crime scenes? Oh, and there's also the little matter of me withholding evidence from Gekas while also messing up a third crime scene.

Or is this no longer about Gekas? Am I after something else? Do I want to be one of the guys that take him down? Am I that much of a self-absorbed ass?

Then I remember Sheri—and her smile and how it catches me off-guard when I close my eyes before I sleep. Most of it I remember, but some things, like the way she looks in profile, or the colour of her hair in the sunlight, have slipped into a shadowy corner of my mind. I struggle to connect my memories together into a whole, one I can hold onto, but the more I try, the more it falls away.

It's been less than two weeks. Only. What happens in a month? Or a year?

The phone quits ringing and I know it's gone to voicemail. I put it down while Charlie continues to stare at the screen.

"It's the construction site."

A small breath escapes me and I look at him. "Where Maggie died?"

He nods.

I see the tent surrounding Maggie's body. I see Bonnie's dead face staring at me. I try to remember Sheri, but I just can't see her clearly enough.

I make the decision.

"Let's go."

chapter 77

I drive and Charlie navigates.

"It should take us about fifteen minutes to get there." He's focused on the map on his phone.

I kick around the idea of calling Gekas again but let the thought roll right out my head. With Gekas comes questions and a long sit-down in her office. We don't have time for any kind of a sit-down, long or short. If he's there—and I hope he's there—this isn't the time to wait around, wasting precious minutes trying to explain ourselves. We need to go now and sort things out later. If we get a face, or, better yet, we get *him*, we'll have all the time in the world to answer Gekas's questions.

The radio plays quietly but I don't recognize the song. We turn onto Lewvan Drive, leaving the residential neighbour-hood behind us. We pass big box stores to Ring Road, and skirt the edge of the city. The streets are humming. People are out for Saturday shopping, brunch—all the ordinary things normal people do. I think about my parents, likely down at the Farmer's Market, heading home, making lunch, maybe wondering where I am.

A plane flies over the highway, coming in from the south-east for a landing at the airport.

Yesterday, for a brief moment, I was a student again, not the boyfriend of a missing girl—a lost girl. A dead girl.

A new thought forms: Sheri's body, dead, cold, grey, lying in dirt and worms, her eyes gazing milky white at me. I can't remember the way her smile looked or how her hair fell across her face, but this thought, *this* damn thought, sticks.

"Turn at these office buildings."

I follow Charlie's instructions.

"Keep going 'til you hit the edge of the city."

I nod. "Do you think he's waiting for us?" It's a legitimate question. The camera didn't get to the construction site by itself.

"Probably."

"So, when we get there—?"

"I don't know."

"You're kidding! You don't have a plan?"

"No!" Charlie snaps. "I don't have time to run all over the city, investigating every possible damn crime scene!"

This is the first time I've seen even a sliver of nervousness.

But I'm nervous too and I need some assurances. "So we don't have a plan?"

"No. No, we don't, Shepherd." He rubs a hand over his mouth, looking out the window. "We're going to play it by ear, okay?"

This is not reassuring, but the only thing that's kept me on this course of action is that Charlie hasn't led me astray—yet.

We hit the end of the road and I take the last street. Charlie shuts the radio off, and I hear him let out a long and slow sigh. He leans forward in his seat, watching the construction site as we approach.

"Keep driving."

He watches out the window as we move past a temporary blue fence that runs along the premises. The shells of houses rise before us in different stages of assembly. New ones with siding and yards of dirt give way to plastic-wrapped shells and plywood roofs, then wooden skeletons sprouting up from open cement forms.

"'Kay, slow down along here…"

We cruise in silence, scanning the buildings and empty lots as we pass, but it's the weekend, so there is no sign of anyone. No truck, no car, no one in sight. If the killer is here, he didn't drive, or if he did, he's done a damn good job hiding his vehicle.

We come to the end of the road, circle around, and pull over to the side. I'm staring out the windshield, waiting for our next move, when Charlie climbs out of the car. I undo my seatbelt and follow.

The place is quiet, and there's nothing discreet about the two of us wandering around here. I look over at him. "So, in the front, like we own it?"

"Yup."

I shoot Charlie another look. Whether he got my dig or not, he doesn't care—he isn't going to hide.

I sigh and lock the car door. It chirps.

If the killer is here, he knows we've arrived.

chapter 78

Charlie checks his phone.

"It's somewhere inside there, halfway down the road."

We walk across the road and down the newly poured side-walk to a gate in the temporary fencing. A heavy chain holds it shut. A big sign—KEEP OUT—hangs on it.

"After you," Charlie gestures.

"D'you think there are guard dogs?"

"If there are, you should be extra quiet."

I bend and wiggle through the space in the fence, hoping not to rattle the gate. Charlie follows and slides in much easier than I did.

We walk between two rows of houses, down what looks like it'll be the backyard. It's an eerie, sound-less space, and although I try to shake it off, my imagination gets the best of me. I can't help but think of the crime scene just beyond the last row of buildings, where they found Maggie. Charlie says the killer grabbed her at school—but what if he brought her here, for some ritual or something that we aren't aware of. What if *we're* the next victims?

I'm almost convinced that whoever brought the camera out here is waiting for us, hiding in one of these buildings, just waiting for us to go past. He seems to kill people at close range—the news said Maggie was strangled and we know Bonnie was—so he doesn't seem the kind who would shoot us with a gun. Then again, he *is* a killer—and I'm guessing that once you've done it a couple of times it doesn't really matter how you do it.

This is really stupid. "We should call Gekas."

"Wow, Shepherd, that's a new record for fastest chickening out."

I'm trying to play this cool. I'd like him to agree. "It's just common sense, right? We step out of this now, we call her, we wait, and make sure no one leaves."

"Fine," Charlie says, "head back to the car."

But he keeps walking.

"I'm not leaving."

"Good."

"How can you be so, so *indifferent* about this?"

"What's he gonna do? Attack us? If he's here, he's trying to figure *us* out as much as we're trying to figure *him* out. Sure, he might attack, but he likely just wants to know who he's dealing with."

"And then do what?"

"Toy with us. Get inside our heads. Then, maybe, kill us."

"Oh, great—"

"Relax, Shepherd. This is a meet-and-greet." He stops.

"What?"

He stares at his GPS, looking at the two nearly finished homes in front of us. He turns toward first one, then the other.

"The camera *is* here, right?"

Charlie gives me a firm nod. "It is. But this is about as close as I can get us." He slips the phone into his pocket. "From here on out, we'll have to use our astute powers of observation."

I glare at him and he shrugs. He kneels down and picks up a rock and pockets it. "Which one, boss?" he asks.

I sigh, giving in, and point to the house on the left. We climb up onto its deck. The patio door is locked.

He smiles. "Guess your powers of deduction need some sharpening, huh?" He jumps over the railing and moves around the side of the house.

I follow.

When I get to the front, he's already working at the lock to the garage. He slides what looks like a key into the keyhole and bumps it with the stone he picked up. It pops open like magic and he goes inside. I go in too, well aware I've just added unlawful entry to my list of recent felonies.

The interior of the house is half finished. Wiring and drywall have been installed, but there's no paint or flooring. Signs of the construction crew are everywhere—tools, extension cords, water bottles, empty coffee cups, and a paint-splattered radio litter the place. The kitchen opens to a dining room that wraps around into the living room. Everything is open and spacious and our feet echo between the walls. We do a quick inspection of the kitchen cabinets and find nothing.

"You check the second floor and I'll check the basement," Charlie offers.

"No, we're not splitting up."

He gives me a dismissive look. "Fine." He goes up the stairs to the second floor landing that overlooks the kitchen.

"What does someone do with all this space?" Charlie asks. It's a sincere question.

"People like big houses. They don't like to feel crowded."

He walks to the edge of the balcony and looks down at the stovetop island. "I could spit in my mac and cheese from here."

I shake my head. "That's just gross."

"So's the mac and cheese at my house."

I follow him into an empty bedroom, wondering how anyone could screw up such a simple meal. The doors haven't even been installed, so we move down the hall. A quick look tells us what we need to know. No one except carpenters have been here. Basement next.

The stairs are still only boards and lights hang by extension cords from the ceiling joists. The basement is unfinished walls, studs, and cement. It smells a bit damp. Light spills in through the wide basement windows and we're able to see to all the back corners easily.

Charlie turns for the stairs. "This place is a bust."

"What if the person who took the camera—"

"The killer."

"Okay, the killer—what if he only wanted to hide it out here. You know, getting rid of the evidence."

"Well, if we find it, then maybe you can take it to Gekas for fingerprints."

"And if not?"

"We'll search for a bit and leave it at that. Back to square one."

I step into the garage. "But judging by your tone, you don't really think he's just trying to get rid of it."

Charlie follows, turning to lock the door behind him. "No. I think it's been turned on for us to find."

"Why would he do that?"

"That's what I'm here to find out."

chapter 79

We walk across the dirt lot to the other house. This time, we skip the patio doors and go straight to the front of the house. I don't like being exposed to the street and the rest of the city, and hope Charlie gets the lock open quickly.

He turns toward me, eyebrow raised. There's a small scratch along the wood of the door jamb.

"Someone's been here who wasn't invited."

He unlocks the door with his bump key and lets it swing open. We both stay on outside of the door frame, listening for movement. After a second, he walks inside. Again, I follow.

This house mirrors the first one and we move into the kitchen, careful to not bang around too much and announce our presence. There's a piece of wood in the hallway and Charlie picks it up, holding it like a club.

This time, we go to the basement first and look down the staircase. Again, the treads are unfinished and the stairwell is open, but in this house there's drywall up along one wall.

Charlie takes the first step down and the wood groans. We wince at the sound. Not much we can do now, though, so we continue cautiously, ready for anything.

At the bottom, the smell of rot hits us hard. There's something nasty down here. We check the corners and go into what will one day likely be a den. A hallway runs off one side of the room, leading to three closed doors.

I hate this—the whole thing feels like a trap—but I know Charlie's going into every one of those rooms whether I'm here or not, and I'm his only backup. We go to the first door and the smell gets worse. Charlie doesn't even wait for me to be ready and opens it quickly.

Nothing—it's empty—and he's on to the next.

"Wait—!"

But it's too late and he swings it wide.

"Shit, stop," I whisper, but he ignores me and goes into the room. The smell is horrible now and I want to puke. I'm pretty sure I hear buzzing but nothing's going to stop him so I go too. And it's bad.

A dog, at least what I *think* is a dog, lies against a wall, cut open, its guts spilling out. I can't handle the sight and walk back out, down the hallway into the den. I take deep breaths and try to stop my lurching stomach, but it isn't working. I vomit. I want to get out of here.

"Shepherd!"

I hear him call and wipe my mouth. I look down the hall and can't see Charlie, but I realize that he's opened the door to the room at the very end. "What?"

"You need to come here."

"Can't we just go—?"

"No, you need to come here now."

I don't like the way he says it—there's an urgency I've never heard in his voice before, like taking a breath can wait until he pushes the words out.

I hold my breath and move down the hallway, keeping my eyes averted from the dead animal as I pass, and go into the room where Charlie is.

chapter 80

Charlie's standing in the middle of the room, staring at the wall behind the door. I can hear the buzz of the flies swarming the dead dog in the room next door and wish it would stop. I turn to see what he's looking at. Suddenly, I'm not breathing and cold sweat runs down my neck.

Us.

He's looking at a collage of us—made from newspaper clippings and photos—circled and coloured with red marker—or what I hope is red marker. Underneath is written: A GOOD BEGINNING MAKES A GOOD ENDING.

"What's the hell is this?"

Charlie leans in, inspecting a particular image. "I don't know."

"Why are there pictures of me?"

"Something's not right—"

"Hell, yeah, something's not right," I exclaim. "He's got pictures of me. He knows who I am."

"I'm in a few too—"

I point. "Look, that's my address. He knows where I live."

"I see that."

"Why does he know where I live?"

Charlie shrugs. "He looked you up in the phone book?"

A switch flips and I punch him hard in the cheek. He stumbles, taking the blow.

"You think this is funny?" I yell.

He charges me, pushing me, and we collapse backwards. He's short and strong, but I'm mad. He rolls over me, struggling to get on top, like a stupid wrestler. I grunt and push him back, kicking against the floor, swinging my arms at his sides. He fights to hold me down, but I'm long and wiry and throw him off balance. I climb on top and he rolls me over again. I'm face down and he grinds my face into the cement with the flat of his hand.

"It doesn't make sense, okay? I agree with you," he says. "Calm down."

I'm breathing fast and hard and I don't want to listen. It's like all the anger of the last two weeks is pouring out right now.

Charlie twists me in a hold. "I'm going to let you go but you have to calm the hell down. Okay?"

I don't give in but he gets off, releasing me. I kick back but he's too far away. I drag myself to my knees.

"Don't you get it? It's too neat. Too clean."

I stare at him, still angry, but start hearing what he's saying.

He continues, "When did he do this? This weekend? Workers probably were here until Friday. So he came in, dumped the dog in that room, and put the pictures up in here. For what reason?"

I wipe the sweat off my forehead and catch my breath. "So, what? It's all a setup?"

"He's trying to scare us. And right now, it's working."

I stare at him and see the red mark on his cheek. It will probably bruise.

"I mean, honestly, it's good to see you got some fight in you, Anthony Shepherd. Who knew?" He looks at the wall. "But the proof ain't in the pudding."

I stare at him before looking at the wall myself, and my senses finally come back. I feel good—not about hurting him—but about knowing I have the ability if I need it. I stare at a picture of me in a news clipping taken sometime during the search for Sheri last Saturday. It seems so long ago. I don't even remember seeing anyone from the press around.

I look over at my address. Seeing it up there doesn't make me feel safe at all—and then there's my parents and sister.

"Do you think he'll come to our houses?"

Charlie's left the room; I didn't even notice.

I step out of the room to ask again—

And come face to face with the killer.

chapter 81

He stands in the hallway, hoodie pulled tight around a white, smiling mask, Charlie facedown on the ground behind him.

He rushes me, plowing into my chest. We stagger backwards and he slams me hard into the wall. The plasterboard cracks—or maybe it's my bones—and I fall to the ground. He stomps at my head and I try to deflect, but it's useless. I take a couple of kicks to the face and before I realize it, he's on top of me, slamming my forehead into the cement. I'm seeing stars and I struggle to get my arm out from under me to stop him. He drops his knee full force onto my back and it knocks the wind out of my lungs. He swings again and again, fighting like an animal, and I can't get my arms up to defend myself.

My vision blurs and I must have gone limp because at some point he's off me and moving away. I hear Charlie yell out. I try to call to him, but it feels like my mouth is full of cotton. I push up with my arms but the hallway spins and all I see is darkness.

chapter 82

"Shepherd."

The cold cement feels good on my face and I'd rather not open my eyes.

"Shepherd?"

I smell the rotting flesh of the dog and hear the buzz of flies. I feel my whole body rebooting from some distant place.

"Tony!"

"What?" I mumble, not moving, waiting for the pain to go away.

"You alive?'

"Maybe."

"Well, you look like shit."

I open my eyes to see Charlie leaning against the wall beside me. He's got a fat cheek, most likely from me, and also a bloody lip and a cut above the eye.

"So do you."

"What...?" He rubs his face with the back of his hand and sees the blood. "Oh."

"Where'd he go?" I can hardly think, but it seems like that might be important.

"He took off when I went after him. I don't know where."

"He must have hit you pretty hard to knock you down."

I drag myself off the ground and everything hurts. If my hangover was almost cured before, there's no hope now. My ears ring and my whole head throbs. My face feels like someone took out my skull and used it as a basketball—I will definitely be a shade of purple mocha tomorrow.

"Actually, he pushed me down the stairs," Charlie says, so matter-of-factly that I wonder how many other times it's happened. "He was waiting for us."

"That surprise you?"

"No. But it sure felt like he knew how to take us out."

"Well, he's been watching," I say.

"Yeah. About that..."

"What?"

"Some of what he has about me in that room..." Charlie trails off.

"Yeah?"

"It's like he knows me."

"I know what you mean."

"No, I mean he's someone close."

"Goes to your school?"

"Yeah, maybe." He knocks his head back and forth against the wall between answers.

"It would explain why Sheri was the first victim."

"But it doesn't make sense."

"Why?" I want to know.

"Everything he's done—the places he's attacked, staying on the edges of the city—have always made it seem like he's trying to cover his tracks."

"You said he probably followed Sheri home."

"Maybe, but—"

"Seems like he's smarter than to work in his own backyard."

"Yeah," Charlie agrees.

We stare at the crack where my body split the drywall.

"You took some good hits, Rich Boy."

"Can you quit with that, please?"

"Fine."

I've never been in a fight like that, so hearing the compliment from someone who's likely been in a few more brawls than me feels good. We sit in silence for a little longer.

"I did try chasing him."

"Yeah?" I can't help but be impressed that he got up after being thrown down a flight of stairs.

"Almost had him at the start, but he was too fast."

"Did you get a look at him?"

"Not good enough."

"What was with that mask?"

"Not sure."

He grabs the man purse beside him and dumps it on my lap.

"His?"

Charlie nods as I open it. "It doesn't tell us who he is, but—"

I pull out a book—*Bluebeard* by Kurt Vonnegut—and a map.

I unfold it.

All the victim's schools have been circled.

"Holy crap."

"Yeah."

"It looks exactly like yours."

"Yup. Exactly—" He points.

On the right-hand side, south of the industrial area, is a circle around the other school Charlie considered.

He drags himself up the wall and it looks like he's hurting more than he's letting on.

"Do you need a doctor?" I ask him.

"No. How about you?"

"Probably, but I'm going to give it a day or two and see. The less I have to explain to my folks, the better."

"Just tell them I beat you up."

I laugh and it hurts.

"You sure you're okay?" He actually seems a little concerned.

"Yeah, I think so." I can't let him be the only tough guy. "He really pushed you down the stairs?"

Charlie nods as he helps me up.

"Seriously, what is your head made of?"

"I drink lots of soy milk."

"Really?"

"No, it tastes like chalk. Now, let's clean up what we can and get the hell out of here."

chapter 83

We gather up all our pictures first and spend the next half hour searching the house for the camera, working our way downward from the top floor—where, thank God, we can no longer smell the dog. We move slowly, like a couple of grandpas trying to climb up the stairs. We search the bedrooms and find nothing and descend to the main floor.

This takes a little longer, checking all the kitchen and bathroom cabinets and reaching to the back of all the closets. When the camera doesn't show up, Charlie checks his phone again to make sure it's still here. A big blue circle surrounding the houses signals that the GPS is still close, so we go back down into the stench of the basement. We check the den, opening the ceiling tiles and looking in the rafters, before moving on to the rooms. By the second room, we've already guessed where the killer left the camera.

"Who's doing it?"

Charlie holds up a fisted hand. Looks like we're doing this democratically.

"One... two... three."

I do paper and Charlie plays rock—I win.

"Damn."

He takes a deep breath and enters the room with the dead dog. I don't want to watch, staying back as far as I can from the smell. Moments later, Charlie rushes out of the room, gagging and retching, his hand covered in blood—but he's holding the camera.

Once clear of the room, he mouths, "Upstairs," and we get as much distance as we can from the nastiness.

Charlie finds a leftover paper cup of coffee in a corner and takes it outside to wash off. As he pours it over his arm, an old cigarette falls out.

"That is all-around disgusting."

He agrees. "Today pretty much couldn't get any worse."

By the time he's washed off and scrubbed dirt over his arm to get rid of more of the stink, it's mid-afternoon. Walking back to the car, Charlie studies the map and I open the killer's bag to see if there's anything else of interest.

"The fact that he's plotted them out like this still doesn't make sense," Charlie says.

"Because of the connection you think he has to your school?"

He grunts, not looking my way.

I search all the pockets and find nothing. I toss it over my shoulder and flip through the book.

Charlie looks up and smiles. "Looks good on you."

"Shut up—!"

Something falls out of the book, catches in the wind, and blows across the road. I race after it, leaving Charlie standing in the middle of the street. The thing catches in the tall grass that rises at the end of the block, flickering like a play-ing card on a bicycle spoke.

"What is it?"

I pick it up and flip it over. It's a picture of a pretty brunette with a big smile.

I look at Charlie. "Do you think—?" I point toward the map he holds.

Charlie's already there.

"We *have* to take this to Gekas," I say.

"Agreed."

I look at him, surprised and relieved.

"Look, we got our asses kicked today. But you've got to do it."

"Why?"

"She's got too much on me. I don't need her finding my fingerprints on this thing."

I nod.

Charlie looks up and sees two seagulls flying overhead. "If I get shit on, I'm gonna to find a bird to punch."

I laugh as we hobble to the car.

chapter 84

I sit in Detective Gekas' office, once again waiting for her to see me.

People are shuffling around behind me, but I don't turn to look. There are a lot more folders piled on her desk since the killer has claimed another victim. Whatever BS she said in her television interview, she's juggling Sheri's missing person's case and the murders of all the other girls. I can also read the top page of a stack of papers that appear to be reports and tips from nervous citizens or wannabe cops about every kid walking down the street with their hood up.

I'm nervous and can't stop wiggling my foot. Somewhere behind the cushion of the chair, there's a hard bump, like a loose screw, that digs into my back.

Only a couple of weeks ago, I was sitting in that uncomfortable plastic chair in the principal's office, waiting for Gekas, not really aware of the messed-up things people are capable of. I believed Sheri was still alive and the world was safe. But now, nothing is the same—not the office, or the chair, or me—except for the weird, uncertain twist in my guts. And maybe Gekas's unwavering hunt for answers.

I feel someone enter the room and unconsciously sit up straight. It's another detective, a man, adding another file to the shaky heap.

"You waiting for Gekas?" he asks absently, not really caring for an answer, but I give a him a nod anyway.

"Do you want anything? Water?"

I try to say, "No, thanks," but he's already gone, leaving with as much apathy as he brought in with him.

The whole department must be under pressure. Listening to the chaos of ringing phones, buzzing printers, and chattering clerks down the hall, I'd think I was in the office of one of Dad's clients. The police station isn't like in the movies. There's no excitement, no eureka moment that moves the case forward. They're doing the tough slog of gathering pieces of evidence, hoping that something will push the case along or crack it wide open. I hope that what I'm about to tell Gekas will help, but I know it could also blow everything up.

My offering is, unfortunately, complicated.

I shift in my seat and reach into the pouch of my hoodie. My muscles twinge sharply as I pull out the picture of the girl. It's gonna take a while to recover from that throwdown.

I flip it over and stare at her, this girl I don't recognize. My memory kicks me in the head, and I think of the disgusting remains of that poor dog in the basement. Immediately, I think about Sheri. I don't like how these two thoughts run together and I try to close a mental door on both of them.

How should I best proceed here?

Do I tell Gekas about my run-in with the masked killer?

Or do I only tell her about the construction site and the dead dog and the room full of images of Charlie Wolfe and me. Maybe I keep it simple, tell her that I have a hunch, or that I somehow came across this information, or that someone left it anonymously on my locker with some cheesy note like FOR SHERI written on it in red marker.

I scoff, knowing the answer. I've placed myself at the centre of the most ridiculous cliché. For every lie I'd tell, there would be too many questions that would have to be answered.

It's all or nothing.

"Anthony."

I jump.

Gekas comes around to the other side of her desk. "Did I startle you?"

"No. I was just distracted." I slide the photo back into my pocket, hoping she doesn't notice.

She sits down and leans forward in her chair.

The sun isn't in my eyes this time. Although I feel like Gekas and I should be on a level playing field, I'm not at ease.

"You hung up on me this morning." She looks tired, but it seems like she's trying to soften her face with a slight smile.

"I know."

It's not my style to be rude and I feel bad, but then again none of what I've been up to is my style. "I just really thought you should look at the surveillance cameras."

Gekas nods. "What happened to your cheek? And your eye?"

I'm really grateful I'm not a white kid right now because the bruises don't look as bad as they actually are.

"I had a little too much to drink at the party. Dumb, I know."

Crap—the lies begin.

She watches me. And I see the edges of her lips tighten and the smile disappear.

I try to move it along. "So the cameras at the mall?"

"We're looking into it. It's all procedure. Why did you hang up so suddenly?"

"I apologize. It was rude."

"I'm not looking for an apology, Anthony." She sits back in her chair and glances at the mess of paperwork sprawled over her desk. "I'm concerned. You see, you have an alibi and so does Charles Wolfe, but your recent decision to sniff around crime scenes has me worried."

She's still gentle, but I can feel her firming up.

"This isn't a game, Anthony."

Really? I must have missed that while worrying that my girlfriend's missing, likely dead, that my life's been turned upside down, and that I've recently been shit-kicked by the killer!

"I know it's not a game." It comes out much more subdued than it feels.

"And I know you're not a suspect. So, what brings you here?"

I'm silent. My finger runs along the edge of the photo in my pocket. Do I tell her the truth?

"Anthony, do you see this?" She gestures to the files on her desk. "I'm busy. If you're just here to hang out, you need to go somewhere else. Try home or the gym."

I pull out the photo of the pretty brunette with a big smile on her face and lay it on her desk.

Gekas looks down at the photo.

"What's this?"

"I think it's the next victim."

chapter 85

"Pardon me?"

"I think this is a photo of the next victim."

She doesn't pick it up. She looks at the girl smiling up at her.

"Do you know her?"

"No."

"Does Charles know her?"

"No."

"Are you sure?"

"Yes. I'm sure."

She opens a drawer and pulls out a blue crime scene glove and slips it on. She picks up the photo by a corner, turning it over to look at the back.

"How do you know she's the next victim?"

I don't answer. Silence is better than lying.

"Where did you find this?"

"In a book."

"In the library?"

"No."

"Anthony—?"

"Charlie and I were messing around a construction site."

She drops the photo as she looks at me. I can see the upside down face of the mystery girl I'm trying to save.

"Anthony, you didn't...?"

I sheepishly shrug my shoulders but then interject, "We didn't disturb your crime scene." Which is accurate, but not precisely truthful. We did disturb *a* crime scene. It's just one she doesn't know about yet.

"Everything out there could be a potential crime scene. Why do you think we put a fence around it?"

The whole thing dawns on me and I realize how deep I'm in it. "We didn't know."

She sighs, trying her best to move on. "So—you found a book?"

I nod. "And a dead dog in the basement of a house. Its guts were torn out. I've—I've never seen anything like it. It wasn't normal."

"And this?" She turns the image toward me.

"That fell out of a book."

"You've lost me."

"We found a book inside the house, near the dog. I picked it up and a photo fell out of it."

Gekas leans back. "Just like that, huh?"

"Yes."

She lays it down and picks up a pen. "Did you find anything else?"

"No." Lying to a cop, especially Gekas, who's really trying to help, doesn't feel right, but I can't imagine telling the truth right now.

"There was nothing else at that house?"

She's testing me and the lies I've spun. "Nothing."

She points at my face. "And that?"

"Like I said, hurt myself at a party. You know how dumb us teenagers can be."

"Yeah, absolute fools."

She leans back in her chair, fiddling with the cap of her pen, watching me. I know she doesn't believe me, but I also know that she doesn't exactly know what the truth is. I'm sure she hasn't guessed we had a run-in with the killer, but she's smarter than I'd like her to be at the moment, and I can't be certain she doesn't already suspect the truth.

"And where's Charles in all this?"

"He's at home, I believe."

"I mean, does he know about this?"

"Yes."

"He knows you came here to give me this?"

I nod. "Actually it was his idea. I mean, we agreed on it."

She smiles. "Well, isn't that chummy of you two. He wasn't the one who happened to do that to you?"

"No." I say it too quickly, too easily, before realizing it only narrows her list of suspects even more.

"So why isn't he here then?"

I try Gekas's own tactic and lean forward in my chair. "Because you don't like him."

She inhales and nods slightly in agreement. "He does make it a bit of a challenge."

I smile. You and me both, lady!

"You bringing this photo to me, saying this girl may be the next victim—if she winds up hurt, or worse, suspicion may fall back on you."

I hadn't really considered that possibility but it's too late now to dwell on it.

"Detective Gekas, will you help me, please? Will you find her? Keep her safe?"

She nods. "Anthony, you can trust me. And when he comes looking for her, we'll get him."

It's the best thing she's ever said to me.

chapter 86

I'm sitting in my backyard—it's cold but the sun is shining—when Charlie comes through the gate. Ollie gets up to greet him, tail wagging.

"You used the gate. I guess I've housebroken you."

"Who says I didn't break into the front and help myself to your dad's wall safe?"

I shoot him a look and he smiles. "Well, now I know your family has a wall safe."

Charlie hands over a to-go coffee cup and grabs a leafy lawn chair, plopping himself down without clearing it off beforehand. It's little things like this that I find strangely interesting about Charlie Wolfe.

"Thanks, man." It's hot and sugary, and I appreciate it.

"Don't thank me. After the soy milk you gave me, for Pete's sake, it's the least I can do." He takes a loud glug of his own drink, then says, "Your face looks better."

I crack a smile—it doesn't hurt too bad anymore. "So does yours."

Ollie comes over to me for some attention and I scratch the back of his neck deeply.

"So, how'd it go? Are we going to jail, or just me?" He rolls the warm takeout cup between his hands. "Since we're both sitting here, enjoying this tasty beverage, I'm guessing you're no longer a righteous boy and told a few lies?"

"Actually, a bit of both. Sometimes the truth is just as good."

He snorts. "I'll maybe have to try it sometime. Did my name come up?"

"Yup, but I think you're good. You're not really her focus."

"For once. Did you tell her about our masked friend?"

"No, but I wondered if I should."

"Nah, our psycho Marcel Marceau will probably announce himself soon enough."

I don't get the reference but Charlie seems to think it's funny and snickers at his own joke. I shift in my chair and wince as pain shoots through my body. "Man, I'm sore."

"You'll be okay. Give it a couple more days. Our masked friend just likes to play a little rough."

It's clear that Charlie's had different experiences than me, especially given the way he defines what happened to us. "Playing rough" is a huge understatement.

We sit in silence for a moment. I should be able to relax but I can't. I don't feel like things are over with the girl in the picture. It's just a feeling but it's solid. I try to shake it out of my head. Gekas is on her way to find her and she'll be taken in and made safe. Still, something's not right.

I turn to Charlie. "You don't think he's done yet, do you?"

Charlie shakes his head. "No, I don't."

chapter 87

I put my coffee down. "What are you thinking?"

Charlie stares up at the remaining leaves in the trees, finger flicking the edge of his lid.

I wait quietly.

He sets his coffee on the ground beside him and reaches over to rub the dog's head. Ollie follows the love and parks his butt down on Charlie's toes.

Charlie continues to rub behind Ollie's ears, then asks a question of his own, "Why?"

I don't answer because I know if I give him enough time it will come.

"Why her?" He looks over at me, like he's actually waiting for me to answer, but I know better. "I mean, who is she? Why choose her instead of someone else? And why that school? Why plan so specifically? Were all the other girls chosen?"

He pauses and I step in. "You said he tracked Sheri from your school."

"Yeah. But am I right?" He's never questioned himself and it surprises me. "No, he *can't* be from around my school."

I follow his train of thought from earlier today. "Because it's too close to home."

"Exactly! And that's the other thing: a photo of me? At my school? But if he's not from there, then why'd he follow me there?" He shakes his head.

I think Charlie's right—it's not lining up.

He falls silent, so I pick up the thread, "So, if the pieces don't fit, then what are we missing?"

Charlie leans forward. "Three girls. Gekas can only confirm two deaths."

"But all are connected based on a hunch."

He looks over at me and I can tell he doesn't like to be challenged, but then he nods and says, "True. If I'm wrong about Sheri, then what else am I wrong about?"

"Two murdered girls, possibly connected, and Sheri, who's still missing—and possibly dead." I hover over that statement before adding, "And now a potential fourth one."

"Right. Not that we know for sure, but all the attacks seem connected to bathrooms. But for what reason?"

"Some weird fetish?"

Charlie shakes his head. "It *is* weird, I'll give you that. And the intimacy of strangulation sure puts it into fetish territory, but it feels like there's more to it than that…"

He trails off again and I can see he's frustrated.

"It's like I'm missing something in front of my face, something right there that I can't see."

I change the question. "Why the mask? Is it just to remain anonymous?"

Charlie lets go of his own thought to pursue mine. "It reminds me of those happy/sad masks you see in a theatre."

I consider this as he grabs his phone out of his pocket and does a quick search. "Here's something. Masks like that represent the ancient Greek muses. Melpomene is the muse of tragedy, and the one our dude was wearing is Thalia, the muse of comedy."

"Comedy, huh? Not funny."

"I don't think he's trying to be ironic. That video of Bonnie—he was performing for us."

"So what? You think he's making a movie?"

Charlie doesn't answer.

I look over. "What?"

"That first day, when we walked the trails, we went into the bathroom..."

"Yeah?"

"I went through the motions, like, I tried to kill you."

I nod. "And?"

"I could see myself in the mirror the whole time. I saw you and I saw myself and I could have watched me kill you."

"All the bathrooms—"

"Have mirrors."

"He wasn't performing for *us*—"

"He was performing for himself."

chapter 88

Bzzz.

My phone hums on the table between us. I look down at the number. "Gekas."

Charlie looks at me with sincere interest, but I hesitate. "Answer it."

I hear a sliver of impatience in his voice, just a sliver. I pick it up and shoot him a look. "You've got to be less bossy already."

The phone stops ringing.

"See! You took too long."

I feel a little bad that I took a moment to tell Charlie to back off rather than to answer Gekas's phone call. I bluff. "Don't worry. She'll call back."

Immediately, the phone rings again and I feel like I've won a tiny victory against Charlie. "See," I say nonchalantly while he gestures frantically at the phone.

I pick it up. "Hello?"

"Anthony?"

Charlie leans in to listen.

"Yes."

"Is your buddy there?"

Charlie shakes his head, but I ignore him. "Yup."

He shoots me a look.

"Put me on speaker phone."

I ignore Charlie's further protests, push the button, and put it between us.

"Hello, Charles."

His face scrunches up at the sound of her voice but he follows through, "Hello, Detective."

"I'm calling to let you two know that we've found her. We found the girl."

A tension that I hadn't realized had been gripping my heart releases. "You did?"

"Yes, we did."

Charlie leans back in the chair.

"I wanted to call you both personally and let you know."

For a split second, I wonder what her motivation is, but I ignore it in favour of gratitude. "Thank you."

"You're welcome."

I should be happy that we have protected her, but after everything Charlie and I've been talking about, I feel a strong wave of doubt.

"Detective, who is she?"

"I can't tell you that, Anthony—"

"I know what she looks like and I know she goes to Greenville High. It won't take much for a couple of resourceful guys like us to find out."

Charlie shoots me a look, wondering what I'm up to. I don't like pushing against Gekas like this—in fact, I feel *way* outside my comfort zone—but I'm as certain about my actions now as I am on the court.

Gekas's sigh comes through loud and clear over the phone line. "Her name is Tamara Seller. She graduates this year."

"How did you find her?"

"Contacted people at the school board office, talked to the principal, and tracked her down."

"Was she at home?"

"Where are you going with this?"

"Was she at home or at work? Does she have a job?"

"What—?"

"Please, Detective."

"We went to her house. She doesn't have a job."

I look at Charlie, expecting him to know what I'm thinking, but for once, he has no clue.

"Is Tamara safe?"

"Yes. She's at home, with her parents and two officers."

I'm relieved for her but it's too easy—everything else has been a struggle. I'm silent for too long.

"Are you okay, Anthony?"

"Yes. Thank you for letting me know."

"Anthony—?"

"Thank you, Detective Gekas."

"Don't you dare hang up on me—!" she yells.

I turn off the phone. "She's not the one."

"What do you mean?"

"It's Saturday and she doesn't have a job."

"So?"

"Where is he going to get her? He's never gone to a house."

Charlie picks up on my line of reasoning. "He needs a public space, especially a bathroom—"

"With a mirror—"

"Because he needs to see himself—"

"Perform."

He stares at me. "She's *not* the one."

I nod.

"So, what then? Until he makes a move—?"

"I hate to say it, but we have to wait."

chapter 89

He sits in his car, looking down the street at the police cruiser parked outside the house.

He was proud of how he'd directed the scene, moving the players around his stage, doing what he wanted them to do. Everything had happened so quickly and he'd had to improvise so much, yet he'd been able to make it all work.

When he'd realized the dark-skinned one was the boyfriend of the first girl, it all came together. He'd begun gathering the newspaper clippings and found photos on the internet. As for the other loser, simply breaking into the school yearbook office gave him all he needed. He had kept the dead dog in a heavy-duty garbage bag in the garage, and once he had his car back from the impound, he loaded everything up and headed to the construction site, appreciating the symmetry of his actions.

Yet, until he'd seen them walk across the space between the houses, he'd never realized how tall the boyfriend was or how solid the loser was. He knew he'd have to take them down separately, knock one down the stairs and keep tight and close to the other. He just never expected the loser to survive the fall and come after him again so quickly. He was lucky this time; he would have to make sure not to let it happen again.

The clue that had led both them and the police to this girl's house had been a series of fortuitous coincidences. Early on, after moving to the new city, he had found the book and picture in an upscale coffeehouse on the east side. He'd held on to them both, unwilling to sever their connection. It had been pure serendipity—he took it as proof that he was following the right path—that the school he'd circled on his map had actually been the girl's school.

The body in his trunk rattled back and forth and he knew it was time to move on.

Five-minute warning. Flash the house lights, everybody take your seats. The performance is about to begin.

part 4

I wake the next day with a heaviness in my chest. It's not the same pain as my sore body. That hurts too. It's a thick and unsettling feeling. Waiting is horrible. I'm afraid that what I'm waiting for is another tragedy. I suppress a shudder as I stand in front of the mirror in my room. My face is kind of a mess. There are deep bruises on my lower abs just above my boxers. A few weeks ago, I was vain about my body and now I have a strange respect for what I know it can take. I turn and look over my shoulder into the mirror at the bruises on my back, but it aches to do this.

Tap. Tap. "Tony."

It's Dad.

I snatch up my shirt and pull it on as fast as possible, not wanting him to see me like this because he'll tell Mom. She's a doctor and a mom and is going to freak out way, way more than Dad.

"Yeah?" I say as casually as I can even though my heart is pounding.

The door opens. The blinds are down. My room is dark.

"Are you okay?" Dad asks, taking a look around my room. I can see he's assessing everything. Nothing is out of order so I don't worry about his curiosity. I do, however, turn my back to him, averting my face, pointlessly moving a stack of schoolbooks from one pile to another.

"Are you on your way down?"

"I was going to do a little homework first. I'm almost caught up."

"Good. I mean, I'm glad. It just makes things easier on you later if you take care of business now." He smiles and nods. "Come down."

He's gentle but firm. I can't say no. I shouldn't say no. Things are slowly sliding toward being better. He looks at my face but says nothing. Can he see the bruises? Did he notice?

"I'll be right down."

"Your mother made some seriously unhealthy but delicious buttermilk pancakes." Dad walks away, leaving my door open.

The fragrance of pancakes, coffee, and bacon waft up into my room.

I need a lie. I can't avoid them until my bruises are gone. I'm going to have to come up with something.

I head down the stairs with more noise than I normally would to make my entrance a little jollier sounding. It's just the three of us. Heather is out with friends. The table has a great spread of a Sunday brunch on it. I wonder what Charlie's Sunday morning meals look like. I sit down at the table and pour a glass of orange juice.

"Good morning, sunshine." Mom says as she walks by me and sits down with a stack of pancakes.

We settle in.

I fill my plate with pancakes, fruit, whip, and bacon, and just as I am about to start eating, Mom says, "Detective Gekas called this morning."

I pour syrup on my food.

"She said you went to see her."

I nod.

"About?"

"Just checking in." I highly doubt she'd give my parents information about an ongoing case, so I risk the lie.

"She's concerned."

"Oh?"

Then she sees it. Her fork clinks as it drops to her plate.

"Anthony. What happened to your face?"

I have a mouthful of breakfast and although it should be delicious, I don't taste one morsel. It's all just mush and I chew it slowly as I plan my piece of fiction before swallowing.

"I don't want to sound like a jerk but you may have noticed that my life has recently fallen apart?" It comes out harsher than I expect. "And I decided that after all this garbage I needed to cut loose a little, so I went to a farm party with Mike on Friday."

"That doesn't explain the bruises on your face."

She moves to get a closer look at me and I pull back instinctively.

I wonder how they'd respond if I said, *Well, Mom and Dad, I was wandering around with a guy from the wrong side of the tracks and we found a death shrine to us and a dead dog and a photo of a potential victim. Oh, and we were both completely beat up by the masked killer. Thank you. Have a nice day.*

"I drank too much." This is not going to go well. I have made it to Grade 11 without any incidents. My parents stare at me from the other side of the table. "And I think I fell off the porch there. I'm not sure. I can ask Mike."

I stuff a large amount of pancake in my mouth and wish Heather were here. Even for a little back up.

They wait. Dead air hangs between us.

I swallow. "It's not as bad as it looks." And I take another drink of juice. I wish it had whiskey in it. There's irony for ya.

"And drinking is a good idea?" Dad steps up when I really thought Mom would take this one.

I shrug.

"The answer is no. Drinking is not a good idea. Drinking in excess is *never* a good idea. Drinking to the point you don't even know how you hurt yourself is the *worst* of ideas."

My heart starts beating a little faster.

"How did you get home?" Dad continues the questioning.

"Mike... I think."

"You *think*?" Dad's on me and I really don't want to cross him.

Mom sits there, arms folded. I've disappointed them badly.

I try a dose of humour. "I guess if you didn't hear me stumble up the stairs, it couldn't have been that bad, right?"

Mom's face twists in a disparaging smile—her perfect son has taken a turn and is heading for a smack in the head.

I try to fix it. "Look, I know it's a bad idea. All of it. I do it so little that it was completely unintentional."

Now I feign defensiveness. "I really just need you to back off for a while and trust me, okay?"

They grill me with their silence. Oh, man.

"I won't do it again. There. Happy?" I've never fought so hard over something that never even happened. "Are you going to ground me?"

Mom finally speaks. "We love you. We're all trying to get through this. You understand that?"

I nod.

"Grounding you won't solve anything, but can you promise to be more responsible and take care of yourself?"

"I'm sorry. I mean it. I'm really sorry." And I do mean it.

They both sit back a bit and the tension between us vaporizes.

Dad takes a sip of his coffee. "Detective Gekas asked us to keep you close. She cares."

I want to laugh but I hold it inside. I nod solemnly.

"Do you want me to look at your bruise?"

She's being more mom than doctor right now—I think she can tell that my face is just the tip of the iceberg.

"I'm fine. For real."

"If it doesn't start improving in the next day or two, I'm looking at it whether you want me to or not."

I roll my eyes and sigh. "Fine."

I hope this is the end of the discussion. I just want to go back up to my room, but I need to stick around and make it look like I am trying.

"No turkey bacon, Dad?"

He shakes his head and grins as he gets my loving dig at his healthy ways.

chapter 91

The rest of Sunday passes peacefully. I stick close to home and tend to my broken self to keep my parents happy. I send Charlie a text message to check in.

You alive?

His reply is delayed and brief:

Yup.

I imagine his Sunday is quiet too, perhaps a different kind of quiet than mine. I do some homework and watch an old movie with my parents about a guy stuck on an island with a volleyball.

Monday morning I drive to school early to see Coach Davies. I'm in no condition to train. My back is stiff and sore. My right hip is black and blue. My face is a wreck. I stand in the door of his office for a while, waiting for him to finish what he's doing.

I clear my throat. "Hi, Coach."

He looks up. "Shepherd."

Then I see him focus on my face.

It feels better but looks worse today. Mom told me that's how bruises heal, making their way to the surface. Charlie said it would make me look a little more badass.

"Your face?"

"That's what I wanted to talk to you about. I was doing some work with my dad in the garage. We were building a shelf and it fell." The more I open my mouth, the more I twist my own lies.

"Anyway, I'm pretty sore and think I need a day or two to rest up. I can get my parents to write a note if you need—"

Shut up, Tony! They'll never write you a note.

"That's fine, Anthony." Coach trusts me—we have a long enough history so the bluff works.

"If you've got plays or something you want me to look over, I can do that."

He nods his approval and hands me the playbook. "You'll know what to do with this."

"Thank you. I think I'll be good to go by Wednesday."

I force myself to walk away stoically from Coach Davies' office, pretending my body doesn't hurt as much as it does. Books in hand, I head to first period, knowing all too well that whatever my idea of normal was, it is now forever changed. It feels like something is always lurking in the periphery of my sight. Corners hold menace. Every blind turn might mean seeing the killer again, coming to finish the job.

Slap! Somebody strikes me hard on the back and it takes everything I have to not crumble. I turn, ready to fight back, but it's just Mike.

"Hey, man! Good party Friday night!" He has a huge, innocent smile on his face. "Whoa! Whose fist did you run into?"

"Long story—"

He waves it off. "That's cool. I got Chrissy's number."

I fake interest. "Great. Who's Chrissy?" I don't really care but figure I should try.

"Remember the super cute brunette from the movie theatre? She's also a cheerleader!" He elbows me in a naughty Dad-joke kind of way. He opens his phone and proudly shows me a selfie of him with yet another girl. She's cute—a long, dark pony-tail and a big smile.

"Good for you."

"You got a little tanked, huh?" He takes another friendly swing with the palm of his hand to tap my shoulder. I step out of the way.

"That I did. How did I get home?"

Mike pauses and shrugs. "Dunno. I was busy wheeling Chrissy."

"What about—?"

Mike ignores me. "Yeah, yeah! It seems there's enough Mike around here for *all* the ladies." He shifts gears. "Where were you Saturday? I sent you a couple of texts. Figured you were nursing a hangover."

Scenes flash like fireworks in my head: the strangled girl, the buzzing flies, the beatdown in the basement, and my third heart-to-heart with Gekas.

"I took it easy."

"Panty," Mike teases.

The bell for class rings.

"Catch you later!" Mike yells with infectious enthusiasm from halfway down the hall. How different he is from Charlie.

Second period history class comes and goes, and I go through the motions. My phone remains relatively silent. I'm waiting for Charlie, but I can't help thinking of when it used to be Sheri.

I miss her.

English is third and I settle in. The teacher starts by handing back our assignments for *Animal Farm* and I get mine. A low D. I'm not surprised. I'm going to have to negotiate a rewrite at some point. The notes come up next. We all start writing from the PowerPoint on the projector screen.

Bzzz.

My phone startles me. I discreetly pull it out of my pocket and look. It's a Snapchat message from—shit—comedymuse.

I raise my hand and cut the teacher off mid-sentence, "May I go to the washroom?"

He nods his permission and I hurry from the class, leaving my books behind. In the stairwell, I take a big breath and swipe open the app.

It's a girl—bound and gagged in the trunk of a car. The photo is carefully cropped above the licence plate.

I feel sick to my stomach.

Her eyes are wide with terror, her face dirty and bruised. That's when that feeling in my gut rushes in. I recognize her.

It's Chrissy, the girl from Mike's selfie.

chapter 92

I take a quick screenshot before the image disappears.
I bring up Charlie's "Hot Diggity" and text him.

It's go time.

What?

Message from comedymuse. It's bad.

I'm almost out of the school when I realize I need infor-mation. I text Mike.

Meet me in the commons.

dude. in class.

now

He doesn't respond.

I text again.

NOW

Minutes later, I see him heading down the hallway toward me.

"What's going on?"

I'm not sure how to approach it, so I barrel in because there is no easy way around this. "That girl you met at the party—?"

"Chrissy?"

"Yeah. Where does she go to school?"

"Man, what are you getting at? You trying to get something on the side?"

"Mike, I need to know."

"What is *with* you?"

"Mike!"

He stops and stares at me. "You know, ever since Sheri, I've been trying to help get your mind off things—but you're not you. You're never around, you're skipping practice. It's like you've just given up."

He's talking but I can't comprehend what he's saying through the chaos in my head. Frankly, I couldn't really care less, and if I did, I'd likely punch him in the face. I hold it all in, trying to calm down and focus on what's going on.

"Mike, I'm sorry you feel that way, but I think something's happened to Chrissy."

"What are you talking about?"

I don't want to explain myself and I sure as hell am not going to show him the picture.

"Just tell me what school Chrissy goes to."

He eyes me, squinting like it's going to help him see the reason for my craziness.

"Mike, I think what happened to Sheri is happening to Chrissy." I hope that's enough to get him to cooperate.

"Why would you—? What makes you...?"

I let him wind down.

"Guthrie," he finally says.

Sheri's school.

"And what's her last name?"

"McIntyre."

"Thanks, Mike. Don't worry. I'm going to do my best to keep her safe."

chapter 93

I realize what I said and that it may have sounded arrogant, but I don't care. I meant it.

I leave him and the school behind, texting as I go.

Girls from your school.

It doesn't take long for Charlie to reply.

Wat?

I start typing but Charlie interrupts:

How do u know?

I erase my message and type:

Long story. Gekas?

The typing indicator bubbles, then:

Yes.

I'm pretty sure he went back and forth on that. Charlie texts again:

I'm there in five.

I didn't know he had a car. Or worse yet, he doesn't but he'll find himself one. Either way, he's not at school because no one gets across town to the east side that fast.

I bring up Gekas's number from my recents—it's been used far too many times as of late.

She answers on the second ring. "Anthony?"

"He's got another one."

Silence but I don't have the patience to wait. "Detective Gekas, can I send you the picture he sent me?"

"He contacted you?"

"Yes." I need her focused and on track. "I'm sending it now."

I put her on speaker, click "attachment," and go to my photos. It's the first one and I can't even look at the thumbnail. The idea that I have something like this on my phone bothers me.

"Sending it now."

"I need that phone, Anthony. Maybe we can trace it."

"He sent it through one of those self-destructing photo apps. There'd be no trace."

"Maybe a bit of code, something to find him?"

"Sure, Detective." I doubt it though, and I think she does too. "You get it yet?"

"It's still downloading..."

"She's from Sheri's school."

More silence. "How do you know? Did he tell you?"

"No. A friend of mine met her." I think about my home address on the basement wall. "Detective Gekas, do you think he went after her because of me?"

She doesn't hesitate. "No, Anthony. It isn't your fault."

"But—" I'm ready to tell her what I didn't tell her before—about the pictures and the run-in we had with the killer.

"Don't think that way. It's just bad luck."

I'm sure she'll investigate it anyway.

She's quiet now and I assume she's got the picture.

"Her name is Chrissy McIntyre."

"Thank you, Anthony. Anything else?"

"The last person I know who saw her was my buddy, Mike."

"I'm going to have to question him."

"Okay." At this point, I have to do whatever it takes. "He met her at a farm party on Friday."

"Is this the one where you hurt your eye?"

Crap. "Yes."

"You really have lousy luck, Anthony."

"I know, Detective Gekas. I know."

chapter 94

Charlie is outside my school three minutes later. He's got two coffees in his hand and what I can only guess is a bag of doughnuts.

I look around. "Where's your car?"

"Don't have one."

"Then how'd you get here?"

"I was at the coffee shop down the street."

Why do I ever assume Charlie lives a normal life? I wonder if he even goes to school. I hand him my phone and show him the text.

"You say he sent it to you? Text?"

"No, a Snapchat." I don't mention that it seems like he and Gekas are joined at the brain.

He stares at it, not moving, taking it in.

"It's pretty bad, huh?"

He looks at me, shaking his head. "No. I know who the killer is."

chapter 95

Charlie hustles me to my car before he says another word.

"Drive."

"Where?"

"My school." He stares out the window, chewing on his first doughnut, mumbling to himself.

"What?"

"I said, 'It's a stupid day to have missed school.'"

"Why? What's going on? Who is it?"

He grabs my phone and shows me the picture. I can barely look at it.

"What do you see?"

"Chrissy—?"

"No, the *car*. Blue Civic with a busted driver's side taillight."

"So?"

"It's Robbie."

"Who?"

He looks at me like I should know these things.

"*Robbie.* The dude I was with the first day you came and asked for my help."

Now I remember. The kid in the hoodie with the baggie and the glass pipe. And the lost car.

"Robbie?"

"I know. It doesn't make sense. The kid can barely tie his own shoelace without falling over. But...?"

I think about the beatdown we got in the house, trying to match up my earlier impression of Robbie with the figure in the mask. It still doesn't work.

"You really think he could've pushed you down the stairs, taken me out, then got away?"

"No. That's why we've got to find him before Gekas does."

chapter 96

"Is he at school?"

"He has a worse track record for showing up than me."

"Don't you have someone you can text?"

Charlie looks at me. "Unfortunately, most of my connections are superficial. It's easier that way."

I can't help but feel a little hurt, so I stick it right back at him. "That's why it pays to have friends." I hand Charlie my phone as I drive. "Here."

He takes it from my hand. "Who do you want?"

"Look up Jessica's name."

He doesn't even pause as he types in my password and scrolls through my numbers.

"Text her and ask if Robbie's been at school."

"Would she even know?" I can hear the edge in his voice.

"Despite what you may think, she pays attention."

He sends the message off and we wait for a response.

"It really doesn't make sense that Robbie could be a killer," he says.

I look over at him; he's staring out the window, sipping on his coffee, but I don't think he's taking in the scenery.

My phone buzzes. He looks at it.

"She says, 'No.' Do you think she'd know where he might be?" he asks.

"Doubt it. You have any ideas?"

He pulls out his own phone. "He lives just off Prince of Wales Drive. Let's start there."

chapter 97

We pull to the side of the street a few yards from Robbie's driveway. No other cars are there and the place looks empty.

It's a big house, probably built in the late '80s, with the garage on the front. A few small saplings on the lawn have only begun to dream of being real trees. The grass is green and manicured, even in this dry fall. Not a trace of fallen leaves on the property.

We step out of the car. This wide-open street doesn't offer much in the way of a subtle approach. Also, if this turns into a thing, which I expect it will with Charlie around, there's no real place for us to avoid being seen by nosey neighbours.

We stay close to the edge of the attached garage, walking along the wall. I hope it blocks us from view, at least a little, but I know that's just wishful thinking. Charlie puts his face to the window of the side door of the garage, cupping his face to block the bright daylight. I follow his lead and now *I* feel like the nosey neighbour.

My eyes adjust to the dim interior. The car's inside.

"We need to get in there." Charlie rattles the knob of the garage door, but doesn't take his eyes off the car. It's locked.

"Now what?"

He looks around, and I hope to God he's not looking for a rock to throw through the window.

Charlie heads up the front steps. I follow and he pounds on the door. So much for subtle, but at least it wasn't a rock through the window.

No answer. No Robbie, no parents.

Charlie hops down off the step and heads into the tight, narrow gap between houses. At the end is a seven-foot fence that splits in a T between the two properties. He grabs hold and jumps, wedging a foot between the stucco of the house and the corner fencepost. He pulls up from the cross brace and drags himself the rest of the way over the top.

"You coming?" he asks from the other side.

I weigh my options. Either I have Charlie let me in the front door and be seen by someone across the street, or I risk the B&E and follow him through the back.

"Hold on!" I yell as I drag myself not so gracefully over to the other side. I still hurt from Saturday but suck up the pain.

Charlie hasn't once complained about his battered body and I take that as a sign of how seriously he's taking this.

"I'm going to assume it's because you're being a pussy that you made that look as awkward as you possibly could."

Apparently nothing's so serious that you can't give your buddies a hard time. "Shut it," I say.

"I mean, I thought you guys could jump—"

"Shut. Up." I don't know if he's trying to offend me but it's sort of good to see he wants to mess with me, even now.

We move cautiously around the outside of the deck, but Charlie breaks off and makes for the patio door.

"You aren't seriously going through that way?"

"The lock sucks and there's too many eyes around for me to toss a brick through the window." He catches my look. "I know you're thinking I'd do something like that."

"You wouldn't actually, though, would you?"

He smiles but doesn't answer. He goes right up to the back door, then hesitates.

"Charlie?"

His hand slips in his pocket and comes out again, empty. "I don't know. Just... give me a chance to talk to him, okay?"

I nod.

He bangs on the door. "Robbie?"

Silence.

He knocks again, waiting. After all the times Charlie has walked right in uninvited, *now* he wants to watch his manners?

He's about to knock a third time when I stop him.

Charlie stares at me. "What?"

"Really?"

He chews his lip, glaring at me. I know he's pissed but I'm sure it has little to do with me. Still, if he decides to take his anger out on me, I'm ready.

Finally, he sighs and smiles and pulls out his ring of bump keys, dumping them in my hand. "You want in? Have at it."

Unfortunately, I barely have any idea how to use them, except for the time I watched him. I find a key that seems to match and slide it in the lock. Charlie hands me a rock from the landscaped yard and I rap the back end, turning the key.

Nothing.

I try it again and again but still nothing happens. I'm ready to kick the door in.

Charlie sighs and, without a word, shows me the trick. He slides the key in and then, while twisting it, pulls the key back gently so that it's no longer flush to the lock. He pushes it back in and lets me try.

I push it in, twist it, and pull it back gently. I feel a slight click through my fingers and hit the key with the screwdriver. The doorknob turns and I've now officially committed my first break and enter.

I motion to the door with an exaggerated "you first" bow.

Charlie swings his long, curly bangs out of the way and raises an eyebrow at me before taking me up on the offer.

I follow silently, closing the door gently behind us with a small, quiet *click*.

chapter 98

We're in a back entryway, but it's devoid of any pairs of shoes or clutter of jackets hanging from hooks. A small set of stairs leads us to the kitchen. It's open concept, filled with black surfaces and stainless steel.

Charlie stares at a large glass bowl full of fruit on the centre island. He picks up an apple and squeezes it. "Fake."

"Sure looks real."

"Bet they paid extra for real-looking fake fruit."

He opens the fridge and assesses its contents.

"What are you doing? Don't you have doughnuts in the car?"

"What's in a fridge says a lot about someone."

"Anything interesting?"

"Too many condiments. Not enough real food."

He shuts the door.

I stare at the bare fridge door. A magnet for a pizza joint holds a couple of receipts under it. "What's *on* a fridge also says a lot about a family."

"Hey, they only moved here a little while ago."

It feels like he's apologizing for them.

A cat comes around a corner and meows, rubbing itself against Charlie's pant leg. He doesn't kick it away but doesn't pay it any special attention either.

We walk into the dining room where a large picture, if that's what you'd call it, hangs. It's a field of colour—orange—that takes up nearly half the wall. I barely give it any notice, but Charlie stares at it.

"Does it speak to you?" I ask.

He ignores me and moves on into the living room. It's as beautiful as it is hollow, with absolutely no personality. The sofas match the chairs and the white walls are only an extension of the white rugs and white curtains. The paintings in here are more ugly décor store designer art, something Mom has strongly voiced a dislike for. There are no photos anywhere to indicate who lives here.

"Charlie, this family has no soul."

He sighs and nods as he goes up the stairs toward the bedrooms. The cat follows.

I pause. "Wait, why aren't we breaking into the garage?"

"Don't you learn anything I teach you, Shepherd?"

I wasn't aware I was supposed to be learning.

"Let's case the joint quickly, gather whatever we can, then move on."

"But—"

"What?"

"What about the girl?"

He looks at me, his face empty of expression. "What about her?"

"She could be in the trunk of the car!"

"So?"

His answer leaves me cold. When he's on the trail of something, he doesn't let anything stand in his way, but he's ignoring a person's life.

Then I realize what his priorities are. "You're not here for her. You're here for Robbie."

He sighs, like he has no time to deal with me. "He isn't our guy."

"But what if he is?"

I can see he doesn't even want to consider it, but he takes a step toward me. "So, what then? Think you'll get to the trunk and she won't look any different than that dog?"

The image of that poor animal flashes in my mind and I'm not sure I want to face it. Yet, I push ahead, ready to argue.

He cuts me off. "Look, you be the hero and go save the damsel. I'm going to do what needs to be done." He turns and heads up the stairs.

I stand at the bottom while he disappears down the second floor hallway. I turn and spy another dark hallway, certain that it leads out to the attached garage, but I can't get myself to move. My brain swirls with thoughts. If Robbie is our guy, I'm certain I could take him. But whoever went after us on Saturday almost took us both out—this scares me. And *that* pisses me off, but until I can get ahold of myself, I'll follow Charlie's lead.

By the time I get upstairs, he's already moved on from the first room. I peek in as I walk by and see it's the master bedroom. Dark, heavy curtains keep out the light. It's spotless, no clothes on the floor or the chair.

Charlie sees me but goes on to the second room.

"All done, are we?"

I hate showing my weaknesses to him and try keeping it short. "No."

He stops outside the next room and nods. "Good. Whoever is behind all this laid a shit-kicking on us last time, and I'd hate for us to split up so he can finish the job."

I'm not sure if he's saying that for my benefit or if it's what he actually feels, but I choose to believe him. "Hey, what can I say? We're partners."

He looks at me and smiles. "We are, aren't we?"

Using a sleeved hand, he opens the next door.

It's the bathroom, and it's huge. A double sink runs along one wall and there's large standalone tub close to the shower.

Charlie stares at it. "Why is there all this stuff?"

"If you don't want a bath, then you can have a shower."

"Then just have a tub with a shower in it." He really can't understand why anyone would want it like this. "Rich people are stupid." He closes the door and moves on to the last two rooms at the end of the hallway.

"Do you even know where you're going?"

"No."

"Haven't you been here before?" I'm betting he came over for some pot party, but the way he makes friends, I wouldn't be surprised if he'd never been here before either.

"Once, but only in the basement."

I pause. "Is Robbie even a friend?"

Charlie turns to me, his eyes sad. "Not really. But if we don't take care of the rejects of this world, who will?"

He opens the next door and we find a bedroom. It's another soulless room, like the master, but this one is extremely sparse. There is a made bed and a small bookshelf filled with books arranged in order of height. The curtains are open exactly the same amount and the light shines on the closed closet door. A chair sits in the corner. The room is empty. It reminds me of when my oldest sister Jodi moved away for college and slowly took all the stuff out of her room over the years. Probably a guest room, I think.

We shut the door and move on to the last room.

Rrrwow! A grey streak zips out of the bedroom between our feet.

"Another stupid cat?"

"That scared the crap out of me." I lean in to look at the room.

Chaos.

I don't even question that this disaster is Robbie's room. A Skrillex banner forms a makeshift curtain over the window. The bed is unmade, clothes everywhere. A stack of LPs are ready to topple off his dresser. A vaporizer sits next to an autobiography of Henry Rollins and a copy of *Rolling Stone* with Howard Stern on the cover. There's a book on hydroponics facedown and half-read on the dusty dresser. At least he attempts to be well-informed. The room has no focus, no order. It's mayhem. It smells dusty, musty, skunky, and sweaty. I'm disgusted.

I toe an empty pizza box with my foot. "Wow, your buddy's a cliché."

Charlie holds up an LP of Deep Purple. "Well, at least he doesn't have terrible taste in music."

I shake my head—we'll never see eye to eye on this stuff.

"It's gross."

Charlie shrugs. "I've seen worse."

I hope he's not referring to his own room.

"This is not the room of a killer," he says.

I survey this upheaval of a bedroom and can't even begin to fathom the twisted, methodical mind of our killer headquartered in here.

"I agree," I say. "Can we please go look at the car now?"

Charlie nods. He closes the door to the room. Both cats sit at the end of the hallway, staring at us. I'm glad they can't talk. This is the first time in my life I've entered a home without an invitation. Or with a lockpick, for that matter. My worldview is shifting.

We leave all the doors in the hallway as we found them and go back downstairs.

I'm at the garage door when Charlie takes a quick detour into the kitchen.

"Just a minute."

I wonder what he's up to when he returns with a can of iced tea.

"Are you kidding?"

He looks annoyed.

"You're not even thirsty."

"How do you know?"

"You just had a coffee. It's in my car."

"So? I want some iced tea."

"Sometimes I think you do things just because you can."

"He'd get me one if he were home!"

"Yeah, well, he's *not*."

I'm raising my voice as we go into the garage. Perhaps it's nerves from snooping around someone else's house, even if it feels like a soulless showhome, or the thought that Chrissy's life may depend on us, but I feel frustrated.

"You want me to get you one?"

"No!" I shout.

"You need to loosen—"

Thunk.

We look at each other, my heart pounding so loud I can hear it.

Charlie moves toward the car. "Hello?"

Thunk.

"Holy shit."

"The trunk."

I catch my breath and fly into action, running to the driver's side and popping the trunk. I scramble to Charlie, who stands there, speechless.

Inside is Chrissy, bound with duct tape and gagged.

But alive!

chapter 99

She's terrified.

Without missing a beat, Charlie has his pocketknife out and works at the tape that binds her hands behind her back.

"It's okay." He sounds gentle.

"Chrissy?" I ask.

She nods.

"I'm going to take the tape off your mouth. It's going to hurt for only a minute, okay?" Her eyes go wide with fear and I wince before I yank.

She whimpers.

Charlie moves to the tape around her feet. "One more." He pulls the tape away and helps her sit up. "There you go."

She's distant, not focusing on us.

Charlie bends down and places a hand on her shoulder. "You're safe. We're not going to let anyone hurt you." He turns to me. "Call Gekas."

I nod.

He looks back at Chrissy. "Are you okay?"

She's a long way from the selfie Mike took at the party. Her clothes and face are dirty, and she has a scratch on her cheek and a bruise on her forehead. "Get me out of here."

Charlie helps her out of the trunk and her bare feet are bloody. "Do you know where you are?"

She begins to cry. "No idea." She grabs her stomach and manages to utter, "Oh God, I feel sick…" before running to the corner and vomiting.

"You're okay. We're calling the police." I grab my phone and dial Gekas. Busy signal! Of all the times…

Charlie comes over to me. "Tony—"

"I was right."

"Yeah, whatever. Listen, we have to get her out of here and find Robbie."

I'm pissed and ready to express it when—

Bzzz.

"Gekas?" Charlie asks.

I look. "No. Jessie." I read the text:

Asked around. Robbies at Brent Chans.

Charlie shakes his head. "Brent lives down the street from the school. He's a dropout and a dealer—all the kids go to his place to get stoned. God, Robbie, you're such an idiot."

I gesture to Chrissy. "Maybe a bigger idiot than we thought."

"I doubt that."

I dial Gekas again.

This time, she answers.

"Detective?"

"What, Anthony?"

"We found her. We found Chrissy."

I look over to see she's propped herself against a sawhorse, pale and exhausted.

Gekas sounds distracted. "Where are you?"

I look over at Charlie, knowing he still has his doubts, but Chrissy needs help. "3212 Crawley Crescent."

Again, a long pause. "Thank you, Anthony. Can you stay with her until I get some officers over and the paramedics arrive?"

"You're not coming?"

"I'm sorry, no."

"Detective—"

"Make sure Charlie stays around to give his statement."

"Okay, but Detective—"

"Thank him for me, will you? Okay, I have to go. Goodbye." She hangs up.

Charlie looks at me. "What?"

"Something's up."

chapter 100

We help Chrissy out of the house as unobtrusively as possible and wait on the curb. A few cars come down the street, slowing down. We must be quite a sight for this neighbourhood—a black kid, a shaggy-haired troublemaker, and a girl who must look like—well, I don't really want to know what they must think we've done to her.

Charlie gives her the iced tea he's stolen and wanders to the car to get his coffee and bag of doughnuts.

I look over at Chrissy. I have to ask. "Can you tell me what happened?"

She's quiet for a bit. I think she wants to cry but there's nothing left inside her. "I was working day shift at the movie theatre. It was quiet and boring and no one was coming because of all the crappy shows that are out. I was thinking about the party I went to the night before. I met a really nice guy and gave him my number and was hoping he'd call."

I smile a bit, knowing she means Mike.

"Anyway, I had to go to the bathroom and went to the one in the back for employees. No one was around. It was quiet" —her voice cracks—"And then..." She breaks into big dry heaves.

I put my arm on her shoulder and she grabs my hand.

"You don't know who took you, do you? Someone you might have recognized?"

She shakes her head. "He had a mask on. Some creepy thing. I just... I can't."

I nod and squeeze her hand. We see Charlie on his way back and she wipes her eyes, running her fingers through her hair. I let her have her space and go to Charlie, who's on his phone.

"What's up?"

"Checking social media."

"See if there's anything about where Gekas is going?"

He nods. "Damn news moves too slow here." He sits beside us and I watch as he switches through his apps.

Chrissy is staring at us. She's calmed down now that we're out in the sun and the adrenaline's crashed. She nods at Charlie. "You go to my school, don't you?"

"Uh-huh," he mumbles without looking up from his phone.

Seems he's turned off all of his empathy again now that she's safe.

"And you were Sheri's boyfriend, right?"

The question is in the past tense, but I let it go.

"Yes."

She takes a sip of the iced tea. "Are you two some kind of undercover cops?"

I can't help but laugh. I shake my head.

"Then how'd you find me?"

Charlie looks up and his smile changes his face. "Cuz that's our job." He goes back to his phone.

Until he said it out loud, I never thought of it like that, but now I understand his vigilance.

A police car and the paramedics arrive shortly afterward. We stick around to give our statements, but I can tell Charlie is annoyed. Just one more report to add to Gekas's growing file. By the time we're free to go, Charlie rushes me to the car.

"What's up?"

"I found Gekas. I think the cops are raiding Brent Chan's."

"The dealer?" I ask, clipping my seatbelt.

Charlie nods. "Somehow Gekas is onto Robbie."

"He's our only suspect."

"Yeah, but despite all this," his gesture encompasses the cops, the ambulance and Chrissy, "he's not the right one. He's too dumb, too weak, too disorganized. It doesn't make sense."

I tend to agree, but we have no other leads. I pull onto the street, trying not to peel out too quickly in front of the cops.

"How did Gekas get to him?" Charlie pulls a doughnut out of the bag and bites into it. He runs the scenario in his head first, then out loud to me. "She has the photo you sent and sees the car. But there's no licence plate visible, so there's not a lot to go on. Unless the car got picked up after he lost it and it went in the system? But still, that's slim. So they run the description and get a few hits—one of them Robbie." He looks over at me. "When you gave her the address, you're certain she was dealing with something big?"

"She didn't say it, but I assumed."

He glares at me. "For Robbie's sake, I hope you're wrong."

chapter 101

By the time I get close to Guthrie High School, the police have the streets blocked off. We find a place to park and get out.

A bunch of students stand by two cop cars angle-parked on the street. When we push to the front, an officer says, "Stay behind the line for your safety, please."

I can see Gekas farther down the street, talking to another officer, looking at a map spread out on the hood of the car beside them. None of the police have their guns drawn, so despite whatever's going on, the tension isn't too high yet.

I look to Charlie to ask his opinion and realize he's disappeared. Again.

I push through all the milling students and catch sight of him moving toward a side street. I run to catch up.

"Where are you going?"

"I've spent time at Chan's."

"Is he dangerous?"

"Only in his own mind. But if Gekas tries to negotiate with him, she'll just make it worse."

"So, what do we do?"

Charlie stops and looks at me. "You don't need to do this, Shepherd."

I shrug. "No? But then who will?"

He smiles. "You're all right, you know, when you're not being such a whiny baby."

I decide to take this as a compliment and follow him.

We move along the street until we're close to Chan's. There's a police car out front and another cruiser down the block. There's also an ambulance on standby. Charlie moves stealthily alongside the house to the backyard gate, but I hesitate.

The officer steps out of his car. "Excuse me? Where do you two think you're going?"

Charlie turns, acting innocent. "Oh, sorry, officer. I was just heading home."

The officer glares at him. "You have any ID on you?"

Charlie shakes his head. "I don't like to take my wallet to school—I lost it once."

The officer looks at me. "What about you?"

"Sorry, no."

He studies us. "Well, we have a situation and I can't let you go back there. You'll just have to wait down at the end of the block."

I expect Charlie to argue, but he surprises me. "Sure thing, officer."

He closes the gate and the two of us stroll back to the street. As we walk away, Charlie pulls out his phone and flips through his contacts.

"The backyard is covered," he says, "and although we're not gonna get past all the cops, maybe we can diffuse things and bring everyone out to us." He takes a photo of the patrol officer and sends it.

He and I walk back to the intersection.

"Who'd you send that to?"

"Chan's supplier."

"Should I even ask how you have his number?"

"I've been doing some work for him on the side. He figured Chan's been charging more than he's been saying and then smoking the overages."

"Was he?"

Charlie nods. "Remember the second day you came, Robbie was bringing me some proof."

"The pipe?"

"What? No, dude, that was a test tube full of product Chan was selling." He looks at me. "Man, you should seriously get your eyes checked."

I don't believe him and I guess it shows.

"I needed Robbie's help to get me proof that Chan was cutting his supplier's stuff down to a lower grade."

Bzzz—he looks down at his phone. "Yup, it's amazing what you can do with a phone these days."

The doors to Chan's house bust open and stoner kids pour out, scattering everywhere. It's pandemonium and Gekas and her officers reach for their firearms but don't unholster them. The general nature of the stoners is hazy disorientation, and their legs aren't interested in keeping up with the rest of their bodies. I laugh as the police corral the herd into a tight crowd. I look over at Charlie, but he isn't laughing.

"I don't see Robbie."

I scan the group. "Neither do I. You think he went out the back?"

"He's stupid but not that stupid."

The police are moving toward the house, guns drawn now. They go through the open door, and Charlie and I walk up to the police line. No one's talking now, except for the hushed chatter of walkie-talkies as the officers proceed through Chan's house.

Then all at once the air is pierced by two gunshots. The students all duck or hit the ground and freeze. I don't move either, but then I see Charlie's face. He looks scared.

The radios sound off—"Clear." "Clear." "Clear."—then go silent.

Suddenly, a radio crackles. "We need EMTs in here, now!"

Two paramedics race across the street from the ambulance and through the front door, their kits in tow. More cops follow. Gekas comes out the front door and I've got a bad feeling. The radio chatter is all just short bursts of police code, but there's enough to know that someone's bleeding out and someone else is dead.

chapter 102

I find Gekas. She's not thrilled to see me.

"Detective, what happened?"

"This isn't the place for you."

"Is Robbie in there?"

When I see her face, I know it's bad, but she deflects. "Why are you here?"

"Robbie's not the one."

"All the evidence says he is."

It isn't until Gekas looks over my shoulder that I realize Charlie is behind me. "Is Robbie...?"

"It's not good, Charles."

Charlie gets in her face. "But he's too stupid to have done any of those things."

Gekas pauses. "I know, but everything points to him."

"So you shot him?"

"No. By the time we got in there, Brent Chan had a gun on him."

"But you weren't *there* for Chan."

"No, but he was going on about Robbie being a rat, saying it was his fault we were there. Before we could do anything, Chan shot him, then turned the gun on himself."

Charlie stares in disbelief. Gekas reaches for his shoulder before pausing and pulling back. She sighs, shaking her head as she walks back to the house

I stand beside Charlie, unsure what to do. In the few weeks I've known him, it seems like nothing fazes him, and now this guy he barely calls a friend has been shot and he seems rattled to the core.

"Charlie?"

He looks at me, at the house, and back at me before walking off into the enveloping crowd.

chapter 103

I find Charlie a while later, sitting on the curb by the school, his hands propped on his knees, his phone hanging down. I hand over his coffee and the bag of doughnuts I grabbed from the car on the way over. He sets them between his feet.

"You okay?" I ask, knowing it's is the stupidest thing I could ask. I, of all people, should understand how annoying that question is.

"Getting Robbie shot was not my intention."

"Gekas says that—"

"I know what Gekas says. But I sure as hell didn't plan any of this."

I nod. There's not much else I can do.

Charlie grabs the bag of doughnuts, rummaging through them until he pulls out a maple dip. "It just doesn't make sense," he repeats.

I can't imagine how Charlie must feel. It must suck feeling responsible for someone else's near death.

"You couldn't know how Chan was going to react—"

"No, not that. That Robbie is some serial killer."

So much for Charlie's empathy—I never can keep up with him. But I have to agree: Robbie's an unlikely candidate for murderer. If nothing else, stoners just aren't that motivated.

Charlie stares at the asphalt. "What are we missing?"

The siren of the ambulance interrupts our train of thought as it disperses the crowd, zooming down the street toward us. It hits the main thoroughfare, cutting through the red light and speeds off.

"The fact they've got the siren on is a good sign," I offer. "Means there's something to fight for."

Charlie stares down the street for a long time before picking up his coffee and looking at me. "You know, Robbie moved here recently. I wonder why."

Charlie's on his phone.

"He came from some city out west. I've searched his name but nothing comes up." He takes a sip of his coffee, thinking it over.

"Wait a sec." He taps something into the search bar and waits for the page to download. He taps again. "Kingstown! That's where he's from." He scrolls some more. "Oh, look at this."

chapter 104

He hands me the phone. It's a news article, dated a year ago, about a Kingstown senior, unnamed of course, who was attacked in the school bathroom. No one was caught.

"Same mo."

"Yes, but because us teenagers never know when to keep our traps shut..." He works away at his phone.

I can't help but be impressed watching him harness the power of the web.

"A lot of social networks have semantic search engines that query all their big data," he tells me.

Uh... "What are you talking about?"

"I can search age, location, likes, dislikes, relationships—anything."

"So?"

"Soooo, by searching what the teens of Kingstown talked about a year ago, I'm ninety per cent certain that our senior is Jayce Morgan."

"Who?"

He shows me his phone and I look. There's a stock photo from graduation of Jayce—a pretty girl with long dark hair.

He takes it back and searches some more. "And that's likely her phone number."

I see his look and realize what he's asking.

"No."

"Come on. She's our only lead right now."

"It doesn't matter. I can't call a girl out of the blue that I've never met and ask her about an attack in a bathroom from a year ago."

"Well, I sure as hell can't, but you? You're a smooth-talking criminal."

I shake my head at his weak attempt to cajole me.

"Seriously, we need this. *I* need this. To make it right."

"For who?"

He doesn't answer, just waves his phone in my face.

I weigh it out. If Robbie isn't the killer, we must be getting close to figuring out who took Sheri.

"Okay, what's the number?"

chapter 105

I dial Jayce Morgan, shaking my head the whole time. In the last few weeks, I've felt exhilarating rushes and real fear for the first time in my life. I've felt my heart pound and my palms sweat, and I've told uncomfortable, awkward lies that have twisted my stomach into knots. But this moment isn't one of them. Now I might finally close in on the answer I'm seeking.

Ring ring.

Charlie takes a bite out of his doughnut and follows it with a slug of coffee. Everything that's happened today seems to have taken a toll on him and he looks like an old man sitting there on the curb.

Ring ring.

My nerves tighten.

Ring ring.

The phone picks up and a teen girl answers, "Heya—"

"Hi, is this Jayce—?"

"—my phone is way over there and I can't get it, so don't be lame. Leave a message or send a text. Later." *Beep.*

I hang up.

"What the hell, Shepherd?" Charlie spits out the words as quickly as he swallows the rest of the doughnut.

I'm annoyed at him for being on my case, and I'm annoyed at myself for hanging up.

"I got her voicemail," I answer curtly.

"And, what? You couldn't say something?"

"Like what?"

"You don't have to hang up like some... like some freshman trying to get a date with the senior cheerleader."

Charlie has this magical way of disconnecting and pushing buttons to provoke me and I can never tell if he's actually mad.

"What am I supposed to say? Hey, Jayce, it's Tony Shepherd. You've never met me, but I was wondering how you feel about strangulation and bathrooms!"

Charlie gets that 'what the hell?' look on his face. "Geez, Shepherd. Gear down, man."

I glare at him but he breaks into a big grin and I reluctantly smile too.

"Take a minute or two... or ten. She'll pick up eventually."

We walk to the car and get inside. I try a second time. It goes straight to voicemail. Charlie scrolls through his phone, learning what was happening in Jayce's world a year ago.

I try once more, ready to give up, knowing I'm on the verge of acting like the psycho we're hunting.

"Hello?"

It's her. My heart leaps.

"Hello?"

I cough and splutter out, "Hi. Is this Jayce?"

"Yes. Who's this?"

"My name's Tony," I gather in a breath. "I was just wondering if you could help me out?"

"Who?"

"Tony Shepherd."

"Sorry, do I know you?"

"No, but—"

"Do you work for the newspaper?"

"No."

"Are you a cop? How do you know me?"

"I'm not from—"

"How did you get my number?"

"I'm from—"

"I don't know you. Goodbye."

Click.

"Shit."

Charlie looks at me. "That went well."

I hit redial.

Charlie raises an eyebrow. "What are you doing?"

"Calling back."

He may know how to do a B&E, he may know what gadgets he needs to spy on someone, but I know how to talk to people. This is what I do.

Ring ring.

"Look, psycho, I told you not to call me! I'm going to trace your number and the cops will be on your doorstep!"

"I'll give you my phone number *and* my address," I say quickly, before she can hang up. "Heck, I'll give you the

name of a nice detective who'd be happy to help you out...
Jayce, please—I promise, just give me a minute and when
the minute's up, if you don't want to listen anymore, you can
ignore me and turn off your phone. Just one minute. Deal?"

Silence.

"Please? Almost everyone's got at least a minute to spare."

It seems like the longest pause in the world.

"Okay. Go."

"I know something happened to you about a year ago—"

"Stop. We're done—"

"No, no, no. You promised me one minute."

I hear her exhale, but she doesn't end the call.

"I'm calling because the same thing is happening here and
I think they're connected." I hold on a moment, waiting for
what I say to sink in, but not giving her too long. "I want to
stop what's going on, but I don't have enough information
and I need your help. What happened to you was scary—is
scary—and you didn't deserve it either, but I don't think anyone else should go through what you did. I just need a little
more information. Can you help? "

I hear nothing and hope she's still there.

"What do you need to know?"

I breathe again and Charlie gives me the thumbs up.

"Thank you."

"Whatever. Just because I'm giving you more than a minute
doesn't mean I won't hang up."

"Fair enough." I pause, wondering how I'm going to proceed. I decide to jump right in.

"Last year you were attacked?"

"Yes."

"In the bathroom?"

"Yes."

"Did you see who it was?"

"No. Well, not completely. I saw parts of him."

"Him? So, there are things you *did* notice?"

"Why can't you get a copy of the police report and leave me alone?"

"Because you can tell me things the police may not have asked."

"You're really not a cop?"

"No." I'm not sure why she keeps asking this.

After a long pause, she asks, "Then what are you doing this for?"

I take a deep breath. "My girlfriend went missing a few weeks ago. The cops have tried everything but it all comes up a dead-end and I'm trying to find out where she is and what happened to her. I love her and I miss her, and to be honest, I think you may be the only one who can help."

She breathes out. "Okay, Tony. Keep asking."

Charlie leans in and listens.

chapter 106

"Do you know Robbie—?" I realize I don't know his last name. I look over at Charlie and he looks back at me, clueless. I muffle the phone. "What's his last name?

Charlie shrugs.

"What do you mean, you don't know?"

"Why would I?"

"A few seconds ago you were upset that he got shot."

"So? Doesn't mean I know all his personal details."

"You know *my* last name!"

"Yeah, but why do you think I only called you Shepherd?"

"You can't remember my first name?"

"Sometimes I can... on and off. Look, it's not my style."

"It's his *name.*"

"Yeah, if I needed to know, I'd just steal his wallet and look."

I'm dumbfounded. In the background Jayce is wondering what's going on, "Hello?"

I go back to the phone call. "Hi."

"Who are you talking to?"

"Um, my… uh… colleague." The lameness of my answer frustrates me.

"Is he listening in? You didn't tell me—"

I'm going to lose all my hard work if I'm not careful. "I'm sorry, Jayce, I really am. My name is Tony Shepherd and the other guy is Charlie Wolfe." I exaggerate my first name and give Charlie a look. He rolls his eyes.

"We just want to catch the guy we think did this to you."

"And your girlfriend?"

"Yes, and my girlfriend."

Silence.

"What's her name?

"Sheri." Saying it does something to my insides.

Another long pause, but I can't keep waiting.

"There's a boy, Robbie, in Grade…" I look at Charlie and he shrugs again. We have to pursue this, no matter where it leads. "…I'm not sure, maybe Grade 10 or 11. He went to your school."

"I was a senior last year, so I probably didn't know him."

"He's kind of a screw-up. Hanging out with druggies…" I run through what I know and it's really not a lot. I grasp at straws. "He's short—"

Charlie grabs the phone out of my hand. "Hi Jayce, Charlie here. I don't know Robbie's last name but he got shot a half hour ago and he's having a really bad day, so I can't ask him his last name. What I *can* tell you is that he likes Skrillex, Henry Rollins, Howard Stern, the Grateful Dead, Pink Floyd, and Deep Purple. He's also probably and almost certainly got kicked out of school more than once. He was also the kid in bio or chem class that asked about hydroponics a lot, which got him sent to the office a lot because he's a druggie, right? But he actually liked growing strawberries and basil and mint and—"

"Oh my God, are you talking about Catnip?"

We look at each other, confused.

"Who's Catnip?" Charlie asks.

"He was this kid who went to our school last year. Stoned all the time but turns out the old ladies loved him because he'd get all their gardens going great at the start of spring because he'd sell them the best plants. I guess he had a real green thumb," she says.

"Anyway," she goes on, "the rumour was that he was growing small quantities of marijuana in his patch and selling it to other students. Teachers hear about this, they plan to come down hard on him—"

Charlie interrupts, "And they bust him and find out that it's catnip?"

"Better. He found out beforehand and swapped it out. Still got expelled, though, because administration thought he scammed a bunch of students."

"I don't think Robbie is that smart—"

"Nah, they said he had help."

"Who?"

"His brother, I think."

I look at Charlie, who shakes his head. He doesn't know the brother.

He's on it, though. "The brother, he went to your school too?"

"No, he went to some private school that's a feeder program to some of the bigger universities."

"I don't get it."

"You, know—places where Mommy and Daddy pay big bucks to give you a high-end education and you live in dorms and it's all fancy pants." Her cynicism is strong.

"Any idea why he'd help Robbie if he had all that going for him?"

There's a pause while she thinks. "I guess he was in some big play and he was worried Robbie was going to mess it up for him."

This piques Charlie's interest. "He was in drama?"

"Yeah. They'd always force us to see the plays each year."

Apparently Jayce is not a lover of the arts.

"And what grade was he in?"

"Don't know. They didn't really use grades at his school. More about who you were than your grade."

"But if you had to guess his age?"

"Maybe my age, maybe a bit older."

Is this our guy?

Charlie leans into the phone. "So whatever happened to him? Robbie's brother? Did he get to do his play?"

"I'm—I don't know."

There's hesitation in her voice and before I can stop Charlie, he charges on like a bull. "Why not?'

"Because just after that, I got attacked."

I punch Charlie in the arm for being stupid. He seems not to realize how insensitive he's being.

I take the phone away from him.

"Thank you, Jayce. I think you've helped us."

She's quiet again. "You don't think—?"

"I'm not sure. But we're going to find out."

"Okay," she says.

I can hear the worry in her voice, like it's happening all over again.

"Jayce?" I try for one last answer.

"Yes?"

"Do you know the brother's name?"

"Yeah. Connor."

chapter 107

I hang up and look over at Charlie. "So, what do you think?"

"I think we should go grab a sandwich."

"Really? You just finished a bag of doughnuts."

"No, I still have one left."

"You're not going to eat it?"

"Nope. It's special." He gets off the curb and starts walking to my car. When he realizes I'm not behind him, he turns. "You coming?"

"What about Jayce? What about everything she said?"

"Come on, let's go. I'm hungry."

We're so close now, and he wants to eat?

"Why don't you weigh 400 pounds?"

"Cuz." He grins and jogs to the car, as eager as Ollie when he knows a squirrel is in the backyard.

"Can I drive?"

I laugh, imagining what he might do to Dad's car.

"Don't you trust me?"

"Do you even have a licence?"

"Do you think it would matter?"

I pop open the lock with the remote and point to the passenger side. He obliges and takes his usual seat. I climb in and he's got the window down and is already going through Dad's CDs, looking for music. He chooses Bones by Bodhi Jones. He listens to it for a few seconds and slowly grows into the mood, tapping his hand against the roof of the car.

"Where to?"

"South."

There's lots of traffic and the drive is slow, but it doesn't seem to faze Charlie. He's on his phone, but I can't see what he's scrolling through.

"I think he's our guy," Charlie announces.

"How can you be sure?" I don't want to be biased by hope.

"First, the car. When Robbie said he lost it, he called it the car his parents let him and his brother drive. As you pointed out, it's a piece of shit, not a family car—especially not for that family. Maybe it's the second vehicle for the kids. It also explains the difference between the killer's first attacks and the next few. The first were on the outskirts of the city. After Robbie lost the car, the bodies were dumped near the places where the girls were attacked. Then, when he got the car back, he was clearly going to start moving them again."

I pull up to a light, thinking about finding Chrissy in the trunk of that car. I look over at Charlie, watching him work through the puzzle.

"Second, the mirrors and the camera. We thought he was performing, first for us, then for himself. This Connor is a theatre student, and from what Jayce said, a serious one at that." He hands me his phone. "Look at the guy left of centre."

Charlie's brought up a photo from the university newspaper of a recent production by the Theatre Department. Three rows of cast and crew stand on the stage. They're smiling, goofy, having fun—except for one guy.

Charlie flips to the next tab and shows me another image. Production promo photos. Same guy in two photos. Again, the people around him are engaged and laughing. He is stoic and separate.

I look closely—there's a slight resemblance to Robbie, more of a distant cousin than a close sibling.

He's tall with dark hair. He looks utterly boring. Over these past few weeks, I've imagined the person who attacked Sheri, who's been killing all these girls. I imagined the devil, a monster, a sex freak, some hillbilly with a chainsaw full of perversion and bloodlust. I want to hate him, to be scared of him, but I don't know if I can. He's nothing like what I thought he'd be—he's a screwed-up teen, floating along just like everyone else.

Well, maybe not *just* like everyone else, the bastard.

A horn honks behind me and I realize the light is green. I hand Charlie the phone and quickly make the turn. I drive down the block and make my decision.

"We're not calling Gekas on this," I say, confident.

"We're not?" He looks at me, a little speechless.

"No, we're not. Not until we're certain. Not until we are without a shadow of a doubt."

"Well, all right then."

There is no argument from Charlie.

chapter 108

We sit by the window at the sub place. I finish off some potato chips and Charlie chows down on a twelve-inch meatball sandwich. He eats it slowly and with what appears to be wicked pleasure. It's sloppy, but he's careful and tidy—much tidier than when he eats doughnuts.

I think about the comment he made about how the contents of a fridge reflects the household. Ours is stocked with fruits and veggies and carefully labelled leftovers. I wonder what his must be like. Is it empty or filled with food he hates and that's why he seems to eat out so much?

"Good sandwich?"

"Yeah. Thanks."

He's enjoying it and I let him eat in peace. He puts the last bite in his mouth and leans back in his chair.

"We should go to the university." He wipes each finger one at a time with a napkin.

"That's what I was thinking."

We're on the same page. Perfect.

Charlie picks up his fountain drink and slurps the last of it. He takes everything off the table and tosses it into the trash bin. I walk with him.

"Any idea where we're going when we get there?"

"Nope. I don't," he says with his usual certainty.

That's good enough for me.

We agree en route that we should just go directly to the Theatre Department. Asking the Registrar's Office if they have a student named Connor in all the thousands of students would be an exercise in futility, even if they were willing to troll through their files. Going to the Theatre Department where the faculty is small is a much better strategy.

As I drive onto the campus, I realize I have no clue where I'm going. "Been here before?" I ask casually.

"No, you?

"I played a couple of basketball games here, so I know where the courts are."

"But the Fine Arts Department?"

"Nope."

"Nice." Charlie smiles as he says it.

"Really?" I don't know how two clueless teenagers can navigate this scenario one bit.

"Yeah. It'll be an adventure."

Charlie's still grinning and I shake my head, equal parts amused and worried, but I'm game. Besides, nothing in this place can beat what happened in that basement.

I find a parking meter near the Kinesiology Building and park the car. I dig into my pockets for change while Charlie stands there. I don't expect him to contribute—I have a feeling there's no use, whether he can afford it or not.

We walk through the main doors with no idea how far we are from the Theatre Department. I recognize the area, having come for tournaments and summer basketball camps, but I've not strayed far from this one building. While I'm confident outdoors, my sense of direction inside buildings could use some work. I pause, trying to get my bearings.

Charlie pushes past me. "Keep walking," he says quietly.

I speed up to catch him. "But where are we going?"

"If you stop right in the doorway, you look like a deer in the headlights and everyone notices the lost guy. Look around while you walk, and we'll figure it out as we go."

I wonder if this is the mantra that Charlie lives by. It makes sense, like a play on the court. I don't know what's coming, but I can't just stand there like an idiot trying to figure it out.

We get to the end of a hallway and I finally know where I'm going. The pools are to the right and to the left is a long corridor.

We go down it.

Students and adults move past me. I always assumed they'd be self-assured, that I'd look like a kid to them, but most of them seem as confused or stressed or bored with life as I sometimes do. I think about saying this to Charlie, but university might not be his thing—he might not have the money to get in, or, smart as he is, even the grades to get in. I hold my tongue, feeling another difference between us that I'd never considered.

There's a map on the wall that we casually walk over to, but it only tells us where to find things in the building we're in. I'm thinking we should stop and ask for directions, but I know Charlie will ignore the suggestion.

We get to the end of the long hall and it breaks in a T. On the right, the hallway curves up to a set of double doors with another set of doors behind that. A sign above guides us to student residences and the library. Charlie goes left and I follow. It's another long corridor. We turn at a sign that directs us toward the Film Department and walk down a narrow hallway full of closed doors and come out the other side, feeling more lost than we did before.

"Well, that was a bust," Charlie says.

He turns back down the hallway we've just come out of, and we make our way back to the T intersection. This time we turn right and go through the doors.

We're in a bright corridor with floor-to-ceiling windows on the left that takes us between the buildings. It leads to an older section of the campus, with dark brick and tile and another T intersection. I watch the flow of students and teachers moving around me and can't figure out how they know where they're going.

"This place is a maze."

"Haven't you ever played a video game? When you're in a cave or dark tunnels, you always turn left—that way you'll eventually end up where you started."

"What if the Theatre Department is on a right?"

He doesn't want to even acknowledge the question and turns left again.

We walk past the library and zigzag through the hallways.

We get to another T and Charlie asks, "Do you have two dollars?"

"Sure." I hand him some coins and he makes for a vending machine.

"You need a drink?" I ask, incredulous.

As he waits for his bottle to drop down, I realize he's taking stock of our surroundings. He sees me watching him.

"You're sneaky."

He smiles at me. "Like a fox."

A guy not much older than me walks over to us. He's got an accent that I can't quite place. He struggles to ask, "Do you know—how I get upstairs?"

Charlie smiles at him. He points down the hallway where we came from. "Go halfway down, turn left. Go halfway down that hall, and there are a set of stairs that should get you up there."

The student smiles and nods and walks off.

I stare at Charlie.

"What? I pay attention."

Turning left, we walk past a cafeteria packed with students.

"I suppose you'll be here in a couple of years?" he asks.

I'm surprised he brought it up but try to downplay it. "Maybe."

"Oh, whatever. You'll be nerding out with the rest of these geeks."

"What about you?" I ask, hoping to sound sincere.

"I don't think this place could handle this." He gestures to himself like a game show assistant. It seems like a deflection but he says it with such confidence I wonder if part of him believes it.

He veers right and stops beside another map.

"I thought you didn't believe in asking for directions?"

"That's before I realized how disorganized it was here."

We look down the legend on the side and find the Theatre Department. It's somewhere on the bottom left, on the second floor.

Based on where it is and where we are on the map, I can't contain my irritation. "We've almost gone around the entire campus!"

"The whole place is one big square loop, to herd the sheep in circles and keep us from realizing we're being indoctrinated into their system," Charlie states.

He's maybe got a point.

We move across a bright building made of concrete before slipping back to the brown tile and brick. Now that we have a direction, we move with the flow, like we really do belong. We come around a corner and a set of metal stairs rises in front of us.

We take the stairs and are immediately lost again.

"What's *with* these people? Maybe when you sign up, they implant a chip in your skull to guide you around this zoo."

I catch sight of a sign that reads THEATRE DEPARTMENT down the far side of the hallway.

Charlie nods. "Good eyes."

I take the compliment. Although Dad has glasses, I seem to have Mom's genes for good eyesight.

"We need to figure out Connor's last name or at least where he might be, his courses, anything," I say out loud. While Charlie does most of his thinking in silence, it seems to work better if I narrate my thoughts.

"Yes," Charlie agrees. "Follow me."

Isn't that what I always do?

chapter 109

Instead of going into the Theatre Department, Charlie doubles back down the stairs to an open food court packed with people.

"But you just ate, man."

"I know," Charlie smirks.

"You're not eating again, are you?"

He considers it, then answers, "No. Not right now."

He grabs us an empty table in the centre of the crowd. He hands me the student newspaper and I know the drill. I open it and try to look inconspicuous while he pulls out his phone and flips through it.

I look over at him. "What are we doing?"

"Relax. You want to find him, right?"

"Definitely."

"Then we need an access point to figure out more about him and who he is. Look to your three o'clock."

I turn slowly. Sitting a few tables over is a man in his late thirties or early forties, multitasking between his laptop and phone. He nurses a coffee in a travel mug.

"What do you see?"

"A professor?"

"And?"

The professor's eyes are darting around the food court; he's barely looking at his computer.

"He's waiting for someone?"

"Uh-huh. And I'm guessing not for long."

We scan the area, trying to figure out who he's looking for.

Then I see her—a gorgeous, leggy redhead walking down the stairs. I look over at the professor and, yup, she's got his attention.

She strolls along the walkway to an empty bench lining the wall, and although she's trying hard to look older, she's definitely a student.

I point her out to Charlie. "I'm pretty sure *she's* not a colleague."

"Nice work, Shepherd. Just like that ancient Police song, huh?"

I don't get the reference, but he doesn't care. He stands up. "Two cream, two sugar?"

"Um, sure?"

"You stay here and keep watch."

I say, "Okay," but Charlie doesn't hear me and takes off. He walks over to the coffee shop and stands in line, looking around, waiting.

The professor takes one last, lingering look at the redhead before leaning over to a couple of guys sitting at the table next to him. He gestures to his computer and they nod back. This dude can't be that stupid. I'm dumbfounded when he rises and makes a beeline for the stairs, leaving his computer behind.

I watch the silent movie of Charlie shooting out of line. He goes straight over to the computer and takes a seat. The guys beside him glance over and he somehow convinces them that everything he's up to is legit.

I turn to watch the professor and the redhead. His hands are in his pockets, acting cool, and she has a pretty smile but an exaggerated laugh. She touches his arm.

Charlie's now hacking away at the computer, but stops for a moment to take a sip of the professor's coffee. He cringes at the taste and goes back to work.

Meanwhile, the redhead's got her phone out and the professor points at something on it. I look at Charlie and signal that he needs to hurry up. He nods and holds up a finger. He still needs a minute but I'm not sure he's got one.

The professor is done flirting with the redhead and she puts her phone away—I'm guessing his cell is the newest number in her contacts. He's on his way back and I get up to intercept him, but it's too late. He sees Charlie and yells but everyone in the cafeteria turns and looks at him—no one is looking at the kid on his computer. The professor rushes past me, pushing through a bottleneck of hopeful scholars, but Charlie is already out of his chair and on the move.

I can't help but linger.

The professor gets to his computer, asking the students who were supposed to watch out for him who Charlie was and why they let him use it. They all shrug, indifferent to their temporary responsibility for the laptop while the professor was working it with the redhead. I'm sure they heard a convincing enough story from Charlie to not give a crap, either.

My phone buzzes.

Upstairs.

I take the stairs two at a time. Charlie's down at the end of the hall and I catch up to him. We hurry down a corridor, far away from the professor and the lunch crowd, and the noise fades away into the quiet hum of the building and the *tap tap tap* of our running shoes echoing off the bare walls. We're past the Music Department now.

"I got it!" Charlie is exultant. "All his details. Class schedule, marks, how much he paid for his books. By the way, I'm definitely not going to university."

"You're crazy."

"Maybe, but aren't we all."

"Does he have class right now?"

"Nope."

I'm disappointed, maybe we're out of runway on this crazy trip, but something's up because Charlie's got that shit-eating grin again.

"What?"

"He's not around because he's practising for this."

I look over to where Charlie's pointing and see a poster for the Theatre Department's production of *As You Like It* starring, you guessed it, our very own in-house serial killer.

chapter 110

A back stairwell leads us out to the middle of the Theatre Department. Props and sets line the hallways and music resounds from a room to our left. Around the corner, we come to a lounge where students sprawl out in bunches, working on homework or playing on their phones.

I pull Charlie back around the corner before we're noticed. "We barely know what he looks like."

"So? We know enough."

"Yeah, but he knows *us* better. Remember that he spent Saturday afternoon beating the crap out of us?" I don't usually have the pleasure of making Charlie pause, but I did this time.

"Fair enough. What's your plan?"

I don't know if I have a plan. He's never deferred to me and I'm a little surprised. "Well, he's been so busy watching us and setting up his little performances that I think it's our turn to watch him."

"Nice."

I take the corner again, keeping an eye open for anyone who might look like Connor. No sign of him. I do take note of a girl, looking like something between a hipster and a punk, lying on a couch reading a graphic novel, listening to tunes. University doesn't seem that hard.

I tap her on the shoulder, hoping I don't startle her.

She slowly slides off her headphones and looks at me, annoyed.

"Where are the rehearsals for *As You Like It* being held?"

"We're way past rehearsals, dude."

"What do you mean?"

She looks at us a bit more carefully. "Are you even *in* the Theatre Department?"

Charlie takes over. "Are you?"

She glares at him. "Hey—!"

"Hey, yourself." He nods at her book. "Superheroes? Seriously? Why not try something a little bit above your reading level?"

I interject before someone starts swinging. "Can you just tell me where they're practising?"

She sighs and with the most dramatically laborious of efforts, raises her arm and points. "Down the hall, but be quiet. There's a matinee on." She pulls the book in front of her face again, blocking us from sight.

Around the corner is another staircase. We descend a flight to find a locked door. We move back up to another level. And another locked door.

Charlie shakes his head. "What is *with* this place? I'd hate to be stuck here in a fire."

We hear a door shut below. A young guy with spotlights in each hand runs up the stairs. "Hey, can you grab the door for me."

"It's locked."

He looks at us like we're idiots. "No, the one on the next floor."

"Uh, sure?" We race all the way to the top of the stairs and open the door for him to find ourselves on a walkway, high above the stage.

"Thanks."

If he'd paid any attention, he'd notice Charlie and I have wandered in behind him. But he's got a job to do and doesn't even acknowledge our existence.

Down below, the auditorium seats are packed with high school students, quiet but bored in the sparsely lit theatre. I'm sure some are watching the stage, but from what I can tell, I'm positive many are asleep. A beautiful set—a forest with sculpted trees—rises up to the arched proscenium, leaves and branches crisscrossing between them. Two men stand below, speaking to each other, and I'm not sure, but I think the one guy wants to lay down and die.

I look at the guy we followed up here. "How do we get down there?" I point to the seats below.

The guy looks at me. "Don't you work here? Shit, you shouldn't be up here."

Charlie steps in. "Relax. We just got turned around on the stairs."

The lighting guy ushers us out the way we came. "Out the door, down the stairs, through the hallway, cut across to the right and try the door."

Charlie just can't let it be and nods and smiles. "Oh. So, easy, then?"

The guy gives us a look as I push Charlie out the door.

"Can't just keep quiet sometimes, can you?"

He looks at me confused. "What?"

We follow the instructions but, of course, the door is locked. We move farther down and finally find one that's open.

We go in.

We come out on a second floor balcony. Light from the bright staircase outside floods in and I rush past Charlie to get the door closed before we attract attention. It takes a minute for my eyes to adjust in the dark. It's quiet up here and we wander down to the first row and pull down the seats.

The actor on stage says:

How now, monsieur. What a life is this,
That your poor friends must woo your company?
What, you look merrily!

The actor he's speaking to walks out on stage and stands under a spotlight. I stare, blood pulsing loudly in my head. Is that him? All I have to go on is a couple of small, blurry photos, and from up here, it could be anyone. But there's something about him that feels off, over-rehearsed, like he's planned every move, every word, to the point that his very presence is stiff, almost empty.

Connor, or at least, the guy I think is him, speaks:

A fool, a fool! I met a fool in the forest,
A motley fool. A miserable world!
As I do live by food, I met a fool…

I stare at him, trying to imagine him behind the mask, killing Bonnie or Maggie. Or Sheri. It's all a blur of white noise and my head pounds with confusion. This is not the monster I imagined, the ugly evil that disemboweled dogs and murdered women. If this is him, he's a dumb kid, clueless to reality. He's not much different from his brother Robbie, except that his way of dealing with being trapped in a suburban hell with helicopter parents and the pressure to be perfect wasn't to numb himself, but rather to experience the world by destroying it.

O worthy fool! One that hath been a courtier,
And says, if ladies be but young and fair,
They have the gift to know it: and in his brain,
Which is as dry as the remainder biscuit
After a voyage, he hath strange places cramm'd
With observation, the which he vents
In mangled forms. O that I were a fool!
I am ambitious for a motley coat.

Charlie watches intently, his back flagpole straight. I'm not sure I've seen him so hyper-focused before.

It is my only suit:
Provided that you weed your better judgments
Of all opinion that grows rank in them
That I am wise. I must have liberty
Withal, as large a charter as the wind,
To blow on whom I please; for so fools have—

I can't help but think he speaks as himself and not as Jaques.

"What do you think?" I ask Charlie.

He nods. "It's him."

chapter 112

He walks off the stage, pleased with his performance of the last scene, but he's frustrated, because the fool playing Orlando has choked on his lines again. He's not jealous that Orlando has more lines—everyone knows that Jacques is the better role—but every other actor's mistakes trickle down to the delivery of his own.

He doesn't go too far; there's only a brief scene and a half before he needs to return to the stage. He sits in a chair at the back where he can look out and see the audience. He likes the one-way mirror the theatre offers: while on stage, he can be seen but can't see the people watching him, and when he is backstage, he can peer out at them without them knowing.

He tries to focus on the present moment, remaining in this world, in this character, but he struggles, his mind shifting to the girl in the trunk. He's kept her at home, safe from detection, alive—for now. He hasn't quite decided what to do with her.

He took her on Sunday, at a matinee. After the excitement of the past few days, the movie had been boring—a stupid show about a guy fighting his drug addiction—and he left to wander.

A doorway at the end of a hall had led to some stairs and he followed them up to the projector room. The space was long and wide with ten machines spooling film onto big platters. It was dark and noisy, and although he saw someone sitting at a desk hand-cranking a reel of film, they neither heard him nor looked up. Another set of stairs took him down to a staff room somewhere deep in the belly of the movie theatre. A young woman who seemed his type walked by and he felt compelled to follow her. Opportunity only knocks once—and he had fallen into the habit of carrying his supplies with him in his new messenger bag. He'd had to buy another after abandoning his old one in the basement of that house.

He slipped his mask on.

He found her in the bathroom and by now it was nearly routine. In fact, it had become too straightforward, and as he rushed her, he felt an immediate emptiness; the fight was more irksome than elation. Still, he must finish what he'd started—he couldn't, after all, simply bow out and apologize for the mistake. Maybe there was something he could do to heighten the intensity again. As they said, the show must go on.

So he'd punched her in the temple, hoping it would knock her out, and was grateful when she went limp beneath him. His bag held a roll of duct tape and he wrapped her arms and feet and taped over her mouth. After checking the hallway, he'd carried her out of the nearest exit and set her behind a dumpster. He'd walked casually around the building to retrieve his car. He'd finally gotten it back from impound where it had been towed after that stupid dopehead had—

Thinking about it was a waste of energy.

He brought the vehicle to the rear of the building, backing up so the open trunk would shield his actions from any possible witnesses. He moved quickly, tossing her inside, uncertain whether he was seen.

The physical exertion of moving the still-breathing figure, and the possibility of being caught, fired his nerve endings. A new challenge was emerging. He shut the trunk and drove back to his residence.

He no longer felt connected to the people who had raised him. At one time, they'd been Mom and Dad, and that idiot, Robbie, his brother—but ever since he had begun to focus his energy on his new work, those relationships had slipped away. He could never share with them the skills he had acquired, the audacity with which he performed, the agility he was able to display.

Besides, they likely wouldn't have cared.

They only worried about keeping Robbie on the straight and narrow, longing for the day he would correct his course and make it through school so he could get a career just like theirs. He wasn't certain when it had happened, but at some point, his parents had grown blasé about his existence, indifferent to his successes. He had proved to them his ability to achieve and they had become disinterested in his future.

In the quiet times between acts, he'd ask himself why he was following this path. He loved the rush and the challenge, but perhaps there was a deeper meaning to his deeds. Was it a cry for help or a desperate attempt to get the attention that he felt he deserved? When he gave it thought, the answer was always no. There was no corollary between his actions and his parents' approval. He no longer sought their attention—in fact, he was resistant to the ramifications that such attention might elicit.

Now he actually prefers the silence of the vacuum so that he might continue his performance, because what he seeks is perfection.

As he watches the players on the stage, marking their exits and entrances, he decides that murder is an ideal, a refinement of action and reaction. He is above them all: the other actors, the director, the audience, the crew in the wings around him. His role—the greatest role—is to be the force that ruptures the heavens, and his performance will be the shining example for all to remember.

He is perfection.

chapter 113

Connor is off the stage and I watch intently until he returns. I've never been a big fan of Shakespeare, but this wait solidifies my opinion. It isn't until Charlie taps on my arm that my attention is drawn away. Two police officers are standing in the dark shadows along the outer aisle.

"Are they here for him?" I whisper.

Charlie doesn't answer.

"Charlie...?"

"I don't know, Shepherd."

Their presence feels like confirmation that we're on the same page as the law, and that's as great a thrill as it is terrifying.

I'm on the edge of my seat, scanning the audience, wondering if there are more cops. I look for anyone out of place among the teenagers, presuming there might be others not in uniform. But except for the officers at the door, no one seems out of place. In fact, judging by their casual stance, it feels like we're the only ones holding our breath.

They make their way to an illuminated side exit and lean against the wall without urgency, but my eyes dart over to Connor as he returns to the stage. The two women who are playing Rosalind and Celia follow him. I wonder if his character, Jaques, is hitting on Rosalind. Although I know it's only a show, he's so messed up that the thought of him touching another human being, even innocently, is repulsive. It's like he's disinterested in everything, a dark shadow among the otherwise bright, funny characters, and again, I teeter in uncertainty over who I am looking at, Jaques or Connor. Is he the player or the man?

He moves across the stage, stepping into the spotlight near the front.

I have neither the scholar's melancholy, which is
emulation; nor the musician's, which is fantastical,;
nor the courtier's, which is proud; nor the
soldier's, which is ambitious; nor the lawyer's,
which is politic; nor the lady's, which is nice; nor
the lover's, which is all these—

His gaze shifts, his view moving to the police officers. He goes rigid and stops reciting.

Charlie and I sit straight up in our seats.

chapter 114

They are here.

He'd always thought that one day they would catch up to him, and all the work, all the training, all the practice would come down to this one live, unpredictable moment. He feels a steady wave of energy. He is neither nervous nor afraid. All his practice has made him perfect, as the saying goes. On this stage, here and now, he will fulfill the role he has always been born to play.

It's time.

The final performance is about to begin.

chapter 115

We watch as Rosalind and Celia look at each other, confused and concerned.

An awkward cough rises from the audience.

A voice from the wings whispers, "But it is a melancholy…"

Someone giggles.

The hushed voice repeats the line, louder this time, "But it is a melancholy of mine own…"

Raven-haired Rosalind puts her hand on Connor's back. "Jaques, is it a melancholy of your own?"

He jerks, looking at her, swallowing, then a smile, a shift in his face, a change in demeanor. Finally he speaks again.

But it is a melancholy of mine own,
compounded of many simples, extracted
from many objects…

The tension in the auditorium dissipates slightly.

...and, indeed, the sundry contemplation
of my travels; in which my often rumination
wraps me in a most humorous sadness.

Rosalind smiles. *A traveller! By my faith, you have great reason to be sad.*

She turns her back and Connor reaches into his costume. I feel what's about to happen before I witness it. Slowly, he pulls a plastic bag out of his costume, drawing it tight in his fist. He takes a step toward Rosalind.

I look down at the cops. They don't make a move.

"Stop him!" I yell.

The officers turn to look at me and the entire auditorium joins them. It's then that I realize for whatever reason they're here, it isn't to arrest Connor.

Charlie grabs me. "It's up to us, Shepherd!" and I'm shaken out of my stupor. "It's time to move. Now!"

And I'm up, racing toward the exit.

chapter 116

Charlie hits the stairs first, but I pass him on the way down. I break right as he heads for the auditorium doors.

"Get backstage. We'll cut him off!" Charlie yells as he races away.

I sprint down the hallway, balls to the wall, full throttle. Holy shit! I'm chasing after a serial killer. On purpose. I don't even have a plan. What the hell?

Whatever fear had seized me earlier today is now gone. Whatever monster mask Connor wore in my imagination has disappeared. He is flesh and bone and not much older than me. If I catch him, I can make him bleed.

I turn right, then left, and shoot past the hipster/punk girl reading her comic as someone yells at me to slow down. I zip past doors and props and rooms filled with actors dressed in costumes. I turn left again and race through a door into a blackened hallway and the dark wings at the edge of the stage. An actor in period costume glares and shushes me.

On stage, it's soundless mayhem. The actors stare, stunned. Connor's nowhere in sight. I shift, looking for Charlie or the cops, and I can't see any of them anywhere.

A guy with a headset shouts, "What the hell else am I *supposed* to do? End the show?!"

I want to feel sorry for him but I don't have time. "Where's Connor?"

"I have no idea, but when you find him, let me know because I'm pretty sure I'm going to kill him. I can't handle this crap!" He yanks the headset off, rubbing his already messy hair.

I run backstage, feeling the strategy of the court coming to me as I work to anticipate what will come next. I shoot back out into the hallway, checking every door. It's like a drill, using my legs to bolt, stop, start, and my hands to shake every handle on every door I pass. I'll have to thank Coach Davies for all the hard work he's put me through.

Someone yells, "Hey!" and I hear a crash and follow the noise around a corner. There's a pile of hats and fabrics and feathers and a poor stagehand cleaning up the mess.

I hurdle past her.

"Asshole!" she yells after me and I want to apologize but there's no time.

I return again to the large hallway behind the stage and hear the *thuck* of a stairwell door closing. I rush to it, swing it open, and hear the *ratatat* patter of footsteps rapidly descending. I look over the edge—a hand disappears from the railing.

I race after whoever it is, hoping it's Connor.

I spill out into another open hallway, but this one is deserted. I dart left, taking the corner quietly, hoping to hide my position and hear him revealing his. At the end of the corridor is a locked door with a keycode, so I turn back the way I came. There's an office to the right of the stairs, lights on behind its big window. Unless he went through another locked door and is hiding under the desk, I'm pretty sure he's not in there.

Where the hell is Charlie? I could really use his help.

Around yet another corner is a wide hallway, this one with a big, solid bay door on one side and long metal beams with hanging lights above. At the end is a doorway, and I race toward it.

Inside is a small, dark room with only a chair, a wall-length mirror, and a door that says it leads to the stage. I'm about to barge through it when Connor slams against me, sending me hurtling into the mirror, my head cracking the glass.

I collapse to the ground, my body crunching against the daggers of the broken mirror.

Connor plans to deal with me like he did before and swings a leg to kick me in the side, but I'm ready for him this time and hold my arm low to block the blow. As he connects, an intense pain shoots into my shoulder, but I know it would've been way worse if his boot had landed on my ribcage.

I grab hold of his foot as he pulls back to kick again and I yank him down, hoping to knock the brain out of his skull. Unfortunately, he twists onto his side as he topples. I have to push him down, but he shoves against me and I can't get enough leverage to get my weight on him.

He kicks again, catching me in the shin, and it's enough that he's able to get the upper hand. I make a fist and swing, connecting with his jaw. I'd barely been in a fight before I met Charlie—I was always able to talk my way out of them— and now I've been in three. I punch again, but this time *he's* ready and blocks it. He pushes his hand into my face, rubbing my cheek into the broken glass. I feel searing pain as the shards slice through my skin, and I try to push him off, but he's too heavy.

His hands slide around my throat and he squeezes hard. I try to break his grip but it's too tight. He sinks his finger into the windpipe below my Adam's apple. It burns in my throat and I'm gagging and sucking for air at the same time. I can't breathe. I grab at his face, claw at his cheeks and eyes, but he keeps himself far enough away that I can't get hold of anything.

Connor's face hovers above me, wild and bloody, the monster I always imagined him to be. My head throbs and dark spots pop in the corners of my eyes. He's playing for keeps and I'm sure as hell not getting out of this alive.

The spots become bigger, blacker, and darkness closes in.

I can no longer fight. I have no air. I know I'm dying.

But then his weight is off as his hands are ripped free of my throat, and I can breathe again even though I can barely move.

I inhale hard.

chapter 118

Charlie has come out of nowhere, slamming his body into Connor's shoulder and face. I look over and see that he's lifted Connor right off the ground with the tackle, slamming him hard against the wall. They're in a tangled sprawl, but Charlie pulls himself from the heap, pushing the unconscious Connor to the side.

I get up onto my hands and knees, still trying to breathe, comforting my throat by putting my hand on my neck.

"That's for the stairs, asshole!" he yells at the heap that is Connor.

He looks at me. I stand, sort of. Both us are doubled over and breathing hard.

"You okay?" he asks.

I'm only starting to think I can straighten up without barfing all over the place. "Think so. You?"

"Oh yeah. Piece of cake," he grunts.

chapter 119

The two uniformed officers arrive shortly after.

When Charlie rushed the stage, they went after him. He never made it that far, and deked out a side exit instead. Connor had slipped away in the pandemonium. So when the cops showed up, they still had no idea what was going on. They saw an unconscious actor on the ground, broken glass, and the cuts on my face. Charlie was the only one who looked moderately okay. When they rush toward us, I'm pretty sure they're only going to arrest him.

"Wait!" I call out, my throat feeling like I've gargled asphalt. I point at Connor. "He's the one you want. He's the guy who's been killing the girls."

They ignore me to lock down the situation before sorting out the mess. They put us against a wall, warning us that if we try anything, they'll handcuff us all. I try and explain again what's going on, but they tell me to quit talking while they bring Connor around. They're checking his pupils and asking for responses when the door behind us opens.

It's the guy with the headset. He sees Charlie and me against the wall and the cops dealing with a semi-coherent Connor and explodes, lunging at the barely conscious killer.

"You! You piece of crap! You destroyed the play."

The officers react, quickly pushing him back against the wall too.

"I worked so hard and you *ruined* it! I'm going to kill you!"

The absurdity of it makes me want to giggle but Charlie beats me to it.

"Jeezuz!"

chapter 120

Paramedics and more police arrive. After they check Charlie and me over, they stick us in a small theatre classroom somewhere behind the stage. An officer waits by the door.

"Where's the other guy?" I ask.

All I care about is what's going on with Connor. If they don't realize who he is, I'm worried they'll let him go. And I sure as hell don't want to lose him.

The cop ignores me.

I look over at Charlie and he shakes his head. He has no use for police and there's nothing he'll share with them, even if it means not helping me out. I'm on my own.

I try again. "Excuse me. What about the other guy?"

The officer looks at me. He's neither annoyed nor friendly. "Your buddy?"

This riles Charlie. "He's not our buddy!"

"Easy, kid."

"Go screw yourself."

Charlie's cornered and he's doing his best to be a punk. I, on the other hand, only care about making sure Connor goes to jail—well, maybe I'm a little worried about what I'm going to tell my parents and whether or not I need a lawyer—but right now Connor's still my focus.

"Whatever you do, don't let him go," I plead.

"Don't you worry." He looks at Charlie. "Your friend is in the next room being babysat by my partner."

I sigh in relief.

"Can you please call Detective Gekas and tell her what's going on?"

"Why do you want her?"

Charlie pipes up, "Why don't you go shove your head up—"

I step in before he makes it worse, "Can you tell her you're holding Tony Shepherd and Charlie Wolfe? Please?" I suspect he's being difficult on purpose and I have to work around the system.

He scrutinizes Charlie and me until he decides to make the call.

"I'm right outside, so don't try anything."

We say nothing and he leaves the room.

"Charlie, you okay?"

"Yup."

"You nervous?"

"Nope."

"What are we going to tell Gekas—the truth?"

"Are you *mental*? I think we need to be very selective of what we tell her."

I have a sinking, nervous feeling. Connor is our guy and I don't want some loophole or something we did to allow him to walk away.

The officer returns. "Get up gentlemen. Let's go. Looks like Detective Gekas wants a visit with you down at the station.

"What about the other guy?"

"He's coming too."

chapter 121

They have me in an interrogation room that looks nothing like the movies. There's a table and two chairs but no big one-way mirror—just four walls and some fluorescent lighting. I wait for a long time, stuck in my own thoughts and all I can think about is Sheri.

One night, only a few months after we started dating, we hung out at my place and watched a movie. I don't remember what we saw, but I do remember it was awful and we both fell asleep halfway through. I woke, a little disorientated but feeling oh, so comfortable with my arm around her, cuddling. Then, she looked up at me, half awake and half asleep, and she smiled, and I knew she felt the exact same way. I knew then that I wanted to spend a long, long time with her—

Now, that's changed and nothing can be the same. I'm crying and I wipe my eyes with my sleeves. I finally allow myself to let some of this pain go, piece by small piece.

I force myself to think about other things.

I wonder where Charlie is; I'm nervous for him, knowing this place and how he feels about it. I think about my parents and how much trouble I'll be in, depending on how all of this goes. I worry about my future, whether I've ended any hope of going to university or playing basketball someplace without barbed wire fences.

The door opens and Gekas enters, holding a bottle of water. She takes a seat across from me. She notices the cuts on my cheek but doesn't mention them. "Thirsty? Water?"

"Yes, please."

"Sorry it took so long, Anthony. I needed to debrief the officers who brought you in."

I take a long drink before I feel I can speak. "Why were they there?"

"Connor was Robbie's emergency contact."

"Not his parents?"

I feel a sense of judgment that quickly turns to matter-of-factness when I consider how screwed up both Connor and Robbie are.

"When we weren't able to get a hold of him on his cell phone, we tracked him down there."

"Is Robbie dead?" I feel a heaviness.

"No. He's stable."

I'm relieved. "So you didn't know about Connor?"

"None of us had even figured it out."

I feel pride, or accomplishment, or something.

Gekas holds my gaze. It's her only acknowledgment.

I nod in acceptance. "How's Charlie?"

She grins. "From what I've been told, he's taking a nap."

The smile looks good on her and I can't help but laugh. Only Charlie could sleep at a time like this. "And Connor?"

Her smile fades and I expect the worst.

"He confessed."

The moment sinks in. The longest minute of the last few weeks passes between Gekas and me.

"To all of it. All the girls."

That feeling I had weeks ago in the office at school springs right up into my belly, that wicked, familiar, dark feeling in the pit of my stomach, but this time it's not just nervousness. It's real. It's connected to the thing I feared.

I wait for her to say it, holding my breath.

"Including Sheri. He told us where she is."

Everything drops away and the silent clamp around my internal organs releases. I gasp at the shock of it. She's dead. I knew it in my head, but this is a visceral punch to the gut and the leaden feeling sinks in. It's consuming, but at least I now know what happened.

"We barely started interviewing him before he volunteered the information. He wanted to take credit for it, for what he called his 'performance.'"

She pauses, waiting for me, but I don't know how to respond. I want her to stop talking and I want her to tell me everything.

She continues, "With his confession, I think all charges will stick. I don't think he's getting out of it."

I nod. I can't quite believe it's over.

Gekas pushes away from the table and stands. "Good job, Anthony. You and Charles, you helped us get him."

chapter 122

They release Charlie and me later that day. Mom and Dad are there to pick me up.

No one's there to pick up Charlie.

I'm about to say something when Mom asks, "Charles? Do you need a ride?"

Charlie tries to wave away the offer, but he doesn't realize the depth of Mom's persistence. "Nonsense, you're coming with us."

If he tries to say no again, she'll likely drag him and shove him into the car, and I'm pretty sure he realizes this too, so he comes along.

Charlie doesn't talk during the trip home, staring out the window, watching the houses go by. Not even Dad's music seems to change his mood.

It isn't until we're in the southeast end of the city that I consider that I have no clue where Charlie lives. I'm curious to see what his home looks like since all he talks about are trailer parks and his absent mother.

"Do you mind stopping up ahead? I'd like to get a coffee and a doughnut."

Mom and Dad look at him, at each other, at me. It's kind of a strange request, but I nod, hoping to help get him out of his funk.

They pull into the parking lot at the doughnut place.

"I won't be long," Charlie says, before going inside.

We wait in the car and I'm suddenly aware that my parents have me right where they want me. Trapped. I need to beat them to the punch. "Mom, Dad, I—"

Mom interrupts, "Not now."

"But—?"

"Nope. It'll be a conversation for later."

Dad looks in the rearview mirror at me. "Maybe over a cup of tea."

Crap—it's gonna be one of those talks. I sigh, leaning back in my seat.

Ten minutes pass. No Charlie.

I go in and look around the coffee shop and check the bathrooms, but I can't find him anywhere. He must have slipped out the back, out of sight, and into the mystery that surrounds—and maybe even protects—him.

chapter 123

Gekas found Sheri. Connor had taken her only a mile south of the trails and dumped her weighted body into the bottom of a dugout. An autopsy will need to be performed as they continue to build the case against him. She tells me that she and her people will be at it for weeks to make sure Connor is dealt with properly.

Gekas also tells me that officially Shepherd and Wolfe were never involved in the case. I appreciate that. It's a complication I don't want, although I never told her about half the stuff we did. Tampering with crime scenes and evidence is not what my favourite lead detective needs to hear just now. We left a pretty big mess behind us that I'm hoping she'll be able to figure out. In the end, she cut our path of destruction out of her investigation, reducing it to the conversations I had with her and the final incident at the theatre.

A week later, Sheri's parents hold her funeral. They ask me to attend. Although Charlie and I aren't officially connected to finding her killer, it appears that Gekas may have hinted to the Beckmans that forgiveness is in order.

The church is full of Sheri's friends and family. I stand by her coffin, and when I close my eyes, all I see is her big smile. Finally, that thick, heavy weight releases in my gut and the pain rises up. I decide not to hide it this time.

Instead, I let it go.

chapter 124

Mom, Dad, Heather, and I come home from Sheri's funeral and go inside the house. Heather gives me a final hug before she runs upstairs to change out of her dress. I'm thankful for her love.

I sit at the kitchen island and then Mom and Dad are there, a cup of tea brewed and set between us.

"Is it that time?" I ask.

They smile.

"You know, you drove us crazy the past couple of weeks," Mom says.

It's more of a statement than a question, but I nod anyway. I don't want to fight. My strategy is to let them say whatever they need to.

Dad builds on her thought, "You did a lot of stupid, stupid things."

"I know—"

"But you also made us proud."

"You fought for what you believed in. And you fought against something that your Dad and I couldn't imagine."

I look at them, not sure what to say.

"But if you ever do something like this again, you'll be grounded for a very long time."

I laugh, even though I know it's true.

chapter 125

I sit in a chair in the backyard, wrapped in a thick fall jacket, eyes closed, feeling the last rays of warm sunlight on my face. Winter is right around the corner.

"You know if you sit on a cold surface, you get hemorrhoids, right?"

Charlie.

I don't open my eyes right away. "That's only rocks or side-walks."

He sits down beside me. "Really? Hmm... I guess you do know some things."

I look over at him. He's brought me a coffee. "You sure took a long time to get that."

He shrugs. "Yeah, well, it's still hot."

I take a sip and have to agree. It feels good, warms me up from the inside out. "So what happened?" I ask.

He doesn't pretend not to know what I mean. "What? You wanted to see my place? Meet my mom? You serious, Shep-herd?"

Always the deflector, always the joker. Still, he makes me laugh.

"Charlie—?"

"Oh, don't say it—"

"Thank—"

"Here it comes—"

"You."

"Ugh, now it's out there. Next, you'll start with the crying and whining, and I won't be able to get you to stop."

I let him have his moment. I take a sip of coffee and finally sigh. "Good coffee."

"Yup, it is."

"You pay for it?"

"Of course not."

We both smile.

"Oh, that reminds me." He searches his jacket and grabs a small paper bag that he hands to me. "This is for you."

I look inside and find a doughnut—a Boston Cream. I pull it out and take a big bite.

It tastes fantastic.

the shepherd & wolfe mysteries

Along Comes a Wolfe (BOOK 1)
Shepherd's Watch (BOOK 2)
Wolfe in Shepherd's Clothing (BOOK 3)
Shepherd's Call (BOOK 4)
Wolfe's Blood (BOOK 5)

acknowledgments

Thank you to our first readers: Lana LaFontaine, Anna Gane, Kate Gane, Charlene Hilkewich, and Kevin Leflar. Our extreme gratitude goes to Dimitrios Kounios for all his artwork and to Nathan Mader for his excellent editorial work. Thank you to Angie's students and Constable Blair Randall for fielding her many questions. We'd also like to give a special thanks to those early readers who caught our mistakes: Kevin Leflar, Kevin Johnson, Lucas Frison, Michael Hadjimichael, Maria Plastaras, and Maria Makris-Nagel. Thank you for your eagle eyes. And a big thank you to Heather Nickel, who helped us bring this book to life.

Angie would like to thank the Creator for this beautiful, crazy journey.

David would like to thank his family, Kate, Anna, and Peter, for all their love and patience.

about the authors

DAVID GANE is a writer, teacher, and stay-at-home dad. He writes film scripts and fiction, and has also composed poetry, plays, and academic film reviews. He occasionally teaches screenwriting at the University of Regina.

ANGIE COUNIOS teaches by day, and writes film scripts and fiction the rest of the time. When she's not teaching or writing, she's packing a bag for another adventure, completing a goal list, playing with her camera or practising yoga.

Find them at **www.couniosandgane.com**

www.ingramcontent.com/pod-product-compliance
Lightning Source LLC
Chambersburg PA
CBHW050852210726
48290CB00004B/1190